Olivia's
Garden

Patricia Fawcett

ROBERT HALE · LONDON

ISBN 0 7090 7625 8

Robert Hale Limited
Clerkenwell House
Clerkenwell Green
London EC1R 0HT

2 4 6 8 10 9 7 5 3 1

Typeset in 10/13½ pt Garamond by
Derek Doyle & Associates in Liverpool.
Printed in Great Britain by
St Edmundsbury Press, Bury St Edmunds, Suffolk.
Bound by Woolnough Bookbinding Limited

To the old girls of The Park School, Preston 1955-62,
who reminded me of the special qualities of childhood friendships

CHAPTER ONE

Olivia Hayton was a dreamer.

Instead of listening to Miss Parr, who was droning on, Olivia was gazing out of the window on to the lawns that stretched sunnily into the distance. Someone was cutting the grass and the new-mown smell drifted through the open window.

They were promised a treat this afternoon, lessons outside on the lawn, which Olivia knew would be full of bits of grass that had escaped the mower's box. They would end up stuck to her legs, sticky with the sun, and down her socks and up her knickers, tiny bits of grass.

'Are you paying attention, Olivia?'

'Yes, Miss Parr,' she said, frowning at a sharp dig from Rosie, who was herself doodling. Reluctantly, she looked towards the front of the classroom, where Miss Parr was writing on the blackboard. Why did grown-ups scrawl so? Her father had the most terrible writing, all flourishy and huge, and her mother had very small writing, as if she was a tiny neat lady.

To Olivia's embarrassment, her mother was not easily missed. She was tall and beautiful with a ringing voice that was often complaining about something. She had dark hair that she wore long, sometimes pinned up, and brown sparkly eyes. She used a lot of make-up near them, special pencils and shadows that Olivia was not to touch under any circumstances. She had heard it said that her mother had *presence*.

She was called Judith Marguerita Hayton and she adored clothes. She favoured Laura Ashley dresses in pretty sprigged cotton, or plain navy jersey when she was in her 'Jean Muir' mood. It was no use, she told Olivia, going for the same style the whole time, because you had to account for your moods. Sometimes, you might feel totally and absolutely wretched and that was when you needed your red dress.

When Mummy came to school, she would arrive at the wheel of a big car and leave it parked in the place by the entrance, where nobody was supposed to park. There was a big notice nearby – a polite notice – which said as much. It mortified Olivia that her mother should break the rules; mercifully it happened only rarely, for she did not visit very often.

This past school year, both her parents had missed all the important social events in the calendar, including, to Olivia's delight, sports day, which they made such a big thing of here at Slyne Hall. As she was spectacularly bad at sport, she was thrilled that her parents were absent. Her mother was full of apologies and it warranted a specially long phone call to compensate but there it was.

Olivia was not one of the star pupils academically either, but she had it drummed into her that she must do reasonably well if she was to do anything with her life.

'But you don't have a career, Mummy. . . .'

'That's different. I married your father. It's not that I didn't want a career and I would certainly have pursued one vigorously if I hadn't met him but I can't have one now. It all boils down to work permits, darling. Infernal red tape.'

Olivia nodded, not fully understanding about work permits or red tape but not wishing to have Mummy go on and on about something that sounded boring.

'Careers will become much more important to girls like you, Olivia, and men like your father will be thin on the ground by the time you are ready to be married.'

Olivia's father, George, was shorter than her mother by a whole inch or more when she wore her platform heels but he did not mind. He had merry golden brown eyes and a friendly, quiet voice and it was for his sake and the deep-down sure knowledge that he loved her that Olivia was trying her best.

Her mother had made an unscheduled visit recently when she returned from the six-month stint in Vienna, but she could only manage the one day because she was busy preparing to jet off again. She was given permission to take Olivia out of classes and they drove into Chester and had lunch in a restaurant on the upper level of The Rows, which was a bit of an ordeal because her mother kept picking her up about her table manners. She would make a complaint, she said, when they got back, for one would have thought with the ridiculous fees they charged that they could teach the very basics of table etiquette.

As they left the restaurant, her mother dug deep in her bag and fluttered a note on the table, accepting the waitress's thanks with a big smile. 'Always tip lavishly,' she told Olivia. 'it impresses people and you get better service the next time.'

Her mother knew all about impressing people.

'Olivia!' Miss Parr's voice interrupted her thoughts. 'Are you with us at all?'

'Yes, Miss Parr,' she said automatically, ignoring Rosie's stifled giggle, noting that the gardener would soon be finished. She was glad for him, because he looked very tired already, going slower and slower, and there was no shade on the lawn.

'I should hope *everyone* is paying attention,' Miss Parr said with a sniff. 'After all, very soon you will be in senior school and we will all have to work very hard then, so that by the time we come to do our external examinations, we are well prepared.'

They all knew that. People were depending on them not to disgrace the name and reputation of the school and, just at this moment, with the sun streaming in and the sounds of summer outside, succeeding in life, in their chosen career, seemed a very pleasant and easy option.

'Day-dreaming gets you nowhere, girls,' Miss Parr continued, not hearing the tiny sigh that escaped them. 'You can do that when you go home.'

Home? Olivia wondered where it was this year. They did have a house over in Chester, on a wide leafy avenue beyond the station, but they rented it out because Daddy worked abroad on contracts. Olivia had not seen it for ages and when she had gone with Mummy to check those dreadful people aren't wrecking the place, it felt strange and another little girl was using her room and had her things in it.

'It is still *our* house, isn't it?' Olivia asked her mother on the return trip.

'Yes, darling, but it's complicated. A long-term let. I don't know when we'll be living there again. If ever. . . .'

'I wish we were.'

'Now, Olivia,' her mother said briskly. 'None of that. It's the way things are and we can't change them.'

That bedroom, her old nursery room, was one of the things she missed the most. During the holidays, she didn't have a bedroom to go back to like the other girls. Here, she shared a dormitory with several girls, including her best friends, little Rosie Andrews and Anna Farrell, who was a bit of a brainbox.

Rosie was bright and breezy and bewildered to be here at Slyne Hall at all. She didn't like it, preferring the state school she had previously attended, but there had been a thundering row and her parents had 'whipped her out of the system'. She didn't mind telling them that her parents couldn't really afford for her to be here but here she was anyway. She was incredibly untidy and her corner of the room was a tip that she zealously guarded. Nobody was to touch anything and nobody *dare* touch anything, for if she started one of her tempers, she exploded.

Anna never exploded. She never threatened to explode. She was quiet and calm, from a medical family, and she told them that she was destined to go into the profession.

'We've always been doctors,' she said, whispering because it was getting late and they were supposed to be settling down and somebody would be checking what they were up to in a few minutes. 'We don't do anything else.'

'My dad works in a bank,' Rosie said cheerfully. 'He's chief cashier. And my mum works in a department store in shoes and handbags. Here, have a treacle toffee. . . .'

Chewing on her large toffee, Olivia was the first to clamber into bed, wiggling her toes to get warm. Even in summer, this north-facing room was stone cold. Her mother had made a strong complaint, insisting that such austere conditions were perfectly ridiculous in this day and age, but it made no difference.

'You don't have to do the same thing your parents do,' Rosie told them, talking through her toffee. 'I'm going to do something very exciting.'

They'd heard it all before. A film star, an actress or a singer. Before Rosie started on about it, Olivia interrupted, asking Anna if she really and truly *wanted* to be a doctor.

Anna looked at her in surprise. She had a very straight way of looking at you. When she smiled, her whole face changed, and made her very nearly pretty, but she saved her smiles for special occasions. Perhaps that's because she was from what Olivia's mother called a 'broken family'.

'What do you mean?' Anna asked now, puzzled. 'Do I want to be a doctor?'

'Livvy means what she says,' Rosie said impatiently. 'You either do or don't. Yes or no.'

'I do.' Anna's face cleared. 'Ben says it's just great. He had to cut up a cadaver in the anatomy lesson and he says that's the real test. If you faint then, you have to give in.'

Their whispers had become excited.

'What's a cadaver?' Olivia asked, sensing it was something outrageous that she ought not really to know about.

'A body. A dead body,' Anna explained. 'Some people leave their bodies for the students to practise on. Didn't you know that?'

'No.' Olivia frowned, not entirely sure that Anna was speaking the truth because it was so horrible. 'Instead of getting buried, you mean?'

Anna nodded. 'It's called donating your body to medical research. I think it's a brilliant idea.'

'I think it's terrible,' Olivia said, a vision of a body and a knife appearing before her sleepy eyes, causing her to shudder at the very idea and clutch the bedclothes closer. 'Ben must be very brave. Do they bleed when you cut them? Dead bodies?'

Anna shook her head. 'I don't think so. It would be just too messy, wouldn't it? Perhaps they're drained or something. Or perhaps your blood dries up when you die. I must ask Ben.'

Anna looked very earnest as the moonlight shone through the thin curtains and illuminated her face. Her new year resolution had been to stop growing but it didn't seem to be working and her new uniform was already too short. She had thick, dark, springy hair that she couldn't flatten down, try as she would, and muddy grey eyes. She was almost an only child because Ben, her brother, was very nearly a teenager when she was born.

'Cadavers. . . !' Rosie said with a shudder, stuffing the remainder of the toffees in her dressing-gown pocket. She had a pale green dressing-gown over her pyjamas and slippers to match from her mother's department store and, in the night light, her milky skin almost glowed. 'I'll probably have a nightmare now and it will be your fault, Anna Farrell.'

Kindly donated cadavers lying there on a slab, bloodless and dead, and brave older brothers wielding knives were not the sort of thing to be thinking of directly before going to sleep and, like Rosie, Olivia was frightened she might dream about it. Owls hooting and strange shadows darting across the room did not help.

It took her some time to settle off that night.

There was some degree of privacy. Olivia could curtain herself off if she really wanted, and when she did that she was shut away and it was the unspoken rule that the others had to knock at the curtain, a dark red velvety one, if they wanted to come in. She chose quiet times like that to read, an assortment of school stories and classic tales like *Black Beauty* and *Anne of Green Gables* from the library.

Sometimes, Rosie Andrews sneaked in books that were reckoned to be too old for them. Gory adventure stories or even love stories. They talked in whispers, she and the other girls, of what it would mean to fall in love. Olivia could imagine it very well. She saw herself, grown up and beautiful, walking into a room and seeing her own wonderful hero standing there.

Across the room, their eyes would meet.

And that would be that.

Happy ever after.

Rosie spoilt things as usual by saying that falling in love was a daft idea and if she couldn't marry one of the Bay City Rollers, she would marry somebody who was very, very rich.

Poor Rosie. She looked younger than everyone else and reminded Olivia of a picture she had once seen of Peter Pan. Her hair was gingery, orangey red, her eyelashes very pale and sandy, her eyes a watered-down brown, and she looked as if she might break if she bent too far. She was always in trouble and being threatened with expulsion if she didn't pull her socks up.

Olivia refused to listen to her. *She* was marrying for love like Mummy had.

Slyne Hall was all right as schools go and Olivia was used to it. In the early days, in the preparatory school, it was very convenient, for they lived then in Chester. She was a boarder even then and her mother had never been one for visiting much during the term, saying it unsettled her to have Mummy visit. As for Daddy, he just said it was better she battle through on her own rather than have them prop her up all the time, and although she wasn't quite sure what he meant she was sure he meant well, for Daddy loved her.

From term to term, year to year, it was comforting that school changed so little. The teachers were quite nice but what Olivia loved most was the garden. Although it was frowned upon, she did sometimes manage to sneak away to talk to one of the gardeners, a Mr Johnson, an old man with a wheezy cough who smoked a pipe and always seemed to be leaning on his spade in deep contemplation.

Two days to go before the start of the summer holidays and all the other girls could talk about was where they were going and what they would be doing. Knowing she would be spending part of the time here, until her parents were settled in the new posting and could send for her, Olivia nonetheless entered into the spirit of things. She could outdo the lot of them if she tried, for she had been to so many places she had lost count.

But it was when nearly everyone was gone, piled into cars, their belongings pushed in with them, waving, laughing their goodbyes, it was when it was suddenly very quiet in the corridors, when the chairs were stacked on desks in the classroom, when the other girls were gone, when she had the whole of the big bedroom to herself, that Olivia dared admit to loneliness.

One of the teaching staff, a Mrs McAdam, and the housekeeper were remaining behind to keep an eye on her and the half dozen others, who, for various reasons, could not go home immediately. An army of cleaners arrived, busily cleaning for all they were worth, and with school restrictions loosened, if not lifted completely, the atmosphere was fairly relaxed, although a couple of the younger girls were showing signs of homesickness.

When Olivia found them beginning to cling to her, wandering round the grounds with her, she thought it time to have a chat. She wanted to be sympathetic but that would only end with all three of them in tears.

'It's no use crying,' she told them, for one of them was unable to eat her meals without snivelling. 'Crying's a waste of time.'

'You don't cry, do you, Olivia?'

'No,' she said stoutly. 'You lose energy when you cry.'

The little girls looked at her and seemed to believe her. After all, nobody could see when it was dark and she had learned over the years to cry quietly and not in great unseemly gulps like some of the others. If she felt particularly sad, she just allowed the tears to flow, hot and wet against her cheeks, dampening her pillow, but by the morning it was dry again, the tears gone, her morning face none the worse. Nobody ever *saw* her cry.

The two weeks she spent at school, when school was not quite school, passed by quickly and the part she enjoyed most was being able to chat to Mr Johnson and not be ticked off too much for it.

'Gardeners all, my family,' he told her proudly. 'We've got potash running through our veins, I tell you, miss.'

She smiled at him, knowing that was a joke. Still, *everybody* in the family gardeners – no wonder Mr Johnson was so pleased with them. It was just like Anna Farrell's family – everybody doctors.

'Why did you move from Chester, Mr Johnson?' she asked, knowing he lived down in the village with his wife.

'My Gwendoline wanted to look out on to fields,' he said, tapping his pipe. 'And you always have to do what the wife wants or she makes your life a misery. You ask your dad.'

Olivia smiled uncertainly at that. She was not sure her father always did what *he* was told. After all, her mother complained all the time about living abroad, so it was not what she wanted to do but they did it anyway. She decided not to say anything to Mr Johnson, because it was private and her mother had drummed into her that you did not discuss private matters with all and sundry, especially gardeners.

Mr Johnson switched about a lot between talking about his family and gardening matters. He was always on about composts and manure and Olivia was quick to learn. She asked her mother if she might have a gardening book but her mother bought her a poetry book instead to broaden her horizons.

'Poetry?' Mr Johnson said, scratching his head when she showed him the book. 'I was never one for poems, miss. I tell a lie – isn't there one about a host of golden daffodils?' He smiled a little. 'Now, I like that one. Who's it by?'

'William Wordsworth,' Olivia said at once, feeling herself flush as he looked at her in admiration. She hadn't meant to show off. 'It's called "The Daffodils",' she added gently. 'I know the first verse off by heart already.'

A few days later, he brought her a gardening book, wrapped or rather hidden in a brown paper bag. He handed it over gruffly, saying that she wasn't to say anything to anybody, because they might get a bit shirty at school if they knew because, by rights, they weren't supposed to be carrying on a conversation at all.

Olivia understood that, and smuggled the book back indoors, tucking it away in her locker. It was a beautiful book, with coloured pictures of the flowers, and pictures, too, of borders and beds. It was also an old book, some of the pages yellowing, and she was extremely careful how she handled it. She was fascinated, quickly learning that gardening was all about timing. Get the timing wrong and you were knackered for the rest of the year, Mr Johnson told her. Gardening never waited for you to catch up with it. Sometimes, he explained earnestly, the weather could bugger you up completely. A wet spring and that was you gone for a Burton for the whole summer.

Olivia lapped it up, even though she looked worryingly at Mr Johnson's dirty fingernails. Mummy said you judged a person by the state of their fingernails – that, and their bank balance.

'You'll be a proper gardener one day,' he told her with a little satisfied nod.

'Like you?' she asked shyly. 'You're a proper gardener, Mr Johnson.'

'That I am,' he said, replacing his old cap on his head, grinning at her with yellow teeth that clacked when he talked.

She would have continued to lap it all up, except he went away one Friday evening and never came back.

When she enquired of Mrs McAdam, she was told that, during the weekend, he had gone away.

'Where to? He told me he'd see me on Monday.'

The teacher sighed. She wore fat flowery dresses and beads and waddled when she walked. 'He's gone to heaven, dear,' she said.

Olivia stared at her. Just how old did Mrs McAdam think she was?

'He's dead? Is that what you mean, Mrs McAdam?'

It was confirmed that Mr Johnson was dead of a sudden heart attack.

'Instantaneous,' Mrs McAdam said with satisfaction. 'It happened at supper time. Apparently, he keeled over into his bowl of cornflakes. He wouldn't have felt a thing, dear.'

Olivia thought about that. Why was he eating cornflakes at supper time? And just imagine, starting to eat them and dying! She realized she would never ever be able to eat cornflakes again without thinking of poor Mr Johnson.

'Oh,' she said, not knowing what else to say.

Clumsily, Mrs McAdam reached out and gave her a swift cuddle and she was given permission to cry if she wished. Olivia chose not to, not at that moment anyway. And she was having none of this gone to heaven stuff. Forced as she was to attend the church in the village every single Sunday, where they occupied four full pews, she found it boring and she did not like the vicar, who had hairs up his nose and a spitty way of talking through big teeth with gaps. She had decided she did not believe in heaven, although she wished she did just now, and that poor Mr Johnson was up there, doing the garden.

He would like that.

Just in case, in bed that evening, she offered a little prayer up to God to ask him to please look after her friend Mr Johnson. He had been a nice man, even if he did say a lot of naughty words and smoked his socks off *and*, to cap it all, had dirty fingernails.

CHAPTER TWO

Mrs McAdam helped Olivia pack her bags and then, on the appointed day, she drove her to Gatwick airport and handed her over to the lady on the desk.

This time, it was a long flight, a trans-Atlantic flight to the new posting, and she was to be met by car when she arrived. Of course, there wasn't a car waiting for her when she did arrive but she was used to such things. Her mother often got arrangements wrong. Vanessa, the air hostess who had looked after her and seen her through customs and immigration, was getting fidgety and anxious to offload her, and Olivia sensed it, insisting she would be fine now, thank you very much. Vanessa said no, she had to hand her over to a responsible adult, and so Olivia allowed her to tag along, as, quite unperturbed, she found a telephone and rang her mother.

'Is that you, Olivia? At the airport already?' her mother said, aghast. 'What a surprise and how ridiculous because the flights are always late. There seemed no point in checking when I heard the flight was late leaving the UK.'

With weather conditions almost perfect, they had made up the time *en route*, as the pilot had proudly announced, and were only five minutes behind schedule.

At her side, Vanessa shuffled impatiently and enquired if there was a problem, but Olivia, winding up the call, shook her head. She was to sit and wait until her father sent a car for her. He was completely tied up in a meeting, her mother explained, and she had no driving licence here, otherwise she would come herself. However, she would tell the driver to hot-foot it along and he would be there shortly.

Vanessa could barely hide her irritation but sat with Olivia, constantly glancing at her watch and doing that tut-tut that adults do, until at last, looking in no particular hurry, a man arrived bearing a notice that had Olivia's name on it.

'Here he is. About time. . . .' Vanessa murmured, beaming now. 'It's been lovely looking after you, Olivia. Have a great holiday. And don't worry, you'll see your mother in no time.'

She wasn't worried but she smiled anyway at Vanessa's concern, watching as she clattered off at high speed, not knowing that she had a huge ladder in her tights, starting at her ankle and going all the way up probably. Olivia knew that ladies just hated that. Something like that made her mother scream with annoyance.

Just for the briefest moment, she felt a little alone as she looked up into the face of the driver, whom she did not know at all. At least she had known Vanessa for the last eight hours or so.

'Is this your first visit to the island, miss?' the driver said, as they drove across the causeway from the airport.

'Yes. But Daddy sent me a book about it. It looks lovely,' she added politely.

He seemed pleased at that, telling her his name was George.

'That's my father's name,' she told him, perking up. 'My mummy's name is Judith and I'm called Olivia. Olivia Rachel Hayton.'

'I know that, Miss Hayton. It was on my notice. It's a very pretty name.'

'Thank you,' she said, putting up a hand to cover a yawn as tiredness gripped her. It was close on seven o'clock here and nearly eleven o'clock at school, Olivia thought with a sigh, thinking suddenly and longingly of a cup of hot cocoa.

Over 3,000 miles away from Slyne Hall, on this island in the Atlantic Ocean, the sea was a deep evening blue, the coral sands a pale pink and the houses pastel-coloured pink or blue or peach with white ridged roofs shining in a sun that was still as hot as an English midday.

They proceeded slowly and regally, a sea breeze blowing the palms and cooling the interior of the car. The house was up a road close to the beach, an enormous property, like a palace, a pale blue building approached via a lush subtropical garden. The drive curved gently upwards towards the entrance and there, on the steps, her mother was waiting, looking quite cross.

'Gracious me, Olivia,' she said as she kissed her, smelling of the same perfume in the fancy-shaped bottle, which she was never to touch because it cost a bomb. 'Just look at you. You should have freshened up at the airport. You had enough time when you were waiting. And what have they done to your hair? Did I give permission to have it cut?'

'I like it,' Olivia said, touching it. 'It looks grown up.'

'It looks like rats' tails, darling.'

The heat fizzled and prickled against Olivia's tired face. Her mother looked cool and comfortable in a sun-dress with tiny straps over her tanned shoulders.

Looking at Olivia's hair once more, shaking her head in irritation, she clicked her fingers and a tall graceful lady in a long slim orange dress, who seemed to slide along on soft-soled sandals, appeared to carry Olivia's bags indoors. Olivia smiled at her and said thank you but her mother said not a word, sweeping off and leaving them to trail in after her.

'My name's Elisabeth, spelt with an "s",' the lady murmured, winking at her. 'Good evening, Olivia, and welcome to the island.'

Olivia thought Elisabeth was a lovely name. One of her friends at school was called Elisabeth spelt with an 's' too, although she was from Twickenham and had blonde hair and blue eyes and this lady had skin the colour of milky coffee, thick hair in tight curls, big dark eyes that gleamed and shiny cheeks. This Elisabeth was beautiful.

Inside the house, it was cool and their footsteps echoed on the tiled floor. The walls in the living-room were white with exposed beams, the furniture heavy and dark, an oval fringed rug toning with the satin pink of the sofas. Olivia took it all in with a single glance.

'What do you think of Bermuda, darling?' her mother asked, managing a proper smile at last.

'It's beautiful,' Olivia said, glancing out on to a dazzling white balcony and the shimmer of the suddenly darkening sea and sky, as night drew in quickly. 'Everything sparkles.'

Her mother nodded. 'A little too hot for my taste with this dratted humidity and so very small that one feels a bit claustrophobic but there it is. . . .'

Mummy always had a complaint. Paris was scruffy. The Milanese were too fond of smoking and fur coats. Copenhagen was wet and the food abysmal. And so it went on.

'Were you good on the flight? Who looked after you this time?'

'Vanessa. She has blonde hair, blue eyeshadow *and* blue mascara . . .'

'Really?' Her mother yawned, losing interest already.

'She's from Leeds. She was very nice.'

'Nice is not a word I like to use, Olivia. Use another word.'

Olivia's fugged, jet-lagged mind struggled for an alternative, before giving up with a shrug.

'Where's Daddy?' she asked.

'Still at the office.' Her mother sighed and flicked at something on her skirt. 'He practically lives there. That's the penalty, darling, of having the buck stop with you.'

Olivia did not know what she meant by that but knew it was something to do with her father being terribly important in the financial world he lived in.

'What's been happening at school?'

Her mother folded her body on to the sofa, long legs stretched in front of her, the sandals slipped off her feet, showing off silver-tipped toenails. Once this term, Rosie Andrews had sneaked in some nail varnish, three pots, and she had painted their toenails red Boots No.7 Slash of Scarlet. It was swimming next day and they thought they would get into terrible trouble but luckily Miss Arnold was always harassed and didn't notice.

'School?' Olivia said vaguely, trying to think of something other than the toenail episode. 'Oh – Mr Johnson died. Mrs McAdam said he keeled over into his cornflakes. She didn't think it hurt at all. He was a gardener and he smoked a pipe.'

'Really? How sad.'

'He was very old. He –' Olivia stopped, knowing there was no point in going on. Her mother was not interested in Mr Johnson.

'How's that sweet friend of yours?' her mother asked with a smile.

'Do you mean Rosie?'

'The little redhead with the raucous voice? No, good gracious, I mean Anna. Her mother's a doctor. I met her last year.'

Olivia nodded. She recalled the two of them together at speech day, Anna's mother with her hair all over the place in a grey flannel skirt and cardigan and stumpy shoes and *her* mother in one of the beautiful designer suits she brought back from Milan and high heels that made her taller than ever.

'A charming lady, I seem to remember, Mrs Farrell – well, Dr Farrell actually,' her mother said with a little smile. 'Although, between you and me, darling, utterly hopeless with clothes.'

Olivia said nothing. She had liked Dr Farrell. She had a giggly voice and kind eyes that wrinkled when she smiled.

'She told me her son Ben was studying medicine. Is he also going to be a GP?'

'Ben wants to be a surgeon,' she said, remembering something Anna had said. 'It will take ages and ages.'

'A surgeon?' Her mother's smile widened. 'I do so admire Dr Farrell, coping on her own like she does, but then women who choose to become doctors are so resourceful. I expect Anna will be a doctor too. From what I've seen of her, she seems a very determined and capable girl.'

Olivia nodded, unable to stop another huge yawn. 'May I have a drink?'

'You shall have one when you have been upstairs and washed your face and done something with your hair. I shall be making a complaint. I do not pay those ludicrous fees to have them chop your hair with pruning shears whenever they feel like it. Come down after you have tidied up and you may have a drink then. And Olivia . . .'

'Yes?'

'I hope we have not forgotten how to say please.'

CHAPTER THREE

There was a pool at the property. It was below the terrace outside the dining-room, down a small flight of brick steps, and Olivia's mother sometimes took a dip in the early morning, before the sun got too strong.

'That's *my* exercise for the day, George,' she would then say, coming in for breakfast, which they usually had on the terrace. She would be wrapped by now in a white towelling gown and frowning at Daddy, who hardly ever did any exercise at all. He had a problem with his knee which meant he could not play sports of any kind because it was too painful. This annoyed Olivia's mother, for all the other men played golf and she felt they were missing out. They attended social functions as guests, but it would be much better if they were a proper part of it, participating players.

'Why don't *you* play golf, then?' Olivia overheard him say one day, in that fed-up voice of his. 'You can take yourself off any time. You've nothing else to do.'

'That is rich, George,' her mother said, voice rising in annoyance. 'I have everything to do. All the supervising and entertaining. It doesn't get done on its own as you well know. And now there's Olivia to keep occupied too.'

'She's happy on her own. She's not the sociable sort.'

'Is she happy on her own? I do wonder sometimes. It's lucky she seems to have a few friends at school, although I wish she didn't seem so keen on being friends with Rosie Andrews. You remember her? A little red-head.'

'I do remember her and I thought she was very lively,' her father said, a smile in his voice. 'What's wrong with her?'

'She's not our type, for one.'

'Not our type? Oh, come on, you are a terrible snob, Judith, darling.'

'How dare you? I most certainly am not. We'll see how things go but I'm just not going to encourage that particular friendship. And another thing, she keeps going on about this gardener Mr Johnson. He died, you know, just before she

came out. It was one of the first things she told me. Has she mentioned it?'

'No. We've not had chance to speak yet.'

'Well, it seems to have upset her a little. She's such a sensitive soul. And the awful thing is she's got it into her head she wants to be a gardener too. I tell you, George, you'll have to nip that in the bud before it takes root.'

Olivia heard her father laughing at that before carefully moving away from the door, before she could be accused of eavesdropping. She did not keep going on about Mr Johnson. And what if she did want to be a gardener, what was wrong with that? She wished he could have seen the plants here. They looked happy and healthy, enjoying the heat and the sharp showers and occasional thunderstorms. Last night, the storm had raged overnight, her room lighting up, the thunder cracking and rumbling, much louder than it was in England, and it kept her awake, even drowning out the sound of the tree frogs.

She lay half hidden under the covers, trying to stuff out the noise of the thunder with her pillows but hearing it anyway. It seemed her heart thudded in tune as she waited anxiously for the next bang and flash.

Once, she had thought to creep to her parents' room but her mother hated her to do that and she did not want to be accused of being silly, so she stayed put, wishing there was someone to cuddle up to. At school, it wasn't so bad because they could all scream and feel frightened together.

This morning, the storm was over, the sun was out and everything was shaking itself dry. She knew what was different about the weather here – it did not sulk and stay grey and miserable for day after day after day.

Since she arrived, Daddy had been desperately busy at the infernal office, as Mummy said, and it was a couple of days before they finally caught up with each other, just the two of them, her mother having gone into town.

He looked different in shorts and loose shirt, idling over breakfast, sitting for ages with the paper, before coming to sit with her on the terrace under the shaded umbrella awning beside the palm trees.

'Well, Olly . . .' he grinned at her. 'How do you like it here?'

She smiled back. Mother hated him to call her 'Olly' and he was the only person who ever did.

'It's nice,' she said quietly. 'Do you like it?'

He nodded. 'I like it very much and I like the job. Very interesting. I feel a bit guilty dragging your mother all over the place but that's how it is. Are you all right at school? Are they looking after you?'

'Yes. Miss Parr's getting married in September.'

'Is she now?' He reached for a cigarette and lit it. Mummy hated him to smoke and he rarely smoked in her presence. 'Miss Parr. Which one's she?'

'She's my form teacher. She's quite small and . . .' She struggled for something pleasant to say about Miss Parr. 'She wears those crochet waistcoat things.'

'Oh Yes, I know. Good God, getting married, eh?' He inhaled, with great enjoyment. 'Wait until you're getting married. Your mother can't wait. It's going to be at home in Chester, of course. We shall walk up the aisle together, you and me, and your mother will sit in the front pew wearing a big hat. What do you think?'

She nodded. That sounded nice, apart from the big hat. Her mother's big hats were *very* big.

'And after the ceremony, we shall have a reception at The Grosvenor or maybe a marquee at home. And your picture will be in *Cheshire Life*, if your mother has anything to do with it.'

Olivia giggled. 'Will the house be our home then? Will we move back?'

'By the time you're in your twenties? I should say so. I might be retired by then.'

'I'm not getting married until I'm thirty at least,' she told him, remembering something Miss Parr had said. 'You have to get your career off the ground first before you get lumbered with a husband and babies. Once you've got babies, you have to get nannies and everything and it can mess up your career prospects like nobody's business.'

He laughed. 'We shall see, Olly. Are you happy at school?'

She nodded, supposing she was.

'And you have some good friends, your mother tells me.'

'Rosie and Anna. I like Rosie,' she said, casting a glance his way, remembering what her mother had said. 'She wants to be an actress or a singer. She's got a very loud voice.'

'And where does your friend Anna live?' her father asked, not seeming very interested in Rosie's ambitions.

'In a cottage in the country. She's invited me to go and stay sometime,' Olivia told him, testing his reaction. 'May I go if she asks me again?'

'Of course. So long as we know where you are.' He drew himself up and smiled. 'Any problems, come to me. Don't bother your mother with problems. She has quite enough of her own.'

She watched as he lazily smoked his cigarette. He had tanned, hairy legs and not very nice toes peeping out of his sandals.

'What are Mummy's problems?'

'Never you mind.' He sighed as he looked out towards a turquoise sea speckled with froths of white foam. 'Just look at that. That ocean just comes and goes, no matter what. Nobody can change that.'

'It's gravity, daddy,' she told him. 'That's what makes tides come and go. Ebb and flow,' she finished.

'You're right,' he said, smiling at her. 'Clever girl. You got a decent mark for your geography, didn't you?'

She wallowed in that, for praise was rare. Good marks even rarer.

'Life is so easy here,' her father went on. 'A lovely slow pace. So different from Europe. It takes a while to get used to although it annoys your mother that nothing ever gets done. Nobody hurries, you see.'

Olivia nodded. Nobody except her mother. Her mother was always complaining she was too hot but then she was always dashing about, meeting other ladies for luncheon and tea, and shopping, shopping, shopping.

She flicked her hair off her face and held her face up to the sun, unhindered in a blue sky. She heard her father pouring lemonade from the jug, the lumps of ice banging as they hit the sides.

'Those are oleanders, those pink ones,' she said, taking a sip of the cool lemonade, pointing out the flowers in the nearest bed. 'Did you know that, Daddy?'

'No.' He smoked his cigarette. 'You're good with plants, Olivia. Oleanders, eh?' He peered more closely at them. 'I like them.'

'So do I. And the hibiscus. Aren't they lovely?'

'If they're the pink things over there, then, yes, they are lovely.'

'They are so happy here. I wish Mr Johnson could see them. He liked plants to be happy.'

'Did he?' He glanced at her oddly. 'You liked him, didn't you? I'm sorry he died. Your mother told me about him. I don't remember him, I'm afraid.'

'I wanted to go to the funeral,' she said. 'But I wasn't allowed. Mrs McAdam said it was not appropriate.'

'Quite right, too. A funeral is no place for a little girl. Mr Johnson wouldn't have wanted you there either.'

She nodded, not convinced.

They could hear a car and sure enough a moment later it emerged on its way up the drive.

'There's your mother. I'll just get rid of this,' her father said, reaching for the ashtray and taking it indoors. 'I'll ask Elisabeth to bring us some iced tea and banana cake, then we'll see what your mother's bought today.'

*

It was her mother's birthday soon and she had been dropping hints for days, hints that even Olivia noticed, although her father didn't seem to.

'He forgot our wedding anniversary this year, so he'd better not forget my birthday or he's really for it,' she told Olivia, watching as his car disappeared out of the gates. 'He's so caught up with his work that I'm afraid he will. If he dares to forget, I shall come back to England with you, darling, and leave him to sweat it out here.'

It worried Olivia dreadfully, because she knew how awful it would be if he did forget, so that night she reminded him when her mother was out of the room, trying to do it gently by showing him the birthday card she was in the process of preparing.

'I haven't forgotten. I'm pretending I have but it's all in hand,' he told her with a smile. 'The flowers are ordered, and a bottle of her favourite perfume, and there's a special surprise too. Not a word, eh? But she's going to love her present and it will give you and me some time together this weekend. Would you like that?'

He didn't actually tell her what the surprise was but whatever it was it was in an envelope propped against the silver teapot at breakfast on the happy day itself. Olivia had made her card on stiff white paper and drawn and painted a picture of a purple flower on it and yesterday Elisabeth had helped her buy some chocolates and wrap them.

'How lovely! Thank you, darling,' her mother said, kissing her and opening the chocolates at once, and although it was only 7.30 in the morning, they each had one. She opened the box with the perfume, squealed her delight and splashed herself with it, admired the bouquet of flowers before passing them over to Elisabeth to do something with, then she took the envelope, saying brightly, 'What on earth can this be?' and opened it.

It took a few moments for Olivia to realize what it was exactly, but, to her relief, her mother was clearly very happy, giving a great whoop of joy, going round the table and hugging her father and planting a pink lipstick kiss on his cheek, when he was all ready to go to the office.

'George, you tease! Making me think you'd forgotten. Oh, you are such a darling. Perfume, flowers and this. Look, Olivia, what Daddy's bought me!'

The envelope contained air tickets to New York, where she was booked into a big hotel for a couple of nights, and she would at last be able to go shopping properly, she said.

With her mother despatched to the airport next day, she and her father did spend the time together he had promised, a lovely lazy time when they did nothing in particular. They got up late, padded around the house, dipped into the pool and took late afternoon walks along the shore.

They talked and talked. Leisurely. About school. About her friends at school. About what she might do when she left school. He told her just to enjoy school and not worry too much about exams and things, a direct contrast to her mother, who was always on at her to do well.

'Doesn't Mummy like it here?' she asked him, totally amazed that anyone could dislike it.

'Your mother likes city life,' he told her. 'She gets bored somewhere like this.'

'I know. She keeps telling me,' Olivia said, glancing up at him. 'I wish we still lived in Chester,' she said. 'I wish I could come home at the weekend and I wish I could ask some of my friends to visit. But I can't. If I go to stay with Anna, I won't be able to ask her back anywhere, will I?'

'Poor darling,' he said sympathetically. 'But people don't always expect to be asked back. She's asked you because she likes you.'

It was getting uncomfortably hot, the sun sizzling in the bluest of blue skies, and there was no shade here on the beach, just dazzling baking heat, so they turned and headed back to the car.

As they did so, sifting their way up a sandy slope, she reached for her father's big firm hand and held it.

Back from New York, dazed from all the shopping, her mother was in a good mood and, quite out of character, suggested a walk along the beach, just the two of them.

Going for a walk with mummy was not quite the same as the carefree walks she had with her father. Mummy did it because she said the exercise would do her good, but she complained the whole time, her good mood evaporating, saying that the heat was already too much and it was only 10.30 for goodness' sake.

Now, a little later, she was completely flaked out, sitting on a rock in sparse shade wearing a yellow dress she had bought for an exorbitant price in New York, looking at the world through sunglasses. She smelled not of perfume but of sickly-sweet oily sun lotion.

'Sometimes I feel like just setting off in a little boat and paddling off,' she said, as Olivia sat beside her, letting her feet and legs dry off in the sun. 'In that direction. . . .' She waved a weary hand. 'Oh, goodness, I feel trapped in paradise. Sometimes I want to go home so badly.' She sighed and glanced wearily at her watch. 'We'd better go. Elisabeth will have lunch ready.'

Olivia stood up, carefully avoiding a gang of madly scurrying insects. Her feet sinking into the hot pink sand, the scorching morning sun burning into her shoulders, she slowly followed her mother home.

CHAPTER FOUR

The state of the garden at Laburnum Cottage, an unremarkable middle cottage of three on the Welsh borderlands, had helped the village to lose the best-kept village trophy, so the wicked rumours ran.

Eva Farrell, Anna and Ben's busy mum, was no gardener.

She might be no gardener but Ben thought her absolutely marvellous. He'd been nearly seventeen when his dad had walked out on her. Seeing his mother's ashen face, her shock, he'd wanted to kill him; certainly wanted to go after him and ask him, man to man, what the hell he was playing at.

It was all to do with sex, of course, bound to be. The facts were that his dad had shacked up with this younger woman, the usual tale, but wouldn't you think a respectable GP like him would have known better?

Ben had wanted to go after him, have it out, get him to ditch the younger woman and come back to them but Eva persuaded him otherwise. It was too late, she told him, the damage was done and she wasn't sure she wanted her husband back anyway. She'd just thrown herself even more into her work and got on with her life and then, a year later, they'd received the news that Dad was dead. Of a sudden heart attack. Aged fifty-two. The new young wife was apparently devastated.

And so were they.

Another roller-coaster of emotions to cope with. It was a miracle that he'd managed to get the grades required for his medical course but in their family medicine came first.

And now, four years on, he was, in a strange way, enjoying the hard slog. He felt confident enough, secure in the knowledge that he was going to do what he most wanted to do in life. One thing was sure, he wasn't keen on getting married himself in case he found himself doing the very same thing. He did not want to risk doing that to a woman *he* loved.

At the moment, as he studied, Eva was engaged in painting the wall in the sitting-room when the phone jangled. She was rather keen on decorating, and one or other room was usually up for it.

'Get that, Ben!' her voice, deepish with a faint Welsh lilt, yelled out.

He sighed, his concentration disturbed, hoping that Anna would jump to it for Anna was very keen on answering telephones.

The phone sat on a replica eighteenth-century mahogany side table, together with a shrivelled plant, a tiny Egyptian figure and a couple of impassive pot cats. The Egyptian figure had been bought from a cheap souvenir stall in Cairo many moons ago on one of Eva's last romantic excursions with her husband before he took leave of his senses.

'Ben, for Christ's sake, get that damned phone!' Eva yelled again as it continued to ring. She wasn't on call and this number was ex-directory, so it was bound to be a personal call. Very likely for one of the children for she had few friends herself.

Up in her bedroom, Anna could hear the phone ringing, absorbed as she was in finishing off a 500-piece jigsaw of a Cornish harbour scene, filling in the sky to complete the pretty picture. At this point, she knew she could give in for the sky bits were all the same and extremely difficult, but she was not going to. Once you started a thing, you had to finish it. Farrell philosophy, so her mother said. She had distant memories of her father, happy ones despite what he had done, but he was rarely talked about because Ben got really cross and he did not feature in any of the photographs on display in the sitting-room.

She heard her mother yelling at Ben again and, sensing there would be no reply from him, Anna put the piece of jigsaw down and prepared to do her bit as the telephone continued to trill. Leaning on the banister rail, she saw her brother strolling towards the phone at last and her mother standing stormy-faced at the dining-room door, paintbrush in hand.

Ben, finally stirred into reluctant action, reached the instrument as if he had all the time in the world, picked it up, and chanted their number.

A girl's voice, identifying herself as Olivia, asked to speak to Anna. She was ringing, she said, from Bermuda and it was very expensive, so could he find her quickly? Please.

Bemused, he glanced up, spotted Anna and waved her down.

'Long distance. From Bermuda. Somebody called Olivia.'

Anna took hold of the phone as if it were a grenade.

'Is that you?' she said, hearing Olivia loud and clear. 'You sound like you're next door. Are you really there?'

'I've been here days. It's fabulous. Everything's so bright. Was that Ben? He has a nice voice.'

'Has he? Yes, that was him.' Anna smiled as he disappeared back into the dining-room. As usual, the summer holidays were proving to be chaotic. Why Mum had to try to do everything herself, such as painting and decorating, when Ben said they could easily afford to get somebody in was a mystery but that was Mum. She wouldn't let anybody help, not even Ben, because she said only she could do it properly. She never ever sat still. She never watched television, except *Upstairs, Downstairs* which she was hooked on, and rarely had time to read a book. They did have a lady, Mrs Parker, who came in once a week to tickle around with a duster, but her mother did everything else.

Mrs Parker told Anna that, in her opinion, Anna's mother, whom she always called 'the doctor', was nothing short of a miracle worker. She also told Anna that patients especially liked Dr Farrell at the surgery because she always managed to look nice and ordinary and country folk felt comfortable with that. Anna wasn't sure that was a compliment and decided not to mention it to her mother just in case she got upset, although she didn't think she would. Her mother wasn't like Olivia Hayton's, thank goodness: Olivia's mother had turned up last speech day dressed top to toe in lilac, wearing a hat, looking like the queen.

'Don't be long, love,' her mother reminded Anna, sweeping past, smelling of paint and turpentine.

Anna nodded, understanding the need for economy, and for a few breathless minutes all she and Olivia could speak about was Bermuda. The sea, Olivia said, was blue-green and the sand soft and pink.

'It sounds so beautiful. I wish I was there,' Anna said with a sigh, looking out of the window of Laburnum Cottage on to variously shaded green fields, at the rain slanting across them, at the heavy grey skies. 'You're so lucky, Olivia.'

From the window at her house, Olivia looked on to sparkling white roofs, pastel-shaded houses, blue sky and turquoise sea, and blinked back sudden tears.

CHAPTER FIVE

When Olivia was sixteen, she chose, for the first time, not to go out to visit her parents during the summer holidays. Anna had invited her to spend some time with her and it was agreed Olivia would do that rather than fly over to Toronto, where her parents were presently and very inharmoniously based.

'I can't understand you at all,' Anna told her, as they waited at school to be picked up. 'I wouldn't have missed out on a trip to Canada. Mum's just too busy to get much time off. We could afford to go. We're not exactly destitute.'

'I'm sure you're not,' Olivia said hastily, anxious not to pry into their circumstances, as she had been told that prying into other people's circumstances, particularly of the financial kind, was vulgar. 'Waiting around at airports is a pig, anyway,' she added, trying to be kind.

'I suppose you're right but I wouldn't mind finding out.'

Olivia smiled sympathetically.

'I wish my mum would get married again sometime,' Anna went on. 'Do you think there's a chance? She's not exactly pretty, is she?'

'Looks don't matter,' Olivia said, believing it implicitly. 'I like your mum,' she went on firmly. 'And she must meet lots of people in her job.'

Anna grinned. 'You're joking, she only meets sick people. Definitely not at their best. And she doesn't go out socially. So, there's not much chance.'

Olivia had explained as best she could the reason for not wanting to jet off to Canada, without revealing all her family secrets. The truth was her mother had left her father during the spring of that year, coming home to England, making a great fuss, accusing him of not caring and so on and then, after a couple of weeks, she had relented and gone back.

'Your father is impossible,' she told Olivia. 'All he ever thinks about is work. But he needs me. He really can't manage without me.'

But the situation being as it was – tender and fraught – Olivia thought it best to keep well out of the way and Anna's invitation was just what she had hoped for. They were going to be staying here and Anna was full of apologies for that but Olivia was looking forward to it.

'Come on, girls!' Miss Armitage's voice rang out from the corridor. 'Get a move on. Dr Farrell is downstairs waiting for you.'

Anna smiled encouragingly. 'Don't look so worried,' she said. 'Mum won't eat you.'

But outside, parked conspicuously in the no-parking zone, was Anna's brother rather than her mother, lounging against a big dark green car.

He straightened up as they approached and called out, 'About time, too. I thought you'd be anxious to be off.'

Anna, after a little whoop of surprise, flew at him, hugged him, and over her shoulder, he grinned down at Olivia.

Olivia, very into reading lurid romances just now, was bowled over. Dazed almost by the knock-out smile, she slightly lost her grip on her bag and it thudded into her leg, the strap catching her on the shin. She yelled out and promptly dropped it on her toe.

'Hey, look out – give that to me. . . .'

He fussed a minute and she caught Anna looking oddly at her, as if she had done it deliberately, which was ridiculous because her shin was tingling with pain and already starting to swell and bruise. For a moment, she did wonder if he might administer first aid but no such luck. Bashed shins and bruised toes obviously didn't feature high up in medical terms.

Goodness me, if he were the doctor here, she thought, the girls would all be racking their brains for some interesting illness to have. Something that didn't involve you looking completely rotten and being covered in spots.

'Ready? You'd better not have forgotten anything,' Ben said from the driving seat. 'Because I'm on a tight schedule and once we get started, there's going to be no turning back. Understood?'

'Shut up and get going and don't drive too fast,' Anna told him, smiling at Olivia. 'We're very organized, Ben. We haven't forgotten a thing.'

'OK, I believe you,' he said, glancing over his shoulder. 'Do we call you Olivia, Olivia? Or something else? A nickname?'

'Olivia, please,' she said quietly, her voice sounding strange. Only Dad called her Olly and Rosie Andrews had always called her Livvy. At least there would be no more of that. It was strange to think that next term Rosie would not be at Slyne Hall, for she had, for better or worse, got herself a job and said goodbye to them all.

'What are *you* doing here, anyway?' Anna asked him, once they were on their way. 'We were expecting Mum.'

'She got roped into an emergency practice conference,' Ben said cheerfully. 'You ought to be pleased. The landrover has seen better days.'

They laughed and Olivia, quiet, listened attentively to their trivial chat. She knew that Ben was working in a Lancashire hospital whilst he studied for his next qualification. It was a long hard haul becoming a surgeon but in four or five years, he hoped to make consultant, so Anna told her.

Shy of him, Olivia took the opportunity of watching him as he drove, a bit fast on the country lanes but with a lot of confidence. His hair curled long over his collar and she wondered what he looked like in a doctor's white coat. Pretty fantastic, she imagined. She wished she was looking more attractive for him, more grown up, even though she knew she would scarcely register with him, not a man of his age.

Olivia's room at Laburnum Cottage was dominated by a high narrow bed covered in blue gingham. The walls were hyacinth blue and, together with the quiet views, it was very restful.

'You'll just sink into the bed. Mum got it from a patient who died,' Anna told her with a smile. 'It's ages old, probably Victorian.'

Olivia glanced at it, wondering if the patient had actually died *in* it. It was a sobering thought and she decided not to ask in case it was confirmed.

'Mum's worried about whether you will want to go to church tomorrow?' Anna asked her as soon as she was unpacked and settled in. 'We don't usually but if you want to go then she says we'll all have to go.'

Olivia laughed. There was only one answer to that. She did go to church at school because they were compelled to do so and when she was visiting her parents she went because her mother thought they had a duty to represent the British community, wherever they happened to be.

'I'll give it a miss . . .' she said. 'We can have a lie-in.'

'Not much of one,' Anna said with a slight smile. 'Mum's going to go through some papers with me first thing. Old medical stuff. We're going to try to do an hour a day during the holidays. She says it will give me a head start.'

'Oh . . .'

'It's all right,' Anna said quickly. 'I don't mind. It's terribly important to her that I do well and I don't want to let her down – she never got over what happened with Dad. He just left one day, just like that, walked out on us all. I was too little, I suppose, to understand properly.'

Olivia smiled her sympathy, not entirely sure which of them was the worse off. Anna, even though she had no father, had a more settled home life than she did, but the pressure was building on Anna and just now, in an instant, she had let it show, as a shadow passed over her face. For Olivia, her exam results were hardly the end of the world and as she still had not the slightest idea what she wanted to do, their importance was diminished.

At the least, she would make more of her chances than Rosie had.

Olivia had felt a moment's pang as they said goodbye, wondering if they would ever meet up again. Rosie had got a job in Manchester at the television studios, where she intended to work her way up to managing director at the very least. She would still be living locally, so it was possible they might stay in touch, although as her mother said, her pursed lips saying it all, Rosie was best forgotten. That young woman led her life by the seat of her pants.

There was no point in worrying on Rosie's behalf. Somehow Olivia felt she would survive and perhaps even make it. As for herself, she was confident, *fairly* confident, she would do well enough, well enough to be welcomed into the sixth form anyway and those final exams for college were two years away.

Just now, at sixteen, two years seemed like a lifetime.

CHAPTER SIX

Olivia, at nearly eighteen, was the same quiet, thoughtful girl and, despite Judith's encyclopaedic knowledge that she had imparted to her daughter, she had recently lost what little interest she had in clothes, content to muck about – as Judith called it – in patched jeans and baggy tops, a disgusting camouflage jacket, and on her feet, horror of mother horrors, Doc Martens.

Sitting at her desk in the house in Chester, supposedly revising, Olivia tried to damp down a growing panic. The plan, at the start of the Easter break, was that, armed with a bucketful of ghastly addictive Cadbury's creme eggs, she would crack the backbone of the studying, get to grips with it and whip it into shape. But the days that stretched dreamily into the distance at the beginning of the holidays were drawing short. On the positive side, and she clung on to that, she had two more weeks, and tomorrow her parents were flying off on holiday, so she would be no longer distracted by her mother's somewhat late maternal flutterings.

This large, shambling, sloping-ceilinged room and the fact that it was hers, all hers, gave her some comfort. Surprisingly quickly, within months of returning home for good, her mother had made the old house home once more. Dismayed at the state the last tenants had left it in, she had swooped on it, armed with swatches of fabric and wallpapers, and transformed it. Some things remained the same but they were hard to spot, jolting Olivia sometimes as she caught sight of an odd corner and saw herself crouching there as a sort of ghost-child.

Mementoes of their time abroad were scattered round the house. After the stint in Bermuda, there had been lengthy spells in the States, three months in Toronto, and then it was back to Europe and a more mundane period based in

Scotland, in Edinburgh, which her mother thought too grey and Gothic, full of cobbles and Jack the Ripper alleys. However, it did have saving graces and Judith was charmed by the shopping in Princes Street and, for a short while, discovered a Scottish look with kilts and cashmere sweaters.

But it was not all froth and fun.

During the last couple of years, her mother had left her father three times in all, returning home to Chester in high dudgeon, calling Olivia on the telephone on each tearful occasion and insisting on telling all about something that Olivia could have been none the wiser about, for her father said not a word.

When the Edinburgh contract expired, though, there was the chance of an exciting longer term appointment in Perth, Australia. At this, her mother put her foot very firmly down and said no. Soon after that, her father took up a senior post at a company based on the outskirts of Manchester, and if he did regret the loss of their more exciting way of life, he never said.

Shortly afterwards, they returned home to Chester.

'Will you please explain to Mum,' Olivia asked her father, collaring him in the dining-room. 'Tell her there's no way I'm going to get those Bs. I'm going to be lucky to scrape passes.'

Deliberately, with just the slightest of sighs, George Hayton folded and put down his newspaper. He was in his late fifties now and Olivia could never be sure how happy he was with the job he had settled for, following the ultimatum from Judith. Not as happy as he had been, she suspected.

'Poor Judith,' he said. 'Your mother's set her heart on having a daughter who's a doctor or a lawyer or at the very least a top executive. She has plans for you, darling. She had a yen to be a top-class civil servant, you know, all ambition thwarted when she married me, as she likes to remind me from time to time.'

'I know. That's what makes it so awful.'

He patted the seat beside him. 'Sit down and tell me why you think they'll be poor grades. You've been working hard recently. If you need my help, just say.'

'That's OK, Dad. In theory, I've got it all organized. If only I could stick to the plan.'

He smiled his nice smile. 'I never stick to plans. Do what you really want, go where the fancy takes you. That should be your philosophy in life.'

She thought again of her mother's ultimatum, the way she had put a stop to the travelling and watched as the smile faded. Poor Dad. Had a wife the right to stamp down on her husband's ambitions or vice versa? Difficult one, that, and she didn't know the answer.

'Don't worry,' her father said again, and she gave him a grateful smile. 'It's not the end of the world if you completely flunk them. It will be a slight setback, of course,' he added, 'although I don't know how much you want to go to university. Are you going because you want to or because it's expected of you?'

She shrugged. 'Because everybody else is going. It seems the right thing to do.'

He looked relieved at that. 'If you do miss your grades, we'll look into that secretarial course again and that and your personality will get you a job, believe me. After that, it's up to you.'

'I'm not very bubbly,' she said doubtfully. Didn't having a 'personality' mean being bright and shining and making everybody glance your way, even when you had nothing much to say? Rosie had a *personality*, for heaven's sake!

'No, you're not always bubbly,' her father agreed with a fond smile. 'You're rather thoughtful, my love. But you're intelligent – forget about passing exams, that's just technique – and you have a good background.'

'Background,' she said with a sigh. 'You sound like Mum. Does that still matter? What school you went to?'

'Yes,' he said, quite sharply. 'You bet your life it does. Perhaps it ought not to matter but there it is. Trust me. I've interviewed an awful lot of people for jobs and I know what's looked for. Most firms are crying out for young ladies like you.'

She grimaced at that – young lady indeed!

'Young ladies like you,' he went on, unperturbed. 'With a good clear voice, pleasant accent, and, believe me, all your travelling when you were a child will stand you in good stead. It makes for a colourful CV, a talking point, and you must make the most of it at an interview. Anyway, apart from anything else, you're beautiful and that's worth two of a fast typing speed any day.'

She smiled. Every girl's father thought her beautiful!

'You will be all right whilst we're away, won't you?' her father asked, checking his watch and rising. 'Your mother's starting to panic about what you'll be eating.'

'A balanced diet,' she said with a grin. 'Loads of salads and fresh fruit, gallons of orange juice. Tell her that. And then she won't worry. . . .'

'Even if it's not true? Do I hear the rustle of fish and chip papers and take-away cartons already?'

'I won't starve and for goodness' sake don't breathe a word, Dad, or she'll have Mrs Wilson coming in and making me meals, standing over me while I eat.'

'No wild parties, I hope?'

'Wild parties? No such luck.'

'A final word of advice,' he added, on his way out. 'if it comes to an interview, Olly, ditch the Doc Martens.'

She laughed. She had been meaning to do that for a while but was waiting for the right moment, waiting for her mother to stop making such a big issue out of them.

Why did you have to be so frantically busy with exams at such an exciting time of your life? Boyfriends were out for the moment. No time. It was not all innocence and she listened, as wide-eyed as the rest, when one or two of the other girls told *all* about their sexual activities. It amazed her that they could be so open and frank about it, for she was sure that she would want to keep her love life, if she had one of any significance, to herself. There'd been a few encounters, kissing and fumbling in a corner at a party, but nothing to set her pulse racing.

Rosie Andrews was already having a proper affair. She had moved in with this man, according to the letter she had put in Olivia's Christmas card that year, and it was heaven. Not only did she love him to distraction but she had got a promotion at the studios. There was a phone number and a PS asking Olivia to keep in touch.

She had meant to phone, catch up on things, but made the mistake of hesitating, whereupon she managed to lose the number, so that was that. Rosie knew where she was, so Rosie could make the effort if she really wanted. And if *she* really wanted, she could ring Rosie's mum and find out the number.

She admitted to a certain jealousy. It was time, high time, she discovered what it was all about, but it really was not possible to devote yourself with any great enthusiasm to sexual discovery when you were thinking about the essay that should have been in last week. There was also the nagging problem of actually meeting up with a boy she fancied, for most of the boys she knew fell into two categories. Too shy or too sure and all of them were just too physically unappealing. There was nobody in between, unless you counted Ben Farrell, of course. Try as she might, she couldn't quite forget him, even though she hadn't seen him more than a couple of times in the last two years and that merely in passing.

He still strode often into her dreams, however, which was too bad of him. Under a romantic cloud, she had re-read *Rebecca* recently, glued to it when she ought to have been studying. She had read it first as a young girl, loving the beauty of the words, but now that she was older, she understood it more, relishing that wonderful moment when the shy heroine saw him – the hero – for the very first time in the dining-room of the hotel Cote d'Azur in Monte Carlo.

It was hard not to think of herself as that shy heroine and Ben as Max de Winter. After all, wasn't it true that her heart had jumped at the first sight of him? Didn't it still do so, sneakily, whenever Anna mentioned him in passing? Didn't she take note of every move in his career? Didn't she still hold on to some slender hope that, when they met the next time, he would be as transfixed as she?

Sweet silly dreams.

'You need to go out to places,' Judith Hayton said, bringing the vexed subject up, as Olivia helped her pack for her holiday. The hotel was five-stars according to the brochure, and it had better be up to scratch or else. Judith's immediate problem was how many pairs of shoes she could reasonably get away with. Harassed, she held up two pairs. 'Which do you think, darling?'

'Take the silver,' Olivia said instantly, putting no thought into it, wondering if they would ever be finished in time. Every single item had to be assessed like this and every single time Olivia's choice was overruled.

Her mother nodded sagely, as if she was considering the matter, before packing the cream. 'The point is, Olivia, how can you be seen if you stay in the whole time?'

'I'm studying for exams, Mum.'

'As if we didn't know.' She sighed deeply. 'Getting yourself dressed up and going out would do you a world of good. You'd come back to the studying revitalized. You have to circulate. Why do you think they went to Bath in all those Jane Austen novels? Not because they were remotely interested in taking the spa water, but because they were on the lookout for young men. And that was the place to find them. All those wonderful balls.' She trailed beautifully manicured hands over some flimsy evening wear. 'I wish I'd lived in those days. The ladies were so gracious. Peeping from behind a fan. And those dresses were so flattering. They showed off a good bosom.' She eyed Olivia with distaste. 'Look at you. Nobody can tell whether you have a bosom. And hardly any make-up. You just don't try...' She paused, glancing at herself in the mirror. Her hair was shorter now with an auburn tint, medium length, cut at enormous expense because it involved a trip into town plus an elaborate lunch at The Grosvenor and anything else she might pick up from the shops. 'Once you turn eighteen, it's a constant battle against time. Look at me. Who would think I was nearly fifty?'

'No one,' said Olivia gallantly. 'You're wearing well, Mum.'

Judith gave her a look. 'I'm overdue a nip and tuck but I think you ought to grow old gracefully . . .'

'So do I.'

'Of course my skin's not been helped with all those hours in the sun I used to suffer,' her mother went on. 'To think, we once thought sunshine was good for you and now we find that not only does it give you premature wrinkles, it also gives you skin cancer. I tell you, I was permanently frizzled, darling. At least you know where you are here.'

They looked out on to a cold spring day, the sky thick and heavy with cloud, the whole of Chester sitting in a grey haze under it, even the late spring flowers looking very subdued. And here was Mum, packing to go somewhere hot and sunny and complaining in advance.

Olivia knew what she meant, though. She was rooted here, firmly rooted at that, roots spreading deep and wide and gripping and never letting loose. Even if she was pulled forcibly away, tiny bits of her would remain for ever.

After all this time, she still occasionally thought about Mr Johnson, the old gardener at school, feeling oddly that he was up there, watching her. She had seriously considered a horticultural course but her mother was so against the idea – gumboots and dirty nails – and even her father oddly lukewarm, that it was just not worth the hassle of a full-blown family row.

Olivia did work hard the two weeks her parents were away in Cyprus, and there were no wild parties, not even tame ones, but it was all in vain.

Judith was initially devastated, going into hibernation for days after the results were announced rather than face people, but thereafter she quickly recovered.

''Who needs exams, anyway?' she said. 'I don't want you ending up as a hard-edged businesswoman. I've met far too many women of that ilk recently, go-getters, padded shoulders, hard as steel, and it's faintly depressing. Women must never lose sight of the fact that a softer feminine image is a formidable weapon.'

Olivia glanced at her with amusement, for Judith had more than enough suits with outrageously over-padded shoulders, but she appreciated that for once her mother was trying her best to be understanding.

'You're not that sort, darling,' her mother continued firmly. 'You're like your father. He has trouble sacking people and you would find it utterly impossible and that, sadly, is what senior people have to do. You have to have a ruthless streak or you get nowhere in this world. I shall see I will have to find you a man.'

'You will do no such thing, Mother,' Olivia said, appalled.

Her mother took no notice of her indignation and aired the subject again quite cheerfully at breakfast next morning.

It stopped her father in mid-Weetabix. 'Good God, Judith!' he said. 'The girl's perfectly capable of finding her own man and don't forget, she is only eighteen. I would have thought getting married was the last thing on her mind. She told me once that she's not getting married until she's past thirty. Are you, Olly?'

He winked at Olivia as he said it, before returning innocent eyes to his wife.

'That's what I used to say and look at me,' her mother said, exchanging a small private smile with him. 'Nevertheless, there's no harm in casting the net, and who better than me to do the sifting through? Olivia's been too sheltered, spending all her time at that incompetent school. She's far too gullible and too young for her years.'

'I am not,' Olivia protested, saved from being angry by the amused restraining glance her father shot her way.

'And I shudder...' her mother went on, in full flow now. 'I shudder to think how you reacted to Gloria's son. You were downright rude. I know he's a little older but thirty-three is a wonderful age for a man to marry. Richard has adored you from afar for years.'

'Has he?' Olivia asked, totally mystified.

'He has indeed,' Judith plunged on resolutely. 'He's Chester born and bred, from a very good family, as you well know, and he will take over the business eventually. Gloria and Hugh play bridge, for goodness sake—'

Her father jumped in at that. 'What the hell has that got to do with it?'

Judith looked at him with that familiar wifely look. 'It shows the sort of people they are. It's an interesting circuit to get into. There's something very intellectual about bridge. We could play, George, if only you would apply your-self.'

'I could,' he said tartly. 'You couldn't, my darling. You have trouble with snap.'

Her mother managed a tight smile. 'Is that supposed to be amusing?' She turned to Olivia, exasperated. 'What's wrong with Richard? He's reasonably good looking.'

'Nothing's wrong with him,' Olivia said, with a shrug. 'Not exactly. He's a perfectly nice man but a bit boring. He could end up boring me to death.'

'Boring?' Judith huffed. 'That's what marriage is all about. If it's excitement you're after once you're married, you have to take a lover.'

There was a short, ringing silence.

'Leave her, for God's sake,' her father said, smiling and choosing to ignore the stinging rebuff he had just been dished out. 'She's right. He is boring. And he's not good enough for Olly. She needs somebody a bit more dynamic, somebody to draw her out of herself.'

Olivia looked at him gratefully, even if the compliment – if it was one – was a little two-edged. She was aware she was not a life and soul of the party person but it was hard to change your basic personality.

After all, she was her father's daughter.

Anna Farrell achieved the results she expected, straight As, and her place at Leeds to read medicine was assured.

To her slightest disappointment, congratulations from her mother were muted. Anna knew that anything other than A grades would have been a tremendous shock, but even so it would have been nice to be commended, to be told – wasn't this so silly? – that she was a clever girl.

Thank goodness, Ben was a bit more enthusiastic when she rang him.

'Well done,' he said cheerfully when she had duly chanted them out. 'Very well done. Not that I expected anything else but you never know – the examiner can have a brainstorm and mark you down for no reason.'

She smiled, pleased at his obvious delight.

'You're on track, Anna,' he went on. 'In some ways, you've got the worst bit over. All you have to do now is work hard, enjoy yourself, and you're as good as there.'

'You make it sound easy,' she said. 'And I know it's not.'

'Of course it's not easy,' he admitted, sounding suddenly earnest. 'But you wouldn't want that, would you? Aim for the big time, won't you? Don't end up a GP like Mum. She's a cracking GP but it's not for me or you.' He paused. 'You're not thinking of taking a year off before you start, I hope. Get stuck in straightaway before you change your mind.'

'Why should I change my mind?' She laughed at the absurdity of that. 'I might take a year out,' she added, hearing him catch his breath. 'Sorry, but I'd like to do something completely different for a while. Charity work, maybe. Something hard and physical. Something where I feel I'm doing some good.'

His sigh was deep. 'Oh God, I might have known. What does Mum say?'

'She's not happy,' Anna admitted. 'Like you. But she says all right if it's what I want. I have the money I got from Dad, so that will see me through the year. I don't know why you're getting so het up. My place isn't going to go away.'

'All right, do it if you must, but don't for heaven's sake get involved with anybody in the meantime,' he said, taking on the fatherly role he sometimes rather sweetly felt he ought to don. 'You could end up getting married and giving up all thoughts of medicine and, if you do, you'll regret it later.'

'Ben, please, give me some credit,' she said with a little laugh, not at all put out by his concern. 'That won't happen.'

'Sorry. Of course it won't. You're not the sort to go starry-eyed.'

'Mum thinks it's high time you got yourself a serious girlfriend, Ben,' she went on.

He laughed but it was a touch forced. 'I'll do that when I'm ready.'

'I jolly well hope so.' Anna laughed too. 'I'm going to be a bit elderly to be a bridesmaid soon. *Little* girls look pretty but big girls like me can look awful,' she added, a vision appearing of herself in a plum frilly concoction.

'You could be very elegant,' he said quickly. 'It's just a question, so I'm told, of choosing the right clothes.'

She frowned, knowing precisely what he meant. With her shape, she had to go in for disguise.

'Look . . .' he hesitated a minute and then shot on. 'If you want a loan to get yourself some new clothes, you only have to say. I'm not exactly flush just now, not with buying the car, but I can let you have a few hundred.'

'Thanks but no. I wouldn't dream of it,' she said briskly, before she changed her mind.

'How did your friends get on? Any surprises? How about Olivia?'

'Olivia crashed, I'm afraid. But she won't re-sit. Her father's persuaded her to do some sort of secretarial course. I think she's wasted on it. She ought to re-sit.'

'Pity,' he mused. 'Thoughtful sort of girl. Give her my regards if you see her. Tell her it's not the end of the world. Looking like she does, something will turn up.'

'I'm not sure I will tell her that,' Anna said, finding herself more than a little bemused.

She wasn't sure when she would next meet up with Olivia. The thing was, with her planning to go off somewhere and Olivia starting on her secretarial course in Chester, they wouldn't see so much of each other. They promised to write but then Rosie had promised that and there hadn't been a single letter in two years. She'd heard on the grapevine though that she was already involved with a man.

Anna was in no great rush herself. Ben was right. Falling in love would just get in the way of study, but chance, as they say, would be a fine thing too. She had to face the fact that she was plain with a bulky nose no amount of powder could disguise. But that was not the most important thing in life. Far from it.

Trust Rosie Andrews to be the first of them to have a serious fling – but then that was Rosie. As for Olivia, well, Anna was just the teeniest bit jealous of

Olivia's good fortune in being so pretty and having such a sweet gentle nature to boot.

She would try to maintain contact but Anna felt that perhaps childhood friendships were best forgotten. They had to move on, grow up, lead their own lives, let go.

And, with stage one of her plan successfully completed, with her medical course ready and waiting in a year's time, her life was already very neatly mapped out.

CHAPTER SEVEN

Second best it might be but Olivia thoroughly enjoyed her secretarial course and put her heart into it. Entirely on her own merit, she landed a job in an architect's office in the centre of Chester, not quite running the place completely, although her mother liked to pretend she did.

One of her colleagues at work had a boyfriend who worked for Granada studios and he wangled an invitation not only for her but a couple more for Olivia and 'guest' to attend a plush reception to celebrate the setting up of a new television company. The party was just an excuse, he said, for a booze-up and a chance for the girls to wear their posh frocks.

At first Olivia said no. For a start, at the moment she had no 'guest' to take.

She had enjoyed a few relationships over the last couple of years, for no other reason than it was pleasant to be taken out for a meal, to the theatre, to be told she was beautiful, to walk under a starry summer sky and to pretend for a while that it was all romantic bliss. She was still young and there was so much time. There was no need for panic, even if her mother acted as if she was in the last-chance saloon.

For the launch party at the studios, Olivia was finally fixed up – gritted teeth time – with a blind date, and it was only because her mother had treated her to a fabulous new dress, a slinky burgundy number with a daring low back, that she agreed to go.

The blind date was predictably a disaster – acknowledged by them both – and they ditched each other in an agreeable enough fashion soon after they arrived. The room was already crowded and there were a lot of 'singles' hanging around so she would not be conspicuous. Noting that the buffet was pretty sensational, Olivia sidled towards it and was just reaching across when a hand landed on her arm and a voice loudly announced for all the world to hear, 'Livvy Hayton! What the hell are you doing here?'

Olivia spun round. She'd know that voice anywhere.

Rosie . . . Little Rosie Andrews!

She was slight as ever with flame-coloured hair, wild and curly, and eyes large in her delicate face. Despite towering heels. she was still so very tiny but she looked sensational, cleverly made up, her voice raucous as ever.

'What are *you* doing here?' Olivia echoed as they gave each other a delighted hug in a great clash of perfume.

'I work here, darling,' Rosie said, eyes twinkling, a glass in one hand, cigarette in the other. 'It's great to see you. You look fabulous. Very elegant.'

'So do you,' Olivia said with a knowing smile that only very old friends can give each other. 'Where *did* you get that dress?' she added in an undertone. 'I've never seen anything quite like it.'

'Not telling,' Rosie said firmly. 'Or everybody will be there.'

'Hardly.' Olivia gave up the pretence and frowned at it. 'It's certainly different. Is it taffeta?'

'Pure fifties. They were practically giving it away. The charity shop almost paid me for taking it off their hands. They found it stuffed in a cupboard at this old dear's house when she died. Crying shame, isn't it?'

Olivia smiled, tempted to say it might have been better to leave it where it was.

'Individuality,' Rosie murmured. 'That's the name of the game, Livvy. I want somebody – preferably a man with money – to say at the end of this evening, "Who the hell was that gorgeous redhead wearing that shocking-pink ball-gown?" '

They laughed, Olivia deciding that, on second thoughts, her own dark dress was maybe a mite safe.

'Do you see Anna at all?' Rosie asked.

Olivia shook her head. 'I'm afraid not. We seem to have lost touch.'

'Look . . . ' Rosie stubbed out her cigarette on a convenient saucer. 'Lets find a quiet corner. Have a natter . . . or are you with someone?'

'I *was* with someone.' Olivia pulled a face. 'Dead loss. I'd rather talk to you.'

'Good. Grab something to eat and we'll refill our glasses. And I'll fill you in on everything that's been happening.'

It was quite a story, the rise and subsequent fall of her love affair, but then Rosie had always been extraordinarily good at telling stories. How much of it was true was of course debatable but just occasionally she let the mask slip and Olivia was left with the impression that Rosie's tempestuous love affair had been – at least on Rosie's part – very much the real thing.

'The awful thing is we still work together,' Rosie went on with a grimace. 'And how can you take someone seriously if you've had it off with him? We even did it on the office desk once. We knew we would be interrupted if we didn't get on with it fast, so you can just imagine . . .'

Olivia laughed, not quite believing it. Although, knowing Rosie. . . .

'I daren't look him in the eye,' she continued with a sigh. 'Not properly, and I'm still jealous as hell if he so much as looks at somebody else. Crazy, isn't it? How do you mend a broken heart?' she finished with a dramatic flourish.

'I'm sorry, Rosie. I can't help much. I haven't met anybody yet who I'm mad about,' Olivia told her apologetically. 'I've had a few boyfriends but never anyone serious. When you live at home, it isn't easy to bring anyone back for a coffee and things.'

'Jesus, Livvy, you're not telling me you still live at home?'

'Well, yes,' Olivia said, wishing she didn't have to apologize for everything.

'I got out as soon as I could,' Rosie said with a shudder, eyeing her sternly. 'Come on, then, when are you planning to get a place of your own?'

'Next year, maybe,' Olivia said, although she hadn't given the matter much thought.

'Why not now?' Rosie stuffed a tiny creamy savoury into her mouth and licked her lips. 'Hey, I've just had this fantastic thought. I'm on the lookout for something, too, and I could do with someone to chip in with the rent. How about it? You and me? It'd be great, wouldn't it?'

'Yes, but I'm looking for something in Chester,' Olivia said, trying to sound regretful.

'So am I. Home sweet home. I'm sick to the back teeth of Manchester.'

'Oh, I see. You're going to commute, then?'

'Why not? It's no great hassle,' Rosie said, puffing on her cigarette. 'I have an old car that just about gets me from A to B. Do you drive, Livvy?'

'Just passed my test,' she said proudly.

'And I suppose Mummy has bought you a car?'

Olivia glanced sharply at her. Just for a moment, she was reminded that Rosie had always resented that aspect of her life, the one Olivia could not help, the fact being that she was from a family with money. In fact, her *dad* had bought her a car, a brand new small car, and she drove it carefully and still, regrettably, a touch nervously.

'Sorry,' Rosie muttered, sensing the cooling. 'Ignore me. It's just that making your own way in this world when your parents haven't a bean and are always on about it is bloody difficult. I keep telling them they should never have bothered forking out all those school fees for what good it did me. Anyway, the fact is,

Livvy, I have to get a flat soon.'

Later, Olivia was to blame the wine, the party atmosphere and Rosie's infectious enthusiasm for making her say 'yes' to what was on reflection a very dubious idea.

And yet, if she didn't share with Rosie, she would have to find someone else and sharing with a complete stranger was not something she looked forward to.

Better the devil you know had never seemed a more apt saying.

'Good evening, ladies.'

They looked round and up into the face of an immaculately dressed, bearded man, fortyish, someone Rosie obviously recognized because she switched on at once, happily dipping into flirt mode with one very wide pink-lipped smile.

'Henry Chambers,' Rosie said, introducing him to Olivia, as if Olivia should know who Henry Chambers was.

They shook hands. Henry was not especially handsome, although he did have eyes of a fabulous cool blue, but in his handshake there was a firmness and in his manner a confidence that was *very* attractive. He was circulating, working the now sweaty, crowded room and within a few minutes, he was politely and discreetly excusing himself and firing off his charm elsewhere.

'My God,' Rosie said, paling as he left. 'Did I put my foot in it? Did I overdo the flirting? Did I look truly stupid? Oh, Livvy, why can't I be cool and unconcerned like you? You've got a very Grace Kelly look. Has anybody ever told you that?'

'What are you talking about? I don't look the least like her. For one, I'm not blonde.' Olivia stared after the departing figure. 'Who is he?'

'He's what this party's about. He's the head of Chameleon, this new company. Just one of the things he does. He's into communications, electronics, you name it. Multi-millionaire,' she added, lips twitching, eyes shining. 'He was on the list of top earners last year.'

'Oh, I see.'

'He's recently divorced,' Rosie went on, completing the potted history, 'although he's dating a model. She's not here tonight but she's one of those damned blondes with legs that go on for ever.'

Olivia shook her head, trying not to smile at little short-legged Rosie's agony.

'Give it a miss, Rosie,' she said gently. 'Anyway, he must be well into his forties.'

'You're right,' Rosie said with a sigh. 'Although I do have a yen for older men. Mind you, I'm aiming high. No more creeps for me. Now, where were we. . . ?'

The search for the perfect flat took a while but it gave them time to get to know each other again and to marvel at how little they had changed. Rosie was every bit as carefree, and laughed as she said that Livvy was absolutely as *stuffy* and sensible as she had ever been.

'Funny, isn't it? Fate. If we hadn't met accidentally, we'd probably never have met up again,' Rosie said, stopping the car in the narrow street near the race-course. 'Is this it?'

Olivia consulted the paper and nodded. 'Number twenty-four. That one with the blue door.'

'Looks promising. I love that colour of blue.'

Rosie was already out of the car, exuberantly clad in pink and orange, white leather laced boots just showing under an ankle-length hem, an emerald and orange chiffon scarf adding to the general air of colourful confusion. Beside her, in plain black pants and cream top, Olivia felt her usual safe self. Her mother might call them an odd couple but somehow the chalk and cheese effect worked superbly.

And, at long last, they seemed to have hit the jackpot. The flat was fine, the furniture OK, and best of all they would be in charge of the small courtyard garden. That sold it for Olivia and a quick successful haggle about the rent sold it for Rosie.

They were signed and ready to move in within the week.

Her mother was predictably appalled.

'I can accept you moving out,' she said, reluctantly helping with the packing. 'Good gracious, you're old enough and you ought to have your independence. But sharing with Rosie, I ask you!' she shot an impatient glance towards her husband. 'Tell her, George. Isn't she making a big mistake?'

'She's old enough to know her own mind,' her father said with a smile. 'When will you learn to leave her be, Judith?'

Her mother could rant all she wanted but Olivia's mind was made up and with her father helping to smooth the way, her mother at last kissed her and wished her luck, making a sudden unexpected fuss as if Olivia was emigrating instead of merely moving a short distance to the other side of town.

'Congratulations! You've cut free,' Rosie told her that evening. 'At last. God knows how you've put up with her for all these years. Do you remember how Miss Armitage used to scurry after her, apologizing if everything wasn't quite up to scratch?'

'It's just her way,' Olivia said defensively.

'I know. Just teasing.'

Olivia nodded. 'It was a bit hard living at home,' she admitted finally. 'Mind you, she's never in these days, now that she practically runs the council...'

They smiled. Judith had an inflated view of her importance in the local scheme of things, which seemed to involve huffing and puffing her way through council meetings, splendidly attired in a rapidly growing selection of business suits and ominous handbags.

'You've got to grab hold of your freedom and I'm the person to show you how,' Rosie went on. 'And the first thing we're going to do is get ourselves a love life.'

'Easier said than done,' Olivia said gloomily.

Rosie collapsed on to the sofa, legs bent under her in that strangely loose-limbed way of hers. 'Can I let you into a secret?'

'Go on.'

'I'm on a mission. I've decided that love, being in love, is a loser and so I'm on the lookout for a man with money, Livvy. Serious money. And you know why? I'm sick to death of having bugger all in the bank at the end of the month. As for the overdraft...' She sighed. 'Least said the better.'

Olivia did sympathize but, honestly, as she was to find out over the next few months, Rosie spent her money on the oddest things, such as antique jewellery that in no way could be termed essential. She was waiting for the day when she would be asked for a sub to pay the rent and worried a little about that because she wasn't sure how to say no without causing Rosie to go off in one of her spectacular huffs.

As to their love life, that settled very quickly into a 'nothing doing' rut for both of them. Olivia shrugged it off, content enough to be off men for the moment. She looked back on her few relationships – such as they were – as practice sessions for the real thing. After all, you had to know what you *didn't* want before you knew what you did.

Rosie, desperate for travel – anywhere would do – was forever asking her about her many trips abroad.

'Where in the world have you *not* been?' she asked her one evening, a dinner plate balanced on her knee.

Olivia twiddled a piece of pasta on her fork and popped it into her mouth. 'Where have I not been? Lots of places. Africa. India. China. I've been to most of Europe though, the States, Canada and a few other places. Just brief visits mostly.'

'Just brief visits mostly....' Rosie mimicked, tomato sauce on her cheek. 'God, Livvy, I never stepped out of Chester when I was young. I thought you stepped off the edge of the world when you got to the city walls.'

'Liar!'

'All right, I might have gone to places in Wales and maybe Scotland but nowhere else of any significance.'

'Travel is overrated.'

'Oh, sure.' Rosie rubbed at her cheek, making it worse. 'People who say that have got passports full to bursting with places they've visited. When I marry my millionaire, the first thing I'm going to do is a trip round the world. I want to see *everywhere.*'

They subsided into silence, finishing their meal, thinking about Rosie's millionaire.

'But could you really marry for money?' Olivia asked at last, concerned that Rosie might actually be talking herself into the idea. It had started as a joke but was gaining momentum. 'Just think of the problems.'

'And just think of the money,' Rosie said dreamily. 'Obviously it would be quite nice if he was reasonably attractive but that's asking a lot, don't you think? By the time they get to the top rank, they're usually losing their hair and gaining weight round the middle. It's the stress. It's all about ratings, ratings, ratings.'

'But wouldn't it be like . . .' Olivia hesitated, keen to get to the bottom of this. 'I'm trying to think what it would be like to marry somebody you didn't love. What I mean is, wouldn't it feel like—'

'Prostitution?' Rosie butted in bluntly. 'No, it would not. If I do meet him, I'll hold out for marriage. And believe me or not, once I do get married, that's it. Faithful to the end. Playing around when you're in a relationship just doesn't work and I'm talking practicality here. I hope you're listening, Livvy, because that's sensible advice from Auntie Rosie.'

Olivia laughed. 'How old are you? I can't believe you're only the same age as me, Rosie. You act like you're at least *thirty*-five sometimes.'

'A serious relationship puts years on you,' Rosie said soberly. 'I feel thirty-five.'

'I couldn't do it. Get married for money.'

Rosie regarded her calmly. 'No, you couldn't. You're far too honest for your own good and you've also got a rose-tinted view of marriage and romance. It doesn't happen like that. Or, if it does . . .' She sighed. 'Bloody hell, you've made me think of you know who. Thanks a bunch, Livvy.'

'Sorry.' Briskly, Olivia started to clear away. 'I just wish you'd let love stand a chance. You never know who's round the next corner.'

'Come shopping with me tomorrow,' Rosie said, as they washed up. 'I've seen this utterly gorgeous silver brocade evening dress in that nearly new designer shop.'

'Silver brocade? That sounds very practical,' Olivia said with a smile.

'Practical? Who wants practical?' Rosie laughed. 'If I'm going to snare my millionaire, I have to wear something stunning. Why not silver brocade? It'll be just perfect for this little party I'm going to at the studios. Everyone will be there and I'm not going to waste the opportunity. I shall wear sequins in my hair. A little eccentricity gets you noticed.' She cast a despairing glance at Olivia. 'We've got to get you toned up, Miss Totally Beige. I don't understand you. You live in magnolia and that belongs to sitting-room walls.'

'I can't help it. It's a reaction to my mum,' Olivia told her 'You know what she's like.'

'A smart lady.' Rosie shuddered theatrically, tossing the tea-towel aside with a flourish. 'Lord preserve us from smart women with high heels and big handbags.'

Olivia smiled and finished at the sink, looking out on to their tiny courtyard. 'Have you thought any more about plants, Rosie? We could have some troughs and window boxes and hanging baskets.'

'Whatever for? Hanging baskets belong outside olde-worlde pubs, not in back yards.' Rosie glanced at the clock, gave an agonized yell, and flew back into the sitting-room to zap the television on. 'If I'd known you were going to turn out to be so domesticated,' she yelled, 'I would never have let you move in with me.'

Olivia laughed. 'You are an idiot, Rosie. No wonder my mother loves you so much.'

'And I love *her*,' Rosie said. 'She has such presence. She'd have made a great actress, such a carrying voice. Forget Maggie Thatcher, your mother's going to be the next PM. She's already got her toe in the water. She'll be running the council before you know what's what.'

'If only . . .' Olivia sobered. Teasing her mum was all very well but sometimes with Rosie it hovered on the edge of real insult and Olivia was not sure she liked that.

Rosie noticed. She straightened her face, stopping short of an apology.

'Go on, then . . .' She lowered the TV sound a notch and, *Coronation Street* faded momentarily. 'You frustrated gardener! I'll go halfers. But nothing too extravagant and don't expect me to remember to water the damn things.'

'Thanks. I'll have a tenner from you.'

'Ten pounds? For plants?'

'That's being economical,' Olivia told her with a smile. 'Leave it to me. It will look like Kew Gardens come the weekend.'

Rosie groaned. 'What have I let myself in for?' She snuggled on to the sofa in her usual TV viewing position, knees at an impossible angle. 'I could kill for a cigarette. You don't have any, do you, Livvy?'

'You know I don't smoke,' she said with a laugh. 'I thought you'd given up.'

'I have. For ever and ever. Did you say yes to shopping tomorrow?'

'No. I can't afford to buy anything,' she said, declining to point out that, at this late stage in the month, neither could Rosie.

The telephone interrupted them and Rosie somehow flipped forward and reached for it, pulling a face and handing it to Olivia.

'For you,' she said regretfully, silently mouthing the words 'a man'.

'Hello, Olivia, Ben Farrell here,' the man said, and recognizing the voice at once, she very nearly dropped the receiver. 'Sorry to bother you but I rang the only number I have for you and spoke to your mother. I didn't know you had a place of your own, although if I'd thought about it, I might have guessed. How are you these days?'

'Fine, Ben,' she said, hearing her voice squeak, aware of Rosie listening in. 'What a surprise! I haven't heard from Anna for ages.'

'I'm surprised you remember *me*,' he said lightly.

'I remember you very well,' she said, trying to be brisk and businesslike and also trying to ignore Rosie's grin.

'The thing is . ' he said, and she noticed the hesitation, 'I'm up in Chester the weekend after next, and I wonder if we might meet up for lunch on the Saturday?'

'Lunch? On the Saturday?' she echoed stupidly. She was wearing old sweatpants and an equally ancient top, her hair was messed up and she had no make-up on. Somehow, she felt Ben knew this. If she'd known he was going to phone, ridiculous as it was, she would have put some lip gloss on at the very least.

'Shall we meet in Eastgate under the clock? About 12.30?'

'Wonderful,' she croaked, trying to think of something to say, something sensible.

'I want to talk to you about Anna,' he said, lowering his voice as if someone was listening in. 'It's quite serious, Olivia, and I can't think of anybody else who might be able to help.'

'Is she ill?' she asked, as reality dawned. He wasn't asking her out to quench some sort of long-held desire to have lunch with her. The man merely wanted to speak to her about his sister. Nevertheless, the idea that Anna might be ill – serious, he said – was dreadful and brought her swiftly out of her brief romantic reverie.

'No, nothing like that,' he said hastily. 'It's so bizarre that I really can't discuss it over the phone. See you next Saturday.'

Gently, she replaced the receiver, ready for the grilling.

'That was Ben Farrell,' she said before Rosie started. 'Anna's brother. I haven't seen him for years.'

'Anna's brother? Isn't he a doctor?'

Olivia nodded. 'Something about Anna. He wants to talk to me. It sounds serious. He sounded very worried.'

'Strange.' Rosie had caught her mood and mercifully was not being frivolous. 'I hope she's OK. You don't think she could be pregnant, do you? She's just the sort who'd come a cropper at the first fence. My God, that would scupper the medical course, wouldn't it?'

'If she is, I don't see what he expects me to do about it,' Olivia said faintly.

'Surely *he* could sort something out. She's in the right place to get a quick and easy abortion.'

'Rosie! Anna's the last person to do that. . . .'

'You'd be amazed, Livvy, at the people who do,' she said with a mischievous smile. 'And no before you ask – I haven't but you wouldn't be the least bit surprised, would you? Well, I'll have you know, Miss Hayton, that I happen to have strong feelings on that subject and there is no way I would do it. So there!'

'All right.' Olivia smiled at the indignation. 'I'm not arguing. Anyway, Anna's much too sensible to get herself pregnant.'

'Shopping tomorrow?' Rosie asked with a yawn, her earnestness deserting her. 'Or have you got something suitable to wear for lunch with a good-looking doctor next week?'

Rosie had got it in one. She had nothing to wear.

'City chic for you,' Rosie said, reading her mind and looking at her through half-closed eyes. 'But something of a surprise. Lowish-cut suit jacket and *no* blouse. Maybe a hint of lacy bra. What do you think? If I remember, you used to have a bit of a thing for him, didn't you? Come on, admit it.'

Olivia shrugged, trying to laugh it off. 'Is nothing sacred? What if I did? I was a child then.'

'But not any more.' Rosie ran her fingers through her hair and grinned. 'If we play this right, Ben might get more than he bargained for. What does a consultant earn?'

'No idea. Enough, I imagine.'

'But not millionaire status,' Rosie said, pulling a face. 'And he'll always be at the hospital and have no social life. And, if I'm absolutely honest, I don't know that I fancy being caressed by a man who digs his hands into somebody's open body. Huh! So you needn't bother bringing him back here.'

'I wasn't going to,' Olivia said, unconcerned at Rosie's dismissal of him. 'I can't afford a new suit,' she added with a sigh. 'Not a decent one.'

'Oh, come on, Livvy, there's a way out of that, isn't there? Ask Daddy.'

Olivia frowned, fretting a bit, for that had just occurred to her too.

'And you might as well get a new frock for the evening in case Ben asks you out for dinner too.'

'He's not going to do that. It's not a date,' Olivia reminded her. 'Not exactly.'

'Livvy Hayton, do I shoot you or what? There's no point in being half cocked about these things. He sounds a good bet for you. So, we're going to make an effort. What have we got to lose?'

She didn't take much persuading.

CHAPTER EIGHT

At eighteen, Anna was a volunteer assistant at a retreat up in the wilds of Scotland, helping with the cooking and cleaning and so forth. At first, her room seemed so primitive, the short walk to the toilet and bathroom block a deprivation of the highest order. Within a week, she was used to it. Within a week, the comforts of life back home seemed almost decadent.

Ross was one of the permanent staff, underpaid and sometimes undervalued, merely a higher class dogsbody, a big friendly giant of a man with a broken nose and a skill for smoothing things over, for solving problems, for calming the agitated, for sympathizing with the recently bereaved who had gone there in search of solace.

Ross was considered by many to be very nearly an angel.

An angel who fell in love with her.

Anna smiled, holding Ross's hand as they strolled along the shore.

Ross had just asked if she really wanted to be a doctor.

'People are always asking that,' she told him, trying her best not to be impatient with him. 'And the answer's yes. Of course I do. Why would I be going to start the course next year if I didn't?'

'I don't know why and that's what worries me,' he said gently. 'I'm not doubting that you wouldn't make an excellent doctor but sometimes you seem so far away from the real world.'

'I am far away,' she said, bringing him to a stop, so that they could watch the evening waves rippling in towards the shingle. The sun was lowering in the sky, pinky streaks floating in the blue. It was a glorious evening and she was overwhelmed as much by the power of the natural beauty as by the romantic nature of the walk. How could people look at nature, really look at it, and say there was no God? And where on earth had that thought come from?

'Far away and getting further away. . . .' he said in such a sad voice that she glanced at him, surprised.

'You're right,' she said as it slowly dawned. 'There is something I have to do with my life, Ross, and I don't know what it is. The worrying thing is I have a feeling it's nothing to do with medicine. It feels like I'm searching for something. Does that make any sense?'

'Not quite.' He managed a rueful smile. 'if you were a guest here, you could have a chat with one of the brothers about that. He'd put you straight. In fact, I can arrange for you to have a chat with one of them anyway if you want.'

She nodded, liking the idea. The brothers were just like the rest of them, buckling down to some of the more menial tasks with not a monk's habit in sight. In a way, she wished for the plain brown habit, for it might be easier to talk to somebody wearing that rather than an ordinary-looking man in jeans and sweater.

'And you know you can talk to me whenever you want, Anna,' Ross went on, his earnestness very endearing.

'I know I can, darling.'

Overwhelmed by a great fondness for him, she leaned into him as he cupped her face in his big hands and stroked her cheek a moment, looking deep into her eyes, before kissing her. Sweet Ross. She knew with a sense of hopelessness that he was falling in love with her and she with him. It was all a bit quick for they had only known each other a few weeks and it wasn't as if she was greatly experienced with men. On the other hand, what was there to know? They liked each other. They laughed together. It felt good and, if this was love, if this was all there was to it, this lovely warm feeling of contentment, then it was fine.

It was late summer and the beach at this hour was deserted. There was a little stretch that was particularly private and they headed there as they usually did. They might stretch out on the shore and huddle together, fully dressed, and have a cuddle in the softly scented sea air.

Nothing more.

He had tried to unbutton her blouse just the once and although pleasantly aroused, still astonished that a man like Ross could find her desirable, she had stilled his hand and shaken her head. To her surprise, he accepted what could only be considered a rebuff with a small smile and had not tried to take things any further after that, nor had he dumped her either.

Poor man. She knew with a dreadful certainty that she was going to break this man's heart.

She didn't know why.

She couldn't explain.

Just a feeling.

And that night, for the first time, she dreamed the dream.

Afterwards, people asked if she had been 'called'.

That was a real poser. It was as if they somehow expected God to be on the end of a telephone, pestering, insistent, wearing her down. It was a difficult question to answer because in a sense it had been exactly like that. She preferred to think of it as a persistent recurring dream, a dream yet not quite a dream.

Whatever it was, it lodged. Nestled deep within her. And at first, it was easy to shake it off, to tell herself it was ridiculous and to just forget it. She did try to talk to one of the brothers but that was ultimately unsatisfactory because he didn't say what she hoped he would say.

She wanted him to tell her that the feeling had merely come about because of her being at the retreat so long and that she should forget it and go back to the real world now. Instead, he told her to go away and pray for an answer.

She did not know how to. She had not prayed since she was a little girl and grown-up praying was another thing entirely and she was uncomfortable with it.

She told Ross because she had to tell him, to explain why she wanted him to let her go and not come after her. She had to have time to think things through. So she told him that one day, some day, she would become a nun. Just when, she did not know, but she was quite sure she would.

He seemed surprisingly unsurprised.

'I think I knew all along it was something like that,' he said with a look of resignation. 'You have that same look on your face sometimes as the brothers. That's why I didn't want to rush you. I hoped I might persuade you to stick with me a while.'

'If I do that, Ross, stick with you, it's not fair on you. Find someone else. Please . . .'

'I'm not sure I can,' he said and she could scarcely bear his disappointment, the way he was struggling to keep control. 'Will you carry on with your course?' he managed to ask at last.

'I have no choice. I'm going to start it,' she told him. 'Because I don't know when I'm going to do this. But if I do change my mind, Ross. . . ?'

'I'll be here,' he said. 'Or, if I do move on, I'll make sure you know where I am. But you must understand that if you do go into a convent then I really won't want to come to see you. Not there. That will be more than I can bear.' She nodded, suddenly unable to speak.

And watched, her own heart bursting, crying out to call him back, as he let go of her hand and walked away.

In the meantime, while she waited for 'something' to happen, she began her course, keeping her deepest thoughts secret. The work was interesting and she found it not too difficult, although she felt anxious sometimes because other people were so uptight with the workload, a few almost suicidal. She tried to help, to console, to offer comfort, but mostly she was spurned. Being 'top of the class' material was a pain to others and because she was so clearly on another level, envy was the overriding emotion and meant she had few real friends.

If there were turning points, positive or otherwise, then one had to be that weekend at home when she decided to go to church in the small town where her mother practised.

'Church? What for?' her mother asked, stupefied, watching as Anna appeared fully dressed at 9.30 on the Sunday morning. 'I hope you don't expect me to come with you?'

'No. I'd rather you didn't,' Anna said, wondering if her cotton dress and jacket was smart enough for church or if indeed people bothered any more to dress up. She didn't know quite why she was going but she had passed by the church yesterday and found her eyes drawn to it, up the path and towards the entrance porch.

She was transfixed. It was as if the whole place pulsated, and she had stood a moment at the railings, hearing the steady beating of her heart, feeling the pulse too of the building, the awful power of a divine presence.

Weird.

And then somebody had jostled her and the mood was broken. But this morning, waking up, she knew what she had to do.

'Take my car then,' Eva Farrell said, giving in to her daughter's whim with a smile. 'I'm not on call. But I hope you're not going to start taking it seriously, darling, because once they rope you in, you've had it. They do say the new vicar is a bit gung-ho and as for his wife – well, they say she's on another planet. I haven't met either of them yet because they're Donald's patients.'

'You shouldn't listen to gossip, Mum,' Anna said, picking up the keys to her mother's newest acquisition, a battered second-hand Volvo. 'I'd rather make my own mind up.'

If God was indeed 'calling' her, then he was going about it in the oddest way, for that first proper grown-up experience of going to church was hardly a calming one. She had been unsure what to expect and to realize that she could do it, go to church, and feel precious little, was in fact a relief.

How could she possibly have ever thought that she might become a nun? Nuns went to church and must feel holy. *She* went to church and couldn't stop her mind drifting off. She listened to a mother desperately shushing her child, she thought about some tricky medical notes all through the prayers, thought sad thoughts about Ross and exasperated ones about her mother and Ben during the sermon and so on. It was as if she was in some sort of trance and it was a surprise when people started to shuffle and leave. The new vicar, desperate to put names to faces, pounced on her in the porch, but thank God, she was not tempted to tell him anything, smiling but promising nothing when he said he hoped to see her again.

It was a profound *nothing* of an experience and ought to put pay to all those irritating religious thoughts that kept popping up.

Of course it did nothing of the kind.

God was patient.

And all she had to do was wait.

CHAPTER NINE

The suit for the hot date with Ben was cool ice-blue and it meant new shoes to go with it and a small clutch handbag, expenses she could ill afford. It had better be worth it, Olivia thought, as she arrived at the clock and, given she was ten minutes late, he had better be waiting.

He was.

His look told her at once that he liked what he saw as he gave her a brotherly kiss.

'It's lovely to see you again and so good of you to come,' he said formally. 'Sorry to do this to you but we're at our wits' end. Mum says if anybody can talk sense into Anna, you can.'

'Oh dear, that sounds ominous,' Olivia said, allowing him to touch her elbow and direct her onwards through the Saturday crowds in the direction of the cathedral. 'Where are we going?'

'A small Italian restaurant one of my colleagues recommended,' he said. 'I've booked us a table. It's the least I can do, dragging you here like this.'

'It's perfectly all right,' she said, feeling a touch irritated that he should keep on about it. 'I wasn't doing anything else today, other than clean the flat.'

It was true. She was not exactly a martyr to cleanliness but Rosie was so hopeless that somebody had to do something. The last time her mother had 'nipped round' on the off-chance, they had been caught on the hop and the tutting from Judith reached a crescendo before she left, threatening to send her own cleaning lady round to 'give them a quick one-off'.

'Talking of flats, I thought you might help me out with flat hunting of my own,' he said. 'I'm thinking of buying a property but I want to rent a while first.'

'Oh . . . that's nice. You're thinking of moving here?' she asked, trying her best to relax and not quite succeeding.

'I am. I've just got a consultancy post that I'm very happy with, so I'm forgetting about the London option and London house prices,' he said with a smile.

She was very conscious of him beside her, having taken in his appearance in a single glance. Smart casual. Catching a glimpse of herself in a shop window, she was suddenly nervous about her own suit. Goodness, she looked a bit weddingy. All she needed was a matching hat and a carnation!

Still, she would make the best of it. After all, it *was* her colour and supremely flattering and Ben had genuinely smiled as he took it all in.

And . . . oh heavens, wasn't it about time she got a grip of herself!

'This is it,' he said, leading her into the restaurant. 'Do you know it?'

She shook her head.

'Authentic Italian run by Italians, I'm glad to say,' Ben murmured as they passed through a cloud of cigarette smoke. 'But there's not a hope of a no-smoking table. Do you mind?'

'Not really,' she said. 'My flatmate is trying to give up but it's a losing battle. Do you remember Rosie Andrews? Anna will. She was at school with us. Well, you can tell Anna she's sharing with me.'

'Rosie Andrews?' he said, frowning in concentration. 'Vaguely. You were all much the same, just Anna's friends. It's odd you two should meet up again and end up sharing a flat.'

'Yes,' she said, still unconvinced about the wisdom of it, although she was determined to stick it out if only because her mother was so against it.

As lunch progressed, Olivia became ever more curious about this thing with Anna.

But Ben seemed in no great hurry and she let it ride, beginning at last to relax in his presence. Ben had a gift for putting people at their ease, she realized, which was a wonderful attribute for a doctor.

'What kind of operations do you perform?' she asked, over coffee.

'Oh, come on . . .' he smiled. 'Not a subject for discussion, Olivia. I rarely talk about my work and I wouldn't want to bore you.'

'You wouldn't,' she said, stirring her coffee thoughtfully, avoiding looking into his eyes in case he should read something into the look. 'I should find it fascinating.'

'Perhaps someday,' he said, distracted suddenly. 'Olivia, may I come to the point?'

'Please do,' she said. 'I can't think what it is you want me to do.'

'We just hope you can talk some sense into her. Into Anna.'

'How can I help?' she asked, feeling the need to take charge of the conversation because he looked in sudden danger of drying up. 'Tell me, please.'

'She wants to pack in the course,' he said quietly. 'She's having no problems with it. On the contrary, she's doing extremely well. Mum's furious with her. I'm trying to understand but it's very difficult. How can she do it?'

Olivia let out a deep breath. Why was she not at all surprised?

'It's something to do with pressure, I suppose,' she offered. 'I'm sorry if it sounds like I'm interfering but even when she was young, so much was always expected of her. All that extra cramming. Perhaps she can't cope with that.'

'All right. I accept that,' he said, rather to her surprise. 'I suppose we have been guilty of pushing her but it was only because we always assumed that it was in her blood. And we could maybe accept that if she just wanted to opt out and do biochemistry instead but she doesn't.'

'What does she want to do?' Olivia asked, concerned as she caught the anguish in his face. Good heavens, what was Anna up to? It wasn't like her to upset her family like this.

'She wants . . .' He looked round furtively and lowered his voice. 'Don't laugh, Olivia, but she says she wants to be a nun.'

Later in the afternoon, Ben rang his mother from the hotel.

'We had lunch,' he said at once. 'And she's agreed to come over next weekend to talk to Anna.'

'Thank God. Was she surprised?'

'Totally,' he said, remembering how she had looked.

He couldn't stop remembering how she had looked.

And the way she looked at him.

Olivia Hayton would have made a rotten poker player.

'Anna always took notice of Olivia,' his mother's voice sighed over the line. 'So we must live in hope. What is she like now, Ben?'

'She's still pretty,' he said, hearing his mother's laugh. 'Dresses a bit old for her age, I suppose, but she's very elegant.'

'I'm not surprised. I remember her mother always being very well dressed. I suppose it's hereditary. That's why dear Anna's always so shabby.'

Winding up the call, Ben hoped the visit would not be a complete waste of time and that Olivia could talk sense into Anna. In any case, the thought of meeting Olivia again next weekend was exciting and he found himself thinking about her most of the week.

She had got under his skin and, if he were to diagnose the symptoms, he would say that at last – at long last, his mother would say – he was falling in love.

Prognosis? Well, that depended entirely on Olivia.

*

Rosie laughed when she told her.

'Jesus! Is she completely off her head? A nun? Honestly?'

Olivia nodded, still miffed that, after dropping the bombshell, it had petered out to nothing, other than an invitation to the cottage next weekend.

'I'm not sure I want to talk her out of it,' she told Rosie, who was fully occupied with painting her fingernails red, prior to doing the same with the town.

'You should have said no then,' Rosie said, offering no sympathy. 'You only said you'd go so that you'd meet him again, didn't you? Go on, admit it. Isn't it just great that he's thinking of moving here? And as for asking you to help him sort something out . . . what a heaven-sent opportunity!'

'Shut up, Rosie, and I can't afford any new clothes to impress him next weekend,' Olivia said quickly. 'So don't even start on that.'

'I wasn't going to,' Rosie said, leaping up as she caught sight of the clock. 'God, I've got to rush. I don't want to keep this man waiting.'

'This sounds serious,' Olivia said with a smile, for it wasn't like Rosie to be remotely concerned about whether or not she kept a man waiting.

Rosie hesitated and Olivia wondered if she had hit a nerve, if in fact this *was* serious.

'Henry's picking me up. Henry Chambers,' she said, raising her eyebrows. 'Remember him? The big boss himself.'

It took a minute to register. 'The one who runs that TV company? You sly old thing. How did you manage that?'

Rosie laughed. 'By being my own sweet self. How else? It just so happens that we've bumped into each other from time to time, in the corridors of power as it were.'

'Oh yes? Just by chance?'

'You bet,' Rosie said, tearing off into her room and continuing the conversation through the open door. 'He heard that I happened to be interested in ballet . . .'

'What? Rosie Andrews, you liar.'

'So he's got the wrong end of the stick. But how could I say no when he just happened to have this spare ticket? You'd think he could have come up with something more original.'

Olivia edged into the room, watching as Rosie ran now dry fingers through her hair and checked her elaborate make-up. 'You won't be bringing him back tonight, will you?'

'Like hell,' Rosie said, spraying a cloud of perfume round her. 'If I'm to catch *this* guy, Livvy, I have to play it right and that means hard to get. I'm a no-go area until there's a ring in the offing. In fact, I might well insist on waiting until the honeymoon.'

'You think there's a chance?' Olivia moved aside, handing Rosie her bag and scarf. 'Really a chance?'

'Why not? He fancies me like crazy. I've been finding out a few things about his past and he's the sort of man who believes very firmly in marriage. After all, he has been divorced twice.'

'Twice? You didn't tell me that.'

'You didn't ask. Twice divorced with a grown-up daughter.'

'I see.'

Rosie laughed. 'No, you don't. His first wife left him after fifteen years and the second was a big mistake. A businesswoman who tried to bring him to heel and worse, started to compete with him. He's had a string of girlfriends since then but they've all been hard as nails and bitchy. So, I'm going for a softer approach, butter wouldn't melt et cetera.'

'*How* many millions does he have?'

'I'm not sure but more than one, Livvy. Anyway, does it matter? It's amazing how much more attractive a man with money is. Suddenly the fact that he's hardly the most handsome man on the block pales into insignificance. Wish me luck!' Rosie said, as the bell jangled. 'Let him in, sit him down and chat to him a moment, will you?'

'I thought you didn't want to keep him waiting?'

'Changed my mind. A few minutes is exactly right.'

'Rosie! Just look at me,' Olivia grumbled, snatching a look at her reflection as she went to answer the door. She had some nice things which stayed nice because she did not wear them for slopping around.

'Hello, we've met before,' Henry said, directly he was inside, taking a seat on the sofa. A quick, confident smile and then, 'Olivia, isn't it?'

'That's right. She won't be a moment. May I get you a drink, Henry? Or a coffee?'

He shook his head, looking at her, making her suddenly acutely aware of her mismatched ensemble. Damn Rosie. She was doing it deliberately, of course, the Cinderella effect, and not for the first time. When it came to the opposite sex, Rosie knew exactly what she was doing.

Henry looked somehow younger in the more casual clothes he was wearing this evening and the blue of the cashmere sweater under the darker jacket matched his eyes.

'How's business?' she asked, willing Rosie to come and get her out of this.

'Up and down. I just keep my head above water most of the time, Olivia, darling.'

'Don't you believe it, Livvy,' Rosie said, appearing suddenly, a fiery red stole, heavily fringed and shot with gold, over the dress. 'Business is booming.'

In a strangely resigned mood, Olivia settled for her quiet night in. She had a lot to think about and seeing Anna again the following weekend was preying on her mind.

Anna had always been a dark horse but this was bizarre.

CHAPTER TEN

Olivia realized she knew absolutely nothing about nuns. Rosie had been no help at all – all she could think of was Julie Andrews in *The Sound of Music* dancing round that Alpine field. They wore no make-up, had cropped hair, scrubbed faces and smiled a lot. They were kind and good, they lived on frugal meals and they did not have sex.

That was it. The sum total of their knowledge. How on earth was she supposed to persuade Anna not to do it when she knew so little?

Anna was out of the door greeting her as soon as she pulled up, bombarding her with questions before dragging her indoors where her mother was waiting with a smile.

'Take the bags upstairs, love,' she told Anna. 'And I'll make Olivia a cup of coffee.'

It was an excuse to talk privately and Eva wasted no time.

'We're at a loss,' she said, her face bewildered. 'Total loss. Can you believe it, a nun! Isn't it idiotic? And she's on the way to being the top student in her year. What can she be thinking of? I thought you had to be Roman Catholic but apparently there are Anglican convents too. Isn't it strange? You don't know these things until something like this happens.'

'I'll talk to her,' Olivia promised, watching as Eva made the coffee. She had strong capable hands, just like Anna. And Ben.

'Ben won't be here until later,' Eva said with a smile. 'it was so kind of you to agree to this. Ben was full of it when he got back. My God, he said, Olivia's grown up.'

She felt a moment's irritation. 'What did he expect? Me to be a child still?'

'Perhaps he did.' She eyed Olivia thoughtfully, obviously deciding it was time for straight talking. 'It's time he got himself settled. I don't care whether he marries or not – I'm very modern, Olivia – but I would like to see him settled. I don't know why that should be so important for a mother but it is. I expect yours is the same.'

'Oh yes,' Olivia said fervently. 'She's already planning the wedding and I haven't even met a man.'

'Mr Right, you mean?'

They laughed, just as Anna returned, smiling a small secret smile.

'You two had a nice chat?' she enquired.

'You know perfectly well what we've been talking about,' Eva said, pushing a mug of coffee her way. 'Olivia is in total agreement that this nun thing is a mad idea. Aren't you, Olivia?'

Anna sat opposite her at the kitchen table. She looked just the same, although perhaps she had gained a little weight. She wore some make-up and her hair was short but suited her, tucked away neatly behind her ears.

They waited until Eva was out of the room.

'Your mum's upset,' Olivia said quietly. 'Ben, too.'

'I know and I'm sorry. I am also rather annoyed with them. It's obvious why you're here and I'm insulted that Ben should concoct some story about just happening to bump into you.'

'Oh . . . is that what he said?'

'Yes. They're such sweeties, though. I know they're only doing it because they love me and they're upset.'

Olivia remembered the stubborn look of old, a look which was now accompanied with a kind of glow, almost as if Anna was in love. She found herself staring a moment, perturbed by it.

'I'm sorry we sort of lost touch,' she said awkwardly, remembering now that it was she who had failed to reply to Anna's last letter. 'I'm so busy with work and everything . . .' she tailed off, hating herself for making the excuse.

Anna ignored the comment and simply smiled instead. 'You look well, Olivia. Is it really true that you are sharing a flat with Rosie Andrews? I couldn't believe it when Ben told me. Rosie, I said, are you sure she said Rosie?'

Olivia laughed. 'I know. Crazy, isn't it? She hasn't changed a bit. We met again at this party and it was her idea to get a flat together. It was all very impulsive. I can't think why I ever said yes.'

'It obviously works,' Anna said astutely. 'Or you wouldn't look so happy.'

'It works. More or less. We're very different and maybe that's why it works.'

Anna nodded, silent a moment.

'Ben popped in to see us last Sunday and couldn't stop talking about you,' she said at last. 'I think you might have made quite an impression on him.'

'Really? I can't think why. All he wanted to do was talk about you and your plans. He didn't seem much interested in me.'

'Oh dear. Don't you believe it, Olivia. Are you pleased he's thinking of moving to Chester?'

'Yes,' she said, knowing she could keep nothing from Anna's wise eyes. 'And he wants me to help find him a flat.'

'Take it carefully,' Anna said. 'He has had relationships but he always seems to veer off in another direction whenever they turn serious. Maybe it's something to do with Dad running off. I think I was too young for it to have much effect on me but he was seventeen and he thought the world of Dad.'

'It's hard when someone you love lets you down,' Olivia said. 'And seventeen is a terrible age. Remember what we were like at seventeen?'

Anna sipped her coffee and looked over the rim of the mug at Olivia.

'Very intense. And I still feel that way. Do *you* understand what I want to do? What did you think when Ben told you?'

'I wasn't surprised you were packing in the course. But I was surprised that you want to become a nun,' she said. 'It's such a strange idea. Girls just don't become nuns these days. Do they? And you aren't even a Catholic.'

'That isn't necessary,' Anna said quietly. 'And yes, girls do still become nuns, some girls. Oh, Olivia, there's so much I have to tell you.'

They were interrupted by the front door crashing open and Ben's voice announcing 'they' were here.

Ben was accompanied by a beautiful blonde, middle thirties, wearing a short-skirted suit, a long mackintosh draped casually over her shoulders; a woman of such style and confidence she could easily have graced the cover of *Vogue*.

Olivia felt her heart sink into the soles of the trainers she was wearing with her comfortable pants. She had intended to change into something a bit more special before he arrived. She responded to Ben's welcoming smile and his kiss on the cheek with a growing despair, even though it transpired that Helena was merely passing through. They had arrived in two cars and Helena, an accountant, was on her way to meet a client.

Feeling a little awkward and definitely non-family, Olivia stepped back as Helena was introduced first to Anna then to Eva. Ben had about him quite a proprietorial air, even though the lady was cool as the silvery glints in her hair.

Olivia's hopes – fragile as they were – plummeted as Helena was persuaded to stay for a spot of lunch.

Ben, as she might have guessed, was involved with someone else and with Anna – shining-eyed Anna – so obviously on the slippery slope to sisterdom,

Olivia could see this weekend disintegrating round her before it had begun.

It was like old times. Talking after lights out. Olivia, dressing-gowned, on the bed, Anna perched beside it wearing no-nonsense pyjamas. It was past midnight and they were whispering so as not to disturb anyone, although from Ben's room they could hear music.

'I suppose I could have fallen in love with him,' Anna said, finishing telling her about Ross. 'Do you think I did?'

'I don't know, Anna,' Olivia said. 'Only you can know that. Poor man. He must have loved you. How could you do that to him?'

Anna shook her head. 'Don't ask.'

'Has he tried to get in touch?'

She shook her head. 'Not once. I often wonder what's happened to him but it's unfair to try to find out.'

Her eyes filled with tears and Olivia sighed, giving her an encouraging smile. For a minute, she almost wished Rosie was here too because Rosie wouldn't have stood for this.

'I can't really explain how God came to me but he did,' Anna continued. 'No . . . please don't be embarrassed, Olivia. I'm not. And as I keep telling Mum and Ben, I have seven years to think about it before I commit to my final vows.'

'But you're so young and nuns are old.'

'That's what Ben thinks. He thinks I'm going to be living with women of sixty plus and that I'll be old before my time.'

'Maybe he's right. We need to talk to people of our own age,' Olivia said gently. 'What are you running away from, Anna? From Ross? From marriage to Ross?'

'No,' she said, voice rising. 'Absolutely not. I'm not running away from anything. Don't you see, Olivia, that in the community there's nowhere *to* run. You have to confront your feelings. Head on. And that's what I love about it.'

'You've made up your mind, haven't you?'

It was hardly a question and a nod from Anna was all she needed to confirm it.

'I haven't mentioned this to Mum yet,' Anna said as she prepared to go to her own room, 'but I might be accepted into a community in Chester. I liked it very much when I visited and it has a lovely garden looking out on to the city walls. I might work in the garden . . .'

'You? Work in a garden?' Olivia smiled.

'I know. It seems a terrible imposition. I shall have to learn about gardening first,' Anna said, raising herself from her knees. 'Goodnight. I'll let you get some sleep. And thanks for coming. I know you mean well.'

In the dim light, Olivia watched her leave.

For the first time, it occurred to her that nuns were people after all.

People like Anna.

Next morning, Ben had a long-standing golf session with a friend. Olivia was nowhere around as he snatched a hurried breakfast.

'If she can't talk Anna out of it, what are we going to do?' Eva asked, sitting opposite him, morosely drinking coffee.

'What can we do?' He glanced at the clock. 'Got to go. She'll do her best, I'm sure of that, but if Anna's still determined...' he shrugged, picking up his golf clubs.

'Yes but how will I explain to people? It's so odd. It's not as if we've ever bothered with church. People will think her quite mad. I shan't be able to bear the sympathy. It was bad enough when your father left. The sympathy drowned me.'

He left her to it, feeling that the matter was rapidly moving away from them and out of their hands. He still felt strongly that Anna was making a terrible mistake but, short of barring her way or shutting her in her room here, what could he do?

He played a rotten round, his mind not on the strokes but on Olivia.

He'd caught a glimpse of her late last night as she returned from the bathroom and she had blushed, clean faced in her dressing-gown, probably embarrassed because it was a simple towelling thing, not exactly the glamorous type. To him, it was far more sexy than any flimsy wrap could ever have been.

She had looked utterly gorgeous, so gorgeous that she stopped him in his tracks, her hair a little damp, face shiny, grasping the gown tightly as if she was afraid of revealing too much. Modesty – in this day and age!

That memory lingered all round the golf course. He stayed for lunch at the club and afterwards got roped into visiting a friend, so it was after six when he finally got back home.

Olivia, banished from the kitchen where much pre-dinner activity was taking place, was in the sitting-room, reading.

'Good game?' she enquired with a smile, putting the book aside. 'It stayed fine for you.'

'Yes.' He nodded fervently, as if she had just said a most remarkable thing. 'Has Anna said anything?'

'I don't think I'm going to make her change her mind, if that's what you mean,' Olivia said, legs tucked underneath her in the chintz-covered armchair. 'She was always stubborn. By the way, did you know about Ross?'

'Who's he?' Ben sat down on the sofa opposite, flexing tired shoulders, reflecting that his swing needed a serious looking at.

'Ross is a man she met at the retreat she went to in Scotland.'

'That's going back a bit.' He frowned, never having heard of this Ross. 'What happened?'

'I think they fell in love,' Olivia said quietly. 'But she gave him up. She felt she had to.'

'I see. So all this was in her mind as far back as that?'

She nodded. 'And it won't go away, Ben. That's what she told me last night. It must be serious, mustn't it, if she can throw away the chance of happiness like that. I gather the poor man was devastated.'

'It happens,' he said, more curtly than he intended. 'We all get disappointments in love but we have to get on with life.'

She made no reply and he realized that was one of the things he liked about this woman, her ability to stay silent when there was nothing to say. He knew too many women who felt they had to keep the conversation going, no matter what.

'Dinner in ten minutes.' Eva Farrell poked her head round the door, grinning at them. 'It's OK, Olivia, you're fine as you are. Jeans will do.'

'She means it,' Ben said gently, as she closed the door and he caught Olivia's slightly worried look. 'You look great in jeans.'

Over dinner, a relaxed affair, they made no mention of Anna's intentions, but to Ben's annoyance, his mother questioned him or rather cross-examined him about Helena.

'I told you, she's just a friend,' he said in an attempt to make light of it. 'We're not an item if that's what you think.'

Eva laughed, although there was a coolness in her eyes. 'I always think that's such a strange description of a couple. You just seem to have gone to a lot of trouble bringing her to see me.'

'Can't I bring a friend home?' He felt his mother's accusing eyes on him. 'I wish I hadn't done it now. We were both coming in this direction, set off at the same time and we were on for lunch and it seemed daft stopping off at the pub up the road when we could stop off here. You didn't mind giving her lunch, did you?'

'Of course not,' Eva said sharply. 'She was welcome. I just thought there might be an ulterior motive, that's all.'

Across the table, he caught Olivia's expression and realized she was avoiding looking at him.

It was the only hiccup in the evening.

As before, Anna and Olivia drifted off to Anna's room later, and he spent the remainder of the evening listening to music, hearing Anna and Olivia chatting next door, wishing Olivia were there with him instead. Tomorrow, he had to leave early and he wanted to say something to her before he left, to make his feelings known to her.

Just what exactly, he had not the remotest idea.

He went over a few ideas as he lay trying to sleep but they all sounded equally insane. When it came to women and handling them, he felt not like the polished consultant he was but a naive medical student.

Olivia met up with Ben downstairs in the kitchen at breakfast time.

'Sorry about this. Mum's been called out,' he said, a little desperately. 'Otherwise she would have cooked something. Fancy some porridge?'

'Lovely,' she said and would have offered to help but he seemed determined to show her he could manage, fussing around in that comical fashion that afflict most men in the kitchen. At least the men *she* knew.

'Any luck with that sister of mine?' he enquired, with only a thin hope in his face. 'I heard you talking again late last night.'

Olivia nodded. 'I talked to her, yes, but it's no use,' she said. 'It's what she wants to do, Ben, and I think you should maybe accept it. Give her your blessing. She would like that.'

That went down like a lump of the porridge he had just tried to make in the microwave.

'I wish I could believe that but I still feel it's just a whim,' he said, pulling his face and pushing his plate away.

'I'll put some toast on,' she said, hearing Anna coming to the surface upstairs. She'd have to learn to get up at a decent time when she went to the convent. Mind you, as she had explained, she wasn't going to a contemplative order where they still got up during the night twice or more. That must really sort out the true vocationalists.

'The point is, Olivia,' Ben went on, looking more upset than cross, 'she'd better not come running to me for help when she wants out. Getting out of something like that is hell, I believe. Worse than a divorce.'

'She commits for several years at a time,' Olivia said, trying to remember what Anna had told her. 'They won't let her go too fast. She will have lots of time to think. What else *can* she do but think?'

'Pray?' he said, going over to the window and looking out on to the morning dewy garden. 'How can she do this to Mum? She's gone through such a lot.'

Olivia nodded her sympathy.

'I don't know why Dad left us,' Ben went on, determined to set the record straight, it seemed. 'It was between the two of them, something we didn't know about. But when he died, what could I do but look after the both of them? Mum *and* Anna?'

'You have looked after them, Ben,' she said quietly. 'Nobody could have done more and I know Anna's grateful. But this has nothing to do with you, has it?'

'It's everything to do with us. We're family. And we're close. Oh yes, I know Mum's never been very good at putting across her feelings but that's just the way she is. For instance, when Anna got her three A grades, what did Mum say? Well, I can tell you that she didn't exactly offer any lavish praise but that doesn't mean she's not proud of us. And she so wanted Anna to be a doctor.'

'And Anna wants to be a nun,' she reminded him. 'I'm sorry but your mother's going to have to accept it.'

He smiled. 'Very sensible advice but I keep telling you, Olivia, this is a family thing, isn't it? I can give sensible advice to my patients all the time, give them news that tears them apart sometimes. But when it's personal, when it's your sister throwing her life away, I don't feel I can stand by and do nothing.'

Without thinking, she reached across the table and touched his hand.

'You'll come round,' she said. 'Don't let it drive you apart. Please.'

'Fancy a walk before I leave?'

'Why not? What time are you off?'

'Ten at the latest,' he said, reaching for a sweater. 'Come on, we'll walk over the field. You'll need stronger shoes than those,' he said, glancing at them. 'There'll be some wellies in the porch.'

'My sister a nun,' Ben said with a little laugh as they slipped through a gate on to the public footpath opposite the cottage. 'It'll be a talking point at dinner parties, anyway. If I gave dinner parties, that is.'

'From what you were saying last night I gather you are run off your feet most of the time.'

'It's a busy life but I love it,' he said. 'It might sound trite but it really does matter to me that I can help people get better. Not always, of course,' he added, 'but that's the way of things in my profession. Sometimes, no matter how hard you try, you lose people. After all, we are dealing with sick people, desperately ill sometimes.'

'How do you cope with that? Losing someone?'

'It's never the same,' he said. 'But you cope because you have to and you've learned how to detach. Well, that's the theory. I still hate having to go into the room and talk to the relatives. But I don't like to delegate that to anybody else. I carry the can.'

Sensing he wasn't altogether happy talking about it, she led it slide, taking his hand as he helped her over a stile on to the rough path.

A little to her surprise, he held on to her hand once they were over.

'Olivia . . .'

She glanced up sharply, for he said her name a different way suddenly, almost with a caress in it.

'I feel I should explain. That Helena business the other day.'

'Oh, that.' She laughed. 'It's really nothing to do with me and I thought your mother was a bit brisk with you. Just like mine. I can't bring a man home without it being the man I'm destined to marry. In her eyes, anyway.'

'I met Helena a couple of months ago. We've been out a few times but it's all very casual. We decided pretty quickly that we're not serious about each other. She's hoping to get back with her ex.'

'It's all right, Ben,' she said hastily. 'You don't have to explain to me.'

'Oh yes I do. I think it's time you and me got a few things straight,' he went on, his grip on her hand tightening. 'We've known each other for years and for a long time I thought of you as just Anna's friend.'

'And now. . . ?'she dared whisper, uncertain of his meaning.

They were walking along the rim of a field, a field that dipped down to the river, a gushing, rushing river at this point, and in the distance church bells pealed.

'I'd like us to see each other when I move to Chester,' he said in a firm voice that was not expecting a negative response. 'I'd like to take you out to dinner, to the theatre, that sort of thing.'

'Would you?' she said, faint with shock at the suddenness of it all, for he had given no hint. 'Would you really, Ben?'

'Yes, I would, and you needn't sound so surprised. When I saw you again, I very nearly forgot the point of the visit. Isn't this crazy?' His smile was unsure. 'Look, I know we don't know each other very well . . .'

'We can get to know each other,' she said, yesterday's dashed hopes resurfacing with a vengeance. 'There'll be lots of time to do that when you're living near. And it will be nice to get to know each other.'

'Won't it just?'

They exchanged a new sort of smile that acknowledged suddenly and completely what they were both thinking.

'I used to have a bit of a thing for you in the old days,' Olivia confessed, feeling her heart give a little flutter. 'All the girls did.'

'Oh no, don't say that. You make me feel a hundred.'

'I didn't mean to. I don't think of you as old at all. You're just . . . well, you're just you.'

He squeezed her hand, leaned forward, asking a question with his eyes before putting his hand on her hair, drawing her to him with a sigh and kissing her.

'Hmm,' he whispered. 'I've wanted to do that for a long time.'

It was almost too much, too good to be true, and she was totally unable to pretend otherwise, pulling into him and begging with her body for another kiss, a proper one this time.

'Hey, let's take it easy,' he said, drawing away gently. 'I don't know about you but I'm a bit overwhelmed by all this. I can't stop thinking about you. You ruined my golf yesterday.'

'Did I?' she asked with delight, not wanting this little stroll to end but knowing it must. 'We'd better be getting back,' she told him. 'Or you'll be horribly late.'

'You're right. I'm tempted to say to hell with it, take you out for lunch somewhere, just the two of us, and drive back tomorrow, but I really ought to get back. I can see you're going to look after me very well. . . .'

'I am.'

They walked back to the cottage, saying very little, for there was no need for words.

'A whirlwind romance . . . that's what it was like for me,' the other novice said 'It was as if God just swept me in his arms and spun me round and round.'

Anna glanced at her, frowning, thinking she was rather fanciful and that she was unlikely to last the course. It was much better to keep at least one foot firmly on the ground.

They were enjoying the peace and tranquillity of the garden whilst they waited for the hour to strike so that they could go in for their noviciate lesson, where they were learning about the 'letting go' of their previous life and how to cope with celibacy, poverty and obedience, the three essentials for life in the convent. It was a complex business and the study was difficult, theologically absorbing and in some ways every bit as intense as her medical studies of late.

Anna loved this garden and was beginning to understand the joy people found in gardens. It was to her as calming as the cool incense-flooded air of the chapel and, just now, the garden's gentleness and the soft summer sunshine not only calmed her but wrapped itself round her in such a way that she was able to put aside her slight feelings of misgivings about her fellow novice. She hoped she was wrong about the other girl's motives, for having *two* novices in the same year was something of a coup for the convent. She admired the other girl's enthusiasm but, to Anna's practical mind, it had to be coupled with common sense.

The walls that sheltered and enclosed this garden were soft brick, shading from rusty red to palest brown. It was essentially a cottage garden with clumps of flowers dotted here and there and swathes of grassy path threading through.

Anna sighed and the novice beside her, perhaps misinterpreting the sigh, fell silent.

Her poor mother! How badly Eva had taken it, so much so that she said she could not bear to visit yet. Ben made no secret of his feelings, still insisting she was 'shutting herself away from reality'. At the end of every visit, he would plead with her to 'come back into the proper world'.

However, the pull of God was a great deal more forceful than that of her mother and Ben, much as she loved them. She was here, serving her time as a postulant and novice and seven years would be quite long enough to know whether something was right for you.

She started as the clock tower clock pealed the hour and quickly, before Sister Margaret, who was a stickler for punctuality, could come searching for them, they made their way indoors to quiet their thoughts in preparation for their lesson.

CHAPTER ELEVEN

To Olivia's embarrassment and irritation, the first time her mother met Ben was quite by chance. Ben now had a flat in Chester, and she was spending quite a lot of time there, for once begun, their relationship had fairly sizzled along and there was no point, with them feeling as they did, in prolonging the agony. She had allowed herself to be deliciously seduced a few weeks after that weekend at Laburnum Cottage.

With Rosie happy to cover for her when necessary, she really didn't want her mother to know about the arrangement just yet, not until things were more settled. So it was annoying but probably served her right that, whilst shopping, they should just happen to bump into Judith.

'Oh, there's my mother,' Olivia said, aware she sounded less than thrilled but honestly, wouldn't you just know it? She knew she couldn't keep Ben secret for long but she was waiting for the right moment, for she knew that the announcement would be greeted with absolute delight. A cardiologist! My goodness, that would be one in the eye for her friends.

Prior to Ben, Olivia had been in a brief relationship with one of her colleagues. A nice enough man, recently divorced, but when her mother heard where he lived and something of his origins, she decided he wasn't up to it and certainly not worthy of the attentions of her lovely daughter.

So, when Olivia and Ben bumped into her mother as they did, Judith assumed that Ben was this colleague, showing her coolness at once with a look that spoke volumes. Within seconds, the mistake was rectified as Olivia introduced Ben to her and Judith realized who he was.

'Ben Farrell!' she said, as if he was an old friend. 'How lovely! How is your dear mother?'

Her face brightened, a smile beamed, eyes warmed.

It was an instant and regrettably see-through transformation.

And Ben saw right through it.

Judith tried desperately to make amends thereafter, but the back-pedalling never quite washed with Ben. Olivia was irritated by the pair of them, her mother *and* Ben, her mother for being such a terrible snob and Ben for making such a fuss about it.

If it came to it, of course, then she would have to go his way, but she hoped her loyalty would never be tested.

She spent the weekends when Ben was not on duty or on call at his place.

They had just spent a lazy Saturday together and were now in bed at a shame-fully early hour.

'What would Anna say if she could see us now?'

Olivia smiled and shifted her position slightly so that Ben's arm was more comfortable round her shoulders.

'I wish you wouldn't say things like that,' she said. 'She probably wouldn't mind – at least, the old Anna wouldn't mind. I'm not so sure about the new. What is she *supposed* to think now?'

'What is she being brainwashed into thinking, you mean?' he said, a touch bitterly. 'She talks to me about the noviciate lessons but I can't take it in.'

'Well, you're not going to be a nun, are you? And Anna is,' she said with conviction. 'She's being tough on herself, asking herself questions and coming up each time with the same answer. This is something she has to do, Ben.'

'She would like you to go to see her,' he said suddenly. 'Will you?'

She shuddered, watching the curtains as they blew softly in the slightest breeze. 'I know I'm a coward but it's just the thought of it – it's so alien.'

'It would please her and it's not so bad,' he went on, gently tracing a finger along her shoulder. 'In fact, it's all handled discreetly. You're welcomed at the door and taken to the parlour where you have tea and biscuits and nobody disturbs you.'

She considered it. Perhaps she would. She was very happy herself and it was a crying shame not to be able to share that happiness with Anna. She and Ben were in love and someday he would propose and she would accept and at last her mother could get on with the wedding she was secretly planning.

'What's stopping him?' she had asked Olivia. 'For heaven's sake, he can afford to buy you a proper house, get you away from that Rosie. Why he didn't just buy a house outright I shall never know instead of renting an apartment, a man of his position.'

Ben rented an 'apartment' whereas they, she and Rosie, rented a 'flat', in her mother's eyes. A subtle difference.

'Will you go to see Anna?' Ben asked again, interrupting her thoughts. 'All it takes is a phone call. I can ring if that's what's bothering you.'

'No. I'll do it myself,' she said, sighing as he sighed, his gentle touch intensified, fingers lightly and yet scorchingly drifting over her bare skin, sending her nerve ends into turmoil. 'Don't forget you've got an early start,' she told him in a half-hearted attempt at putting him off. 'You're going to be dead-beat, darling.'

'Dead-beat maybe but very happy, my love.'

The following day, she tiptoed cautiously into her own flat, relaxing when she realized there was no sign of a male presence.

Peeping in at her, she saw Rosie was still in bed, at ten in the morning, lying in such an odd position she looked like her back was dislocated. Minutes later, accompanied by the sound of great grumbles, she staggered out of her bedroom, as Olivia, tutting loudly, pottered about in the little kitchen, heaping last night's dishes into the sink.

'What are you doing here?' Rosie asked, rubbing her eyes. She was wearing old shorts and a vest top and looked about fifteen. 'I didn't expect you back until late this afternoon. Leave those, Livvy. I was going to do them later.'

'Quite,' Olivia said tightly, her hands already in hot soapy water, getting sick and tired of doing all the domestic chores. It was supposed to be a fifty-fifty set-up but it was not working. Left to her own devices, Rosie would have the place like a council refuse tip. It was her week to dispose of the papers, cans and bottles into the appropriate recycling banks and, as usual, they just sat on the workbench taking up more and more space. Maniacally shifting them around, wiping under them with a damp, super-clean cloth, Olivia knew she was overreacting.

Rosie grinned. 'Don't take it out on me if you've had a tiff with Ben.'

'We haven't had a tiff.'

'What are you doing back so early then?'

'He's had to go to the hospital. Some patients he needs to see urgently.'

'I did warn you,' Rosie said, hair more tousled than usual, looking much prettier without her heavy make-up. 'That's what doctors are like. Just so long as he's not having a quickie on the sly. Let's face it, he must rate one of the dishiest consultants there. I bet there's a lot of meaningful glances over the bedpans.'

Despite her mood, Olivia managed a smile. Rosie was the limit!

'He wouldn't dare,' she said.

'They all would, given half a chance. Men are men or hadn't you noticed?

They're all bastards of varying degrees, although some are quite nice bastards, I grant you.'

She grinned, drifting out again, not offering to help with the dishes. Thoroughly grumpy, Olivia finished them and washed down surfaces, wishing she could stop acting like a domestic. Her mother hated it too. 'Why you feel the need to flash round with the Domestos is utterly beyond me,' she would say.

Satisfied at last, her hands reeking of disinfectant, she made two cups of instant coffee and took them through. Rosie was lying on the sofa, in her dressing-gown now, still looking half asleep.

Trying not to tut like her mother, Olivia tidied up yesterday's paper and the myriad of supplements, which were scattered like media confetti all over the floor. She would be glad to move out. She might consider moving in with Ben if he wanted her to – he had already hinted as much but she was deliberately holding fire because moving into their own home as a married couple was what she really wanted. As she saw it, *not* agreeing to move in was her trump card just now.

'Stop acting like a housewife,' Rosie grumbled, watching all the activity in a semi-bored fashion. 'All this nest building gets on my nerves. What you need is to get married to Ben and start a family. Then you might slow down.'

'Is that what I'm doing? Nest building?'

Rosie glanced at her, smiled a little. 'What's wrong? Are you worried that he's not popped the question yet?'

'Not worried exactly.' She bit her lip, knowing she was fooling neither of them. 'Well, all right, I suppose I am. What's he waiting for? He's perfectly free. He says he loves me. I love him. Am I daft to keep expecting an engagement ring to appear?'

'Well, he does come from an odd family. What do you expect? I can't think what's got into Anna.'

'Neither can I,' Olivia said, reminded that she had promised to visit. 'Although Ben can't be blamed for Anna. He can't be responsible for what she wants to do.' She glanced at Rosie and saw the suppressed excitement in her face. 'What's the matter with you? You look like the cat that's got the cream.'

'Oh, Livvy, you're not making this easy for me.' Rosie sighed. 'You'd better sit down. This is going to be a shock.'

'OK. What is it?'

'I have the most exciting news.'

'News?' Olivia glanced quickly at her. 'What? You're not pregnant, are you?'

'Christ, no. I'm engaged,' she said, flinging her hand forward and showing off a whopper of a diamond. 'What do you think of that? I'm surprised you didn't notice.'

Olivia sat down abruptly. 'Engaged?' she repeated. 'Who to?'

'To whom, actually. Henry Chambers, of course. Haven't I been seeing Henry these last months?'

'Henry?'

It had never occurred to her that, whilst she was preoccupied with Ben and spending a considerable amount of time over at his place, Rosie had been *seriously* seeing Henry.

'But isn't it all a bit soon?' she asked, staggered at the news. She had never believed, not truly, that Rosie would do it. She had thought it all talk.

'So what? You've only known Ben a few months and you'd marry him like a shot if he asked you,' Rosie said.

'I've known him for years,' she said hotly. 'Admittedly, we've only seriously known each other for a little while but—'

'It's long enough,' Rosie interrupted, unconcerned. 'Henry can't afford to hang about at his age. We're hardly going to have a long engagement whilst we save up for a deposit and some furniture. He has all the furniture he needs. Three houses worth, in fact. I've only just found out he has three houses as well as the flat in London. I knew about two of the houses. The manor out in the country and the cottage in the Loire valley but I didn't know about the other one.'

'Hang on.' Olivia tried to make sense of it. 'This isn't one of your silly jokes?' She glanced at the outsized ring. 'Is that from Woolworth's?'

'No.' Rosie looked a little aggrieved. 'It is not. It's from Boodles. God, they treated us like royalty.'

She ran fingers through her hair, the diamond catching a ray of morning sun and glinting. 'Well. . . ?' Rosie demanded, flashing the ring this way and that and smiling. 'Aren't you going to congratulate me?'

'Congratulations,' Olivia said, trying to be bright herself but failing. 'When's the happy day?'

'Four weeks,' Rosie said. 'Registry office. And we're honeymooning at his house in Bermuda. This is what I've been trying to tell you. I didn't know about that house. He has a house there, bought years ago. Cost him nearly a million dollars even then. We might spend part of the year there when he retires, if he ever does that is. He likes to keep his finger on the pulse. You can come and visit, Livvy. You always said you loved it there.'

'Are you sure you've thought properly about this?' Olivia said, aware her dismay was showing. 'You ought to have told me before now, Rosie.'

'Why? I don't need your permission.'

'No. But I could have given you advice.'

Rosie laughed. 'What makes you think I'd take your advice? You haven't exactly got your own love life organized brilliantly, have you? Never date a man who's reluctant to commit, Livvy. It will end in tears.'

Olivia said nothing. There was nothing to say.

'Henry believes in marriage,' Rosie went on cheerfully. 'He gets it wrong sometimes but, by God, he believes in the institution.'

'All right,' she said irritably. Bully for Henry! 'But four weeks is pushing it, surely?'

'Henry and I do hope you and Ben will be our witnesses,' Rosie went on, surprisingly formal suddenly.

For a moment, Olivia could not bring herself to speak. She took a deep breath, trying to say the right thing. 'You've taken me completely by surprise. I don't know what to say.'

'I can tell that,' Rosie said drily. 'From the way you look, I might as well have said I was marrying a murderer. You might look a bit happier. If you'd told *me* you were getting married, I'd be thrilled for you.'

'That's different.'

'Why is it different?' Rosie asked, her eyes glinting in a way Olivia knew well. She had a temper and it was stirring up.

'Come off it, Rosie. Be honest. I never thought you'd do it. I really didn't. I just hope you know what you're doing.'

'What do you mean?' She uncurled herself. 'Of course I know what I'm doing. I love Henry and I'm going to marry him. He's the most exciting man I've known in ages. He just rockets along and I can hardly keep up with him. He's got the energy of a man half his age.'

'Really?'

Rosie gave her a thunderous look. 'Yes, really. Honestly, Livvy, I might have expected some support from you of all people.'

Olivia could not believe it. Rosie was pretending she was in love with this man. Pretending to *her*?

'You will come to the wedding, won't you?' Rosie said. 'We haven't time for formal invitations and so on and there's only going to be a handful of people there. Small reception at The Grosvenor afterwards.'

'Of course we'll come. I'll have to ask Ben, see if he can rearrange his schedule, but we'll be delighted,' Olivia said, saying the only thing she could say under the circumstances.

'Thanks.' Rosie smiled. 'I'll tell Henry. He'll be pleased too. He likes you. He thinks you're ever so slightly snooty but he likes you.'

'Snooty?'

'Joking,' Rosie said, playfully pulling a face. 'You have no sense of humour, Livvy.'

'Where will you live, when you get back from your honeymoon?' she asked, still dazed by the news. It was pretty hard to swallow. She was going to go through with it. Rosie was actually going to do it. Live with the man. Marry him. *Sleep* with him. Goodness, she knew Ben was older than her but he wasn't as old as Henry. Rosie was young enough to be Henry's daughter and that was a very sobering thought.

'We will be living at the manor house,' Rosie said, unbelievably gracious. 'I shall have to completely refurbish and redecorate. Henry's happy to have all traces of his ex removed. She was an absolute cow from all accounts. Henry's been incredibly generous to her.'

'Has he? Was she the mother of his daughter?'

'No. That was the first wife and we don't talk about her. The point is Henry needs someone to look after him.'

Olivia nearly laughed out loud.

'He's buying me a complete new wardrobe,' Rosie went on happily. 'He wants me to calm down a little.'

'Oh! And you're going to do that?' Olivia asked in surprise, for there had been a time, not too far in the past, when Rosie would have shot a man who suggested such a thing.

'Why not?' Rosie shrugged. 'I'm not going to argue with him.'

'Will it be you, though? Country life?' Olivia asked, thinking about the vicious gossip that would precede the arrival of Henry's new exciting young wife.

'Of course it will be me. I shall adore it,' Rosie said, face closing up. 'We won't exactly be lord and lady of the manor but Henry says it's a close-run thing. We will be expected to participate in village life and the manor is used as a venue for various events.'

Olivia stared. Rosie was a hopeless organizer.

As if reading her mind, Rosie made it plain that they had staff there. Of course, she knew they might feel a teeny bit of resentment towards her when they had grown used to his last wife, but they would come round and, if they didn't, that was just too bad. As Henry said, they were staff and they would have to get used to her or leave.

'There's more to it than that,' Olivia said, remembering her mother's cavalier attempts. 'I can't see you handling staff, Rosie.'

Rosie's face clammed up. 'Stuff you, Livvy, stop being so pessimistic. I shall learn. It's a doddle, Henry says, provided you keep your distance. Staff like to know what's what.'

Amazed at the deadpan expression, wondering just who Rosie was trying to kid, Olivia left it. If that was the way Rosie wanted to play it, then so be it. She must go along with it and keep up the pretence of it being a love match.

'A pale green suit?'Anna laughed. 'But she used to hate green. Said it made her look like an elf.'

They exchanged a smile. Olivia had just finished describing Rosie's wedding in great detail. She glanced worriedly at the large ticking clock on the wall of the visitors' parlour, hoping there was no time limit to the visit for she had spent half an hour there already.

'Should you be doing something?' she enquired nervously, thinking of prayers and chants and chapel. 'Don't let me keep you from whatever it is you do.'

'It's my free time,' Anna explained. 'I work outside for a few hours in the morning and in the afternoon we have our leisure time. We don't have television but we can listen to the radio or one of us will lead a poetry or prose reading.'

'I see.'

'It's Sister Margaret's turn to read today,' Anna said in a low voice. 'She loves *very* lengthy poems and has a very monotonous voice that sends us all off to sleep. I'm not sorry to be missing it.'

'Oh!'

So, Anna had not lost her sense of humour entirely. It brought Olivia to her senses, realising that Anna was still Anna. She might be wearing a 'uniform', for this particular convent was keen to keep the old habit, but underneath that, she was the same old Anna. Rosie had actually invited Anna to the wedding, fingers crossed that she would say no – for where the hell could you seat a nun at the wedding breakfast? In a panic, Rosie wailed that she would put a damper on everything and she would have to warn Henry to watch his language.

Blessedly, Anna regretfully declined.

'Would you like to have a look at the garden?'

'I'd love to. Am I allowed?'

'Of course,' Anna said. 'We like to share it with visitors.'

Olivia stood up, smoothing down the skirt of the simple suit she was wearing. This visit, this first visit, had been planned with military precision. Ben had been no help at all, totally lost when she asked what she ought to wear. In the end, she was forced to ask her mother's advice. Judith had promptly enquired of the vicar's wife, who had cheerfully said, 'Anything goes.' The nuns, she said, were surprisingly modern in outlook these days and it wouldn't matter to them if you turned up in jeans.

Her mother ignored the advice. She was having none of that.

'She doesn't know what she's talking about,' she said dismissively. 'If you can't apply a dress code when visiting a nunnery, when can you? I think a skirt rather than trousers and go easy on the make-up and perfume.'

So, it was a plain suit, careful make-up, and at the last minute she remembered to take off her deep burgundy nail polish. Olivia cared for her hands and loved nail polish. Looking at her naked nails now, she felt odd, as if she was playing a part in a play – visitor to convent.

Beside her, Anna rustled in her dark habit, like a lady of old. She smelt of soap. Clean unperfumed soap. Briefly, Olivia wondered what the bathroom arrangements were here – did they shower in cold water, or worse, just have a wash down with the help of a jug and bowl? She was not allowed to see the private quarters where they slept but she gathered that it was pretty basic. Also, it seemed very un-nunlike to wallow in a deeply scented warm bath as she herself had done last night, surrounded by relaxing aromatherapy candles.

And, afterwards, in the king-size bed in his apartment, she and Ben had made love . . . slowly.

She shoved that inappropriate thought aside, horrified that it should nudge her just now, as she and Anna walked down a long silent corridor with a polished wooden floor, white walls, a simple cross facing them, before stepping out into the garden. She remembered seeing this very garden from the city wall when she was a little girl and had asked to be lifted up so that she could see over. Although it was too far to see a clear outline, someone was walking along the wall now, looking over, and from that vantage point, above and at a distance, it must look lovely.

It was autumn in all its leafy splendour and they stood a moment at the garden's edge admiring it. A cat was sitting on the stone slab in the centre of this part of the garden, a ginger cat surrounded by Michaelmas daisies.

'He likes to sit there,' Anna told her, following her gaze. 'In winter, I'm told he sits right beside the range in the kitchen and the sisters can't get him to budge, even though they worry he might scorch his fur. He chooses not to go into chapel, although we wouldn't mind if he did. Perhaps the smell of incense puts him off. I can't think why. I love it and wish we used more.'

'The roses need dead-heading,' Olivia remarked, glancing at them critically, itching for a pair of secateurs. 'Who does the garden?'

'Sister Bethany but she's in her nineties now and her eyesight's failing. There is a man who comes in a couple of times a week to do the heavy work and I'm helping a little too. Sister Bethany is most anxious that I take over when she dies. She is praying it will be soon. She is very tired, Olivia, and more than ready for the Lord to receive her into his arms.'

Olivia said nothing. She didn't know *what* to say. When Anna started talking like that, it was her no longer, it was the nun in her, and Olivia was uncomfortable with it.

'How are you coping, Anna?' she asked. 'With all this?'

'I am very happy and I wish Ben would accept that. And Mum, of course. She hasn't been near. She says it's nothing personal but it would upset her too much.'

'Ben and I are . . .' Olivia hesitated. 'Well, we're together, Anna.'

Anna smiled. 'I know. You're an item, aren't you? I gather it all started when you came that weekend to try to persuade me to drop all this.'

'I'm sorry. I should never have done that.'

'Don't worry. At least some good came out of the weekend. You and Ben finding each other at last. He is very happy, Olivia, and I see you are too. Will you marry?'

She nodded. 'I hope so. He needs a bit of a push.'

'I'll see what I can do,' Anna said gently.

They did a complete leisurely turn of the garden, Olivia pausing, admiring, telling Anna the names of various plants, and by the time they returned to the parlour, she was more relaxed in Anna's company. Even though there were still traces of the old Anna, the new had taken over and the change was complete. There would be no turning back.

Olivia saw it in her eyes.

She knew Ben still held on to the belief that she would change her mind, see sense, as he put it.

Ben would do well to forget such thoughts.

CHAPTER TWELVE

Anna sat on the warm stone slab beside the cat, and thought about Olivia's visit. She hoped Ben would do the decent thing and marry her, for Olivia wanted children and would make such a good mother. Sometimes, she felt odd stirrings herself, maternal yearnings, and she had talked to the noviciate tutor about these feelings and been assured they were not the least unusual.

Despite everything, she must not forget that she was still a woman, a young woman at that. She was still capable of looking at a man in that way and she still thought often about Ross. She had mood swings and was irritated sometimes with the others, particularly Sister Margaret, but she must learn to overcome these failings.

Patience and perseverance.

The convent of their community of The Heavenly Cross was not so far from the centre of the town, its main entrance half hidden up an unpromising alley off an old faintly neglected square. If it had started off intending to be a secret place, it certainly succeeded.

The clock tower bell pealed, drawing her to prayer, and, at once, she stood and walked slowly down the straight brick path towards the convent. She had to wash and then compose herself for the afternoon Office. She was not to know it but she made a solitary figure and from the city wall, someone watched and pointed out the darkly garbed nun making her way through the hazy patchwork of the garden.

Ginger the cat, making the most of the last of the warm days, roused himself and followed at a discreet distance.

'I told you that girl would come to grief. We can only hope the money will make her happy. It was certainly an obscene-sized engagement ring,' Judith said with a disapproving sniff. 'If I was his ex-wife, I'd kill him,' she went on. 'If your father

'I can't afford to live there on my own,' Olivia said. 'With two of us chipping in it wasn't so bad.'

'You could come back to live here.'

'Thanks, Mum, but . . .'

The laugh was short. 'Oh, come on, Olivia, I didn't mean that for a moment. Your father and I have grown used to being just the two of us, but please don't insult me. It's quite obvious what will be happening. Ben will be moving in with you, won't he? Or you'll be moving in with him?'

'We've talked about it, yes,' she admitted, stung to aggression by the tone but feeling herself flush nonetheless. 'Why ever not? It's silly to keep two places going, especially when I can't afford my flat on my own.'

There was a silence.

She waited anxiously. She had to let her mother think this out, but she hoped she would give a muted blessing to the arrangement. She and Ben had enjoyed a candlelit dinner during the week and, lulled by the romantic nature of it and the way he had treated her over dinner, she had found herself expecting a proposal which, in the event, had not happened.

Instead, he had suggested the far more unromantic notion that they move in together permanently. It was insane not to. Financially and emotionally, for they were quietly going crazy with the present living arrangements. For some reason not quite obvious to her, her flat was preferred to his.

It was all intensely practical but nonetheless . . .

'All right. I suppose we have to move along and it's the way of the world these days,' Judith said at last with an uncertain smile. 'It wouldn't have happened in my day but there you are ... However, I would feel happier, darling, if you had an engagement ring at least. And I must say, I'm rather surprised, a man like Ben, a surgeon of all things – one would have thought he would have certain standards, particularly as his sister is a nun.'

'Anna being a nun is nothing to do with us,' Olivia said, amused at the idea.

'Perhaps not but what must she be thinking? I know they are supposed to be broad-minded but I don't believe a word of that. Anyway, darling, in my experience, once you start living together, there's always the danger that thoughts of marriage begin to drift away. Have you discussed it at all?'

'Mother. . . !'

She waved a hand in apology. 'Sorry – I shouldn't have asked. It's not my business.'

'No, it isn't.'

They exchanged a slight smile, a relieved one in Olivia's case because she had expected trouble or, at the very least, a show of indignation. Sometimes it was as if she did not really know her mother at all. Sometimes, her reactions were totally at odds with what she signalled.

'Go and talk to your father. Tell him. And break it gently. He's rather fragile just now,' Judith said, pulling an exasperated face. 'It's work. Why he doesn't just retire and have done with it, I shall never know.'

Olivia knew why. You only had to look at her mother to know why. But she agreed that he looked tired and wondered if it was all getting a bit much for him. She caught up with him in the garden where he was, uncharacteristically, pottering about.

'I've been sent to talk to you, Dad,' Olivia began with a smile. 'Mum says we don't talk often enough, you and me.'

'Does she now?' He downed tools and reached guiltily for his pipe. 'Do you mind? Or are you one of the smoking Mafia these days like Judith?'

'I don't mind.'

'Thanks, love. They're safer than cigarettes,' he said, damping down the pipe. 'Who says?'

'I say,' he said firmly.

The tobacco smell was rich and memorable and here, in another garden, the memory was ignited.

'Mr Johnson used to smoke a pipe,' she said. 'Do you remember him? He was one of the gardeners at Slyne Hall. He died when I was in the junior school, Miss Parr's class.'

'Good God. Let me think. Mr Johnson . . .' He looked into space thoughtfully, nodding as if he did remember when she was sure he did not. 'He really got you interested in gardening, didn't he?'

'He started it off, yes.' She smiled at the memory of her ten-year-old self. She realized now how Mr Johnson had been incredibly patient with her and she would always treasure the book he had given her just before he died.

Her father's sigh in the soft summer afternoon was deep.

'We messed you about, didn't we? All that travelling. Such a little girl and all that travelling. How could we do it to you?'

'I got used to it. It's only when I think back that I feel scared for what I used to do. What would I have done if something bad had happened?'

He shuddered. 'Don't say that. I'm sure somebody would have helped. But I worried for you, darling. And so did your mother.'

She made a small sound of disbelief and he looked at her sharply.

'Your mother wanted me to pack it all in at one point and for us to come home so that we could see you every weekend. She missed you. You mustn't ever think she didn't care. She cared a lot.'

'Then why didn't she say?' Olivia asked. 'She never does say.'

'People don't,' he said amiably. 'You know that. Especially people from our backgrounds. Stiff upper lip et cetera. I don't go in for that sort of talk either.'

'You don't *need* to say it,' Olivia said, awkward.

He sighed and puffed on his pipe, leaning back on the bench and contemplating his puny efforts in the garden.

'Maybe I should tell you before I forget that I'm proud of you, Olly,' he said. 'Proud of the way you buckled down after that exam fiasco and made something of yourself. Your mother's proud of you, too, but she finds it hard to say. She was brought up, as you know, in a hard-faced family with no love lost between the lot of them. They're a funny lot, your mother's side.'

'And your lot are completely sane?' she teased.

'Absolutely. The Haytons are a splendid bunch. Lucky for your mother I caught up with her, even though she's been a bit of a trial. Remember the times she left me?' he asked ruefully. 'Scared me to death.'

Olivia smiled a little. 'That was a rotten thing to do to you. She never meant it, you know.'

'I know. She's always been one for the grand gesture.'

'Did you fall in love at first sight?' she asked, posing the question gently. 'When you met Mum at Ascot?'

'Ascot? Of course.' There was the slightest pause and she wondered if he would opt out of a satisfactory answer. 'That was a long time ago . . .' he said at last. 'I often wonder what would have happened if I had skipped Ascot that day. Would we have met somewhere else or would she have met someone else? I was rocketing along with my career and destined to stay single.'

'Why?'

'I was shy, darling.'

'Never!'

'Yes, I was. Shy of women. I needed a girl liked Judith. Full of confidence, someone to bring me out of my shell. I noticed her as soon as she came by. I stood on the sidelines and watched her all afternoon. She had a wonderful time that day – she was so lively and excited. Took my breath away.'

Olivia held *her* breath, lest the moment escape him. She wanted more. Sometimes she wondered if they did love each other and it was important to her that they did. Fond exasperation was how best to describe her father's feelings now. Ditto her mother for him.

'I can remember what she was wearing,' he said excitedly. 'A frock with a big skirt. You know the sort of thing – crisp cotton, sticking-out style. It was white and it had great splurges of colour on it – pinks, mauves, blues. It was just like a garden in full bloom . . . Oh, and she was carrying an umbrella to shade her from the sun. One of those fancy ones – they don't do them now. Chinese pagoda shape when you opened it up. That was flowery too.'

'Pretty,' Olivia murmured, finding the floral image difficult to conjure up.

'Lovely. And she was laughing such a lot. Such beautiful dark hair that she wore in a plait then. Thick dark hair knotted together.'

'What? No hat? At Ascot?'

'She carried one,' he said. 'It was tricky for hats – a windy day, if I recall. Anyway, there she was, looking lovely. You know how she sounds when she laughs – people were buzzing round her like flies.'

Olivia smiled at the image. 'And you went over and asked her out?'

'Not immediately. That took some nerve, I can tell you. I can't remember exactly how I got round to doing that.'

But he could remember every detail of how she had looked.

'I proposed to her three months after we met.'

'You didn't? That was a bit quick off the mark, wasn't it?'

'I don't see why. We both knew we'd be happy together, so that seemed to be it. She was young, yes, and that meant I had to get her father's approval . . . '

'Did you? People don't do that sort of thing any more.'

'They didn't much then either but I did. He'd made his money, Judith's father, and he wanted to be sure I was up to it. He wanted no truck with a loser.'

'Honestly? It's like something out of the Victorian age.'

'Maybe.' He puffed reflectively on his pipe. 'Perhaps it wasn't such a bad idea. After all, a father of all people knows his own daughter,' he added, casting a sly glance her way.

'You obviously passed the test with Grandfather?' she asked, slightly uncomfortable in that she had not yet broken her news.

He smiled. 'Yes. I think I impressed him. I was already doing well.'

'What if he had said no? What would you have done?'

'That would have been up to Judith,' he said, thinking on it. 'I wouldn't have wanted her to estrange herself from her own family. The decision would have been hers. But I was accepted into their family and Judith and I never had any doubts.'

Neither did she, she wanted to say, sensing somehow the slightest reproof.

'So, your mother tells me your friend Rosie has got herself married,' he went on. 'It was a bit of a surprise. Your mother thought she was the sort who'd just live with someone.'

'I hope she's doing the right thing,' Olivia said carefully, casting a glance his way. 'She says she loves Henry.'

'And do you think she does?'

'I don't know. I don't think so.' She hesitated. He had popped on his sunglasses, which made it impossible to gauge his reaction. 'Ben's moving in with me, Daddy,' she went on, quickly before she lost her nerve. 'It's financial more than anything. I mean, what's the point of paying two lots of rent? And eventually we'll think of buying a property together. He's doing well at the hospital. They think very highly of him but then he's so conscientious.'

Aware of his silence, she rattled clumsily on. 'Mum wishes we'd get married or engaged and we will, but please give us time. We've lots of time.'

He sniffed. 'He's not exactly young, is he? And he must be in a handsome position financially. So what's he waiting for?' he asked, voice sharp. 'Do you want a family?'

'Yes.'

'Both of you?'

She hesitated and it was enough for him to pounce.

'Don't say you haven't talked about it?'

She realized they had not talked properly for whenever she mentioned it, he skirted round it.

'I'm sure Ben will want a family too,' she told her father, sounding unconvincing even to her own ears.

'Find out and quickly,' he said.

'What's wrong, Dad?' she asked, uncomfortable with his changed manner. 'You do like him, don't you?'

'Well enough. What I don't like is that he doesn't like your mother much,' he said with a grimace. 'He makes it a bit obvious.'

'They got off to a bad start,' Olivia said uncomfortably. 'And she always manages a sly dig at his mother when we get together. He's very protective of his mother.'

'Commendable but he should make an effort. It rattles Judith. I know she can be indiscreet but she tries and she doesn't feel she's getting anywhere. That annoys me. I know she has her faults but she doesn't deserve that sort of cold shouldering and I take exception to it too.'

'You're making much too much of it. Mum's imagining it,' Olivia said quickly. 'Of course he likes you both. Do you really like him, Dad?' she repeated, desperately anxious to get an affirmative answer.

'Stop pushing me, darling, I don't know him very well.'

'You don't try to get to know him,' she said, exasperated, because whenever Ben tried to spend time with him, he either talked about the weather or suddenly remembered he must do something. 'And he's had a tough time with Anna doing what she has done. With his father gone, he feels responsible for her.'

'So he should. And surely, with his sister being a nun, he should marry you. I don't understand all this nonsense of being afraid to commit to marriage. You have to make decisions in the business world, for heaven's sake, decisions that you can't change once made, so why not in marriage. What's he frightened of?'

'Dad . . .' She clicked her tongue in exasperation. 'It's very nearly the twenty-first century. Things are different these days, everyone's much more relaxed. Couples have children now and then get married afterwards. And nobody worries about it.'

'Really? Is that what *you* want?'

That hit the jugular.

'You're making a mistake, if you start to live together,' he continued, puffing with agitation on the pipe. 'You'll never see a wedding ring and it's easier to walk out without one, no matter what all these modernists will have you believe. And where would you be then? Past thirty yourself.'

'What is this preoccupation people of your generation have with getting married?' she said, trying to keep control of her temper. 'Does it matter so much? I love him, Dad, and surely that's all that does matter. And he's moving in tomorrow, whether you like it or not.'

'Is that so?'

'Yes. Sorry to be so blunt,' she flustered, not happy being aggressive towards him. 'I'm sorry you feel this way, Dad, but I think you're being very unfair.'

'Let me make one thing clear . . .'

'What?' she asked nervously, knowing that tone of voice.

'If he moves in with you, lives with you before you are married, then it's quite simple. I don't visit your flat again,' her father said, removing the sunglasses and stuffing them in his pocket, looking at her with sad eyes. 'I'm sorry, too, but that's the way I feel. I have principles . . .'

'Principles?' she laughed, unsure. 'This isn't just a fling, Dad. We're very serious about each other.'

He ignored that. 'And you don't visit here, either, not if I'm here.'

'No.' She tried to laugh at the absurdity of it. 'That's silly. Lots of people live together. They say it's a good idea. Then you really get to know each other before ever leaves me for a younger model, I've warned him what will happen.'

Olivia smiled. This had all been said before, lots of times, often in front of Dad, and it meant nothing. It had also been said a few times in front of Ben which, owing to his circumstances, was indiscreet to say the least and just another nail in the coffin of Ben's attempts to make the best of things.

'Henry has two ex-wives, Mother,' she said, making matters worse. 'Didn't you know?'

'I don't wish to know the gory details. How long before Rosie becomes the next ex?'

'That's cruel. I don't wish that for her.'

Judith eyed her calmly. 'Don't you? We're all jealous of anyone with more money than us. I should know. A lot of people look at me with that look.' She gazed round her elegant drawing-room with satisfaction. 'We have all this but we are not millionaires and Rosie's husband is.' Judith glanced out of the window triumphantly as the sun came out from behind a wispy bank of clouds. 'There! I knew it would come out. Do you want to take tea on the terrace?'

'Here's fine,' Olivia said quickly, anxious to avoid the pantomime involved in outdoor eating. Her mother liked everything to look just as pretty as the dining-room and by the time it was all organized, the sun would very likely have escaped behind the clouds again.

'What is she thinking of?' her mother continued, seeming unable to let Rosie off the hook yet. 'The man's getting on and that's when it all starts to disintegrate. If she's expecting any sparks, she's going to be disappointed.'

'She's invited me and Ben for the weekend when they get back from honeymoon,' Olivia said quickly. 'I understand the manor house is beautiful.'

'I've no doubt. Of course, her husband got a good start in life. He's from old farming stock originally; that's where the money came from.'

'Henry can hardly help that,' Olivia said, feeling an absurd need to defend him in the face of her mother's brittle dismissal.

'No, but it must make things easier when you have money to fall back on. You can afford to take risks then. I have to say I mistrust a man who has been married and divorced twice. It shows either a complete lack of judgement where women are concerned or a far too cavalier attitude.'

'Try telling that to Rosie. She's managed to convince herself she's in love with him.'

'Nonsense. But there's no point in conducting a post mortem now the deed is done,' Judith said, looking at Olivia before asking, voice carefully neutral, if she was going to advertize for a new flatmate.

you get married . . .' She stopped as she saw the look, set in stone, on his face.

'Your mother and I did not,' he said.

'But that was then.' she said. 'Ages ago.'

'Not so long ago,' he muttered. 'You talk as if it was the Stone Age.'

'We move on, Dad. Each generation moves on,' she said, trying her best to be gentle with him, understanding how old-fashioned he was. 'I expect it will be quite different for my children when the time comes and I'll have to try to understand them.'

'Meaning I don't?'

'Well, Mum seems to have accepted it,' she said, catching a glimpse of her mother at the window. 'We'll get married when we're ready,' she went on firmly. 'And not a minute before. I can't believe you're going to make a big thing out of it, Dad. Please don't. Please come and visit us – Ben will be as hurt as me if you don't.'

'No. I've made my position quite plain. You've disappointed me, Olivia.'

Olivia, not Olly. It was the nearest he had come in a long while to a full-scale reprimand and it stung as if he had slapped her viciously across the face.

'You don't mean it, Daddy,' she said, helpless suddenly.

'I do mean it,' he said, getting up and striding away, kicking off his gardening wellies at the back porch and flinging his spade and assorted tools into a corner with an unnecessary crash.

Slowly, side-stepping the spread-eagled tools, she followed him indoors. Her mother was in the middle of preparing a simple tea but Olivia excused herself and left at once. No doubt her father, at present performing noisy and annoyed ablutions, would put her in the picture.

Thinking it over later, she was sure the rift with Dad would be temporary. She couldn't believe he would be so intransigent for long. He would come round – Mum would see to that. But even when he did, it would always be there, a little niggle of resentment.

With a heavy heart, she knew that things would never be quite the same again.

CHAPTER THIRTEEN

Anna was rarely ill, so she did not take kindly to the troublesome cough and sore chest that was aggravated by the windy weather.

Reverend Mother was concerned enough to send for the doctor, a young woman with a most pleasant smile, who, after an examination and questions, advised rest.

'I mean it, Sister. You must have complete rest for a few days,' she said, writing out a prescription. 'Will it be possible for somebody to get this for you?'

'Yes. Sister Marie will walk into town. She does the errands for us,' she explained hastily. People in the outside world sometimes had a strange idea of convent life. People thought they never spoke and that was true of some contemplative orders, of course, but not theirs. Nor did they prostrate themselves on the floor, or survive on bread and water and extreme hardship. And they were not confined here, as if in prison, although in this particular community they ventured out only when necessary and rarely alone.

'You have a nasty infection,' the doctor went on, although Anna could have told her that already, for she had diagnosed it herself. 'It's lucky you're normally healthy and young too. But you need rest and warmth.'

Warmth? Anna smiled a little. Not much chance of that.

'No scrubbing floors either,' the doctor said, glancing round as if she would see this happening. 'And I'm sorry but no outside work. I'm told you've been working in the garden,' she added, rebuke in her tone. 'I'm afraid you mustn't just now.'

'Oh dear. There's the tidy up to finish for the winter.'

'The garden can wait.' The doctor smiled her friendly smile. 'Take care, Sister.'

'Thank you, Doctor, and God bless you and your family.'

'Thank you. I shall tell my daughter I've been visiting. She wants to be a nun at the moment.' She snapped her bag shut and smiled again. 'Last week, it was a doctor and the week before that a check-out lady at the supermarket.'

They laughed together at the ways of children and Anna felt a pang as uncomfortable for a moment as the ache in her chest.

'My mother is a doctor, a GP, and my brother a cardiologist,' she said shyly as the doctor reached for her coat. 'I studied a while, too, but then I had to give it up . . .'

'How interesting! You do surprise me. It must have been very difficult for you to give up the course. What on earth happened? Were you called?'

The same old question!

'I suppose I was in a way,' she said, trying to keep it simple. 'We're not a churchgoing family so it was all very odd. I tried so hard not to listen.'

'But. . . ?' the doctor prompted with interested eyes.

'I tried to forget about it and studied medicine like I was supposed to but my heart wasn't in it. And then I started attending church every week and one week . . .' She paused, remembering it vividly. 'Sorry, I don't want to bore you.'

'Not at all. You're my last patient,' the doctor said, waiting with a concerned face until Anna finished a bout of coughing.

'One week a nun came to church. She sat at the front, the very front where nobody else dares sit, and I watched the back of her head all through the service and afterwards . . .'

'You talked to her?'

Anna smiled. 'I *nearly* talked to her. But when it came to it, I couldn't. She seemed somehow forbidding, I suppose.'

'I must admit I had a few doubts when I first came to visit here,' the doctor said, her honesty refreshing. 'And, believe it or not, some of my male colleagues are more than a little apprehensive at the thought.'

Anna could understand that. The very nature of their calling, the fact that most of the population couldn't possibly do what they did, made them women apart, and the overwhelming reaction was generally respect tinged with suspicion.

'But looking at that nun that day,' she went on, undaunted 'I remembered how serene she was, how happy she looked, and that stayed with me a long time. Eventually, I talked to the vicar. He looked very doubtful about it all. It took some time to persuade him I was genuine before he gave me the names of some convents I might try.'

'And you came here?'

Anna, breathing tightly and still painfully, looked round the little bare room.

'Yes. I came here.'

*

But before she came here, she went to others, convincing herself that the life was not for her. Just as well she hadn't told a soul about it, apart from the vicar, and it was a sudden relief that she was not going to be a nun after all.

She returned to her studies in a carefree mood and for a while she lived life to the full, partying and drinking, very nearly neglecting her work and generally having a good time.

A nun! What an idea! But it refused to go away. It *refused* to go away.

The soul searching continued for many months after that and she secretly visited several different communities, having been told that when you arrived at the right one, you just knew.

Some communities rejected her, thinking her too young, and even told her to come back when she had done something, seen something of the world. It was said in a very kindly way but it was a shock, as she had stupidly imagined she would be welcomed instantly and without question. Twenty-four was the absolute minimum age most would accept and she was not much more than that. For an institution, if you could call it that, that was desperately short of numbers, with convents folding right, left and centre, they seemed picky to the extreme.

The solitary enclosed community she visited in Kent made a tremendous impression on her, even though it turned out to be not suitable for her. There the sisters wore the old-style wimple although there were rumours afoot about ditching it. Anna hoped they did not for they looked wonderful in their floor-length black habits, like something out of a medieval pageant. Just like Julie Andrews and Anna remembered laughing at the thought and telling the sister *what* she had thought!

The sister laughed too and said that when you became a nun you did not necessarily lose a sense of humour. In fact, it jolly well helped on occasions. One sister had quite dreadful pitch and was totally oblivious to it, which used to cause giggles amongst the rest of them but, poor soul, she could not be persuaded to sing a little more quietly, so they had become accustomed to it, rejoicing instead in her enjoyment of singing.

But, all in all, learning about life in the strictly enclosed community, Anna was chastened at the discipline of rising in the middle of the night to say prayers at two in the morning and then again at three. They held seven services a day and, in addition, there were two hours of private prayer which seemed a very long time. She just knew her thoughts would drift and true prayer time amount to a mere fraction of that. But it's a skill that has to be learned, she was told, and once you are at ease with it, then two hours is barely long enough.

The enclosed life was strict and the hardship real. Once their vows were taken, the sisters would not be allowed to receive visits from family nor have any holidays themselves and would only leave the community for medical reasons or when they died. Anna saw it as cutting off completely, too drastically, and in the end she could not do it to herself or her family. Leaving that convent that day, she thought all her hopes were ended and she arranged a visit here – to this place – with a heavy heart, feeling she had somehow failed herself and, more importantly, failed God.

As soon as she stepped through the door here to be greeted by the Mother of the community, Anna knew she was coming home.

She would die here. But not yet.

She must do as the doctor said and rest. She felt ill. She had difficulty in breathing and the wheezing was making her chest hurt. Mother would be most kind, as she always was, and give permission that she stay in her room with her meals brought in. An additional heater would be provided, extra blankets too, and one of the sisters might read to her later in her recreation period and she looked forward to that.

She uttered a silent prayer, long and thoughtful. Then she lay on her bed, from where she could see the tops of the trees and, beyond them, the city walls.

She fretted a little about the jobs she had set herself this week, jobs that would not now be accomplished. The doctor was wrong, the garden did not wait. It tramped along, weeds flourished, and delicate plants struggled without help. There had been almost a week of continuous cold rain which had delayed her going out to work in the garden and encouraged the weeds.

The medicine would help.

She was sure the medicine would help.

She closed her eyes but the garden, every single inch of it, and the swaying branches of the trees, remained vividly in her memory.

CHAPTER FOURTEEN

Olivia knew just how sweet and thoughtful Ben was being and she tried to make it easier, suspecting he would have welcomed a full-blown medical emergency with all hands on deck in preference to visiting Rosie and Henry for the weekend.

She was not entirely sure she was looking forward to it either, although Rosie had sounded fine on the phone, bubbly and bright as usual. But . . . Rosie entertaining! The mind boggled.

She might sound the same on the phone, most of the time, but there was always the danger that a sickening graciousness would come over her and then it was like talking to a stranger, or a not very good actress. Olivia would bet her last penny on Rosie acting a part. She really could not believe that she loved Henry when she had set out – her own admission – to snare him.

But if having an apparently unlimited amount of money made Rosie happy, who was she to judge? She really had to stop thinking she knew what was best for her friend. And perhaps this weekend, seeing the newlyweds at close quarters, she might see how it really was between them. She would not ask. She would wait for Rosie to tell her. The Rosie of old would be telling her everything, including all the juicy bits, within minutes of them meeting again, but today's Rosie might have learned something about discretion.

It was a pretty-pretty village with a wide main street, the houses set well back with an avenue of trees, a green off to one side complete with duck pond and a truly magnificent oak. The sturdy red-brick cottages were softened with creepers, gardens packed full of pastel-shaded lupins, pink and white foxgloves and hollyhocks, all buzzing in the sunshine with honey-bees. In other words, the standard cottage garden of her dreams. It would have made the perfect setting for some TV mystery play, out to capture the US market with its glorious English setting.

Rosie's house was known as The Old Manor and it was smaller at first sight than Olivia had imagined, for she had imagined nothing less than a grand country house. The location was splendid, the house lying in a large bright clearing amongst trees, on a gentle slope within sight and sound of the church. There was an imposing but not too enormous garden with perfectly cut lawn and trimmed edges, dotted with neat colourful beds. It was quite different from the village gardens, the planting much more uniform and controlled. It would have drawn forth a sigh of delight from most people, but to Olivia, although it was pleasing, something was missing, something stopped it being perfect.

It was the garden, of course, and Olivia was quick to spot it. It was tended, efficiently tended at that, by a busy gardener, but not loved.

If The Old Manor were to come on the market, it would be described as a charming small country house with character and large yet manageable gardens. If it were to come on the market, it would very likely be snapped up as a second home by some Cheshire businessman, following in Henry's shiny expensive shoes.

'It's quite something, isn't it?' Ben said, smiling across at her as he stopped on a gravel area to one side. 'I know exactly what you're thinking. Your idea of heaven.'

She smiled. 'Pretty close.'

'I bet the church bells are deafening when they start up,' he said, lifting the bags out of the boot and looking towards the squat square tower.

'Trust you to think of that,' she said, shaking her head, and breathing in the sweet summery smells of cut grass and flowers. 'You should never complain about church bells. It's sacrilegious. Anyway, it's well known that it's noisy in the country. Surely you know that?'

'Yes, but I'm a townie at heart,' he said. 'I need my injection of city air, all that pollution, to keep me sane.'

Rosie was out of the door before they had time to knock, throwing herself on Olivia, dragging them indoors into the hall. It was very tastefully decorated – surely not Rosie – and immaculate down to the elaborate flower arrangements – *definitely* not Rosie.

'Henry's going to be awfully late. Sends his apologies,' she said breathlessly. 'Sorry, I'm absolutely knackered. I've been tearing round getting ready for you. You are my very first weekend visitors since we got back from honeymoon, so I wanted to get it right.'

Her childish enthusiasm was catching, although Olivia caught sight of a cleaning lady hurriedly stashing equipment in a far-off cupboard, confirming her suspicion that Rosie hadn't exactly been floating round with the hoover and polish herself.

'What do you think of it?' she asked, eyes wide with excitement. 'Isn't it fantastic? It's got a very interesting history. It was built in about 1700 for a lawyer and he and his family lived in it for ages before they died out. He's buried now in the churchyard. I'll show you his grave tomorrow. Isn't it romantic? Being buried within sight of the house you lived in for fifty years?'

'Very romantic,' Olivia said, smiling at her. Rosie looked happy enough, only lightly tanned but then she took care with her skin, smart in well-cut beige trousers and a crisp blouse, the only concession to her Isadora Duncan days a filmy, silky scarf knotted loosely round the collar. She was wearing skilfully applied make-up, smelled of some glorious scent, and her pearl earrings were discreet and most certainly the genuine thing. She looked good although the new classic styling aged her. Thinking of the old days, of glamorous second-hand jewellery bought for a song at some flea market, Olivia dared once again to marvel at the whole set-up.

'Come on through,' Rosie said, leading them into a light and airy drawing-room, where big bold daisies sat in a pewter pot on top of a coffee table. It was restful and elegant and not at all Rosie. It cleverly managed to strike just the right note – not too cottagey, not too ornate. On the walls there was an arrangement of interesting paintings and on the mantelpiece two elaborately carved candlesticks either side of a French mantel clock. Recalling Rosie's tendency to put her favourite Mickey Mouse mug on the mantelpiece in the flat, Olivia could not help but smile.

'What do you think, Livvy?' Rosie asked anxiously. 'Have I got it right? I agonized over the colour. It's from the National Trust palette, so it's authentic for the period.'

'It's lovely,' Olivia said, reassuring her. 'Did you do it all yourself?'

'You bet. I planned it before we married and, by the time we got home, the decorators were gone and it just needed a few finishing touches.' She grinned, looking like her old self for a brief moment. 'If Henry didn't consider it an utterly naff career, I might go in for interior design. It's not bad for a first attempt, eh?'

'Not bad at all.'

Rosie seemed on edge now, uncertain what to do with them. Olivia helped her out.

'Would you mind if I freshened up?'

'Not at all. I'll show you up to your room,' Rosie said, happy once more now that she had established what came next when entertaining. 'We've put you in one of the guest rooms at the back. It's up a side staircase that's dreadfully steep, so you'll have to watch you don't catch a heel and come a cropper. Come on, I'll show you.'

The house was bigger than it looked, bits having been added on at a later date, and the side staircase led them up in a curve to the next floor, a broad cream-carpeted landing and their charming room.

Rosie hovered around like a landlady, showing them where the extra blankets and pillows were and taking them over to the window to show them a view of the garden, at the bottom of which they could see a flight of worn stone steps leading to a small brown gate that led directly to the church. Olivia could feel the silence out there and thought of the lawyer who had had the house built, lying there in the graveyard.

She loved it here.

There was a bang-up-to-date bathroom adjoining, Italian tiled, ceiling to floor, and the bedroom itself was dominated by a Victorian brass bed covered in a beautiful patchwork quilt. The walls were pale pink and the smallish window, letting in sunlight, was draped with muslin tied back with pink ribbons.

It was unashamedly feminine and quite simply a delight.

'I'll leave you for a few minutes. Do come down for coffee when you're ready and if there's anything you need that I've forgotten, just ask,' Rosie said, exiting and closing the door gently.

They looked at each other and laughed.

'What has he done to her? Has he hypnotized her?' Ben whispered. 'Is she his slave woman?'

Olivia smiled. 'Looks like it. If I ever start behaving like that, do please tell me.'

He took her in his arms. 'I wouldn't change you for the world. You're perfect as you are,' he said as he kissed her, murmuring against her ear. 'How soon does she expect us for coffee, would you say? That bed looks very comfortable and we ought to christen it.'

She wriggled out of his arms. 'Not enough time for that,' she said cheerfully. 'Nor is it the done thing to keep your hostess waiting. I'll just pop to the bath-room and freshen up and then we'll go back down.'

Coffee and home-made date and walnut cake were waiting for them, as was Rosie, dying to tell them all about her honeymoon.

'You never told me Bermuda was so wonderful,' she told Olivia. 'I can't wait to go back. The house is an absolute dream. Henry says we may go for Christmas, although I'm not sure about that. A barbecue in the grounds sounds fantastic but Christmas is all about cold and snow, isn't it? And we shall have such a lovely Christmas here. Carols at midnight. Mulled wine and mince pies. We shall have open house. . . .'

Sitting side by side on the enormously comfortable pale lemon sofa, looking at the honeymoon photographs, was almost like old times, with Rosie forgetting herself and wrapping her legs round each other in that familiar way.

Many of the photographs were of places Olivia knew and remembered and nothing seemed to have changed that much. It became a cross-fire of talk about what was still there and what had long gone.

Casting aside the solid presence of Henry in most of the photographs, Olivia looked beyond him at the settings. The house of softest pink and white was very impressive, making this house look almost ordinary by comparison, but that might have been the effect of the dazzling sun and the glimpse of the blue-green sea in the background. High sunshine was capable of making the simplest shack look like a millionaire's retreat.

The conversation turned to Anna.

'I still can't believe it,' Rosie said. 'Should I go to see her? Or would it be better for me to remember her as she was?'

'She's not dead,' Olivia said gently.

'Not quite but she might as well be. It's like volunteering yourself for a life sentence,' Ben spoke up with a sigh. 'Maybe I should have asked you to have a word with her, Rosie. You might have been able to talk her out of it when Olivia couldn't.'

'I doubt it. She always took much more notice of Livvy,' Rosie said stoutly. 'Anyway, each to his own. I think she's gone completely nuts but if she wants to opt out, then I suppose we should leave her to it.'

'Olivia's still trying to convince me,' Ben said with a sigh. 'And she'll win me round eventually. She always does.'

He glanced her way and shot her one of his wonderful smiles.

'In that case, Ben . . .' Rosie drew herself up, her manner suddenly indignant. 'Isn't it about time you. . . ?'

'Did you mention the local pub this evening?' Olivia interrupted desperately, anticipating the remainder of the question. 'That sounds a nice idea.'

'Hardly!' Rosie said with a grin. 'It's deadly dull and Henry is not a pub person but he feels quite strongly that he has to put in an appearance,' she explained earnestly. 'Just as I have to be involved with church matters. It's part of the job.'

'What job's that?' Ben asked, all innocence.

'Well, traditionally, this house and the occupants played an important part in village life,' Rosie said. 'The people at The Old Manor have always been looked up to. Henry says we can't abdicate that responsibility just because it's the twentieth century.'

'Quite right. Good thinking,' Ben said, watching as Rosie refilled his coffee. 'I like the idea of lording it up. These peasants have to be put firmly in their place.'

He said it lightly enough but Olivia flashed him a warning glance. 'Take no notice of him,' she said. 'He's just madly jealous, Rosie. He adores this house. Don't you, darling?'

'*You* adore it,' he corrected her, but mildly enough. 'I have a realistic eye. I can see the pitfalls. Old houses mean problems – dodgy plumbing for one, period electrics for another . . . Give me brand new properties any day.'

'Misery,' Olivia said, pulling a face at him, pleased that Rosie seemed amused rather than offended. 'Ben wants to design his own house someday. Can you imagine *that?*'

'No accounting for taste,' Rosie said. 'Brand new means lacking soul, so Henry says. As for the problems, they don't bother us, Ben. Henry just forks out the money.'

And there was no answer to that one.

Shortly, after that, Henry arrived home in a cheerful mood. He had his jacket off, tie loosened and brandies poured before you could say 'lord of the manor'. Rosie's fluttering round him made Olivia want to puke. My goodness, she was going at it for all it was worth. She wondered what the honeymoon had really been like but, until she got Rosie on her own, she was unlikely to find out.

In the meantime, idyllically happy or not, the newly-weds put on a good show between them.

It was almost possible to believe the impossible – that they were in love.

The whole weekend promised to be an ordeal with Rosie in her strange semi-automatic mood, Henry at his suave, unnerving best. However, the food on the Friday evening was simple yet delicious, the service from the housekeeper discreet. The bed in the guest room was wonderfully comfortable and they were wakened next morning by birdsong and the sun pouring through the window.

Finding her way to the dining-room, Olivia found Henry there alone, enjoying coffee and toast.

'Olivia, darling, join me, please,' he said with an easy welcoming smile. 'Rosie hasn't surfaced yet.'

'Nor has Ben,' she said uncomfortably. 'He had a tough week – a full schedule plus a heavy clinic and some emergencies, which is nothing new, of course.'

'I had a tough week too. In fact, I ought to be jet lagged because I was in the States earlier in the week but luckily I can get by with very little sleep,' he said, passing her a cup of coffee and giving her what could only be described as the once-over. She realized what it was about Henry: he had a way with women that made you feel special yet at the same time slightly uneasy.

The look he shot her way, admiring and more than a touch sexy, was enough to make her just a little confused, and she tried to hide it by avoiding a direct look, causing him to laugh softly.

'Are you a morning person, Olivia?'

'Not a bit,' she said firmly. 'It must be this country air. It's woken me up completely.'

'May I say you look delightful,' he told her, giving her his full attention. 'Quite delightful. Ben's a lucky man.'

She managed what she hoped was a gracious smile at the deft compliment, which she was not entirely sure was genuine, because she had heard him dispensing them often enough to other women. It did cause a faint glow of pleasure, though, which under the circumstances was ridiculous. She wouldn't go near Henry, even if they were both free. He was practically the same age as her father, for goodness' sake, and he had a grown-up daughter.

'I might take a wander in the garden later,' she said, just for something to say to break the ice. 'It looks so lovely.'

'By all means,' he said with a smile. 'Glad you like it. Rosie tells me you like gardening. We're both hopeless. The gardener's a good man, though. Local chap.'

'I wish I had a garden to look after,' she said wistfully, looking out at it. 'It's so frustrating when all you have room for is a few plants. I really itch to get my fingers into the soil, to get things planted, to watch them grow. I am a very frustrated gardener, Henry.'

'I've never thought about it,' he said, obviously puzzled by her enthusiasm. 'Would you excuse me. Enjoy your breakfast in peace and I'll go and see if I can rouse that sleepy wife of mine. . . .'

Olivia and Rosie went for a walk after breakfast, the men going off to play a round of golf. Olivia could hardly believe Rosie's country gear – workmanlike cord trousers, sweater and walking shoes – but then she had always possessed the ability to blend in with whatever the situation demanded of her. All she needed was a couple of labradors and the transformation to countrywoman would be complete.

'There's nothing much in the village,' Rosie told her, 'but we do have a shop and post office and, by God, we're going to hang on to that if Henry has anything to do with it.'

'Why? Might it close down?'

She shrugged. 'You know the score. Even the villagers here tend to drive to the nearest superstore when they ought to be buying every damned thing at the local shop. Of course they'll all be up in arms if it does close but by then it will be too late.'

'Do you use it?'

She laughed. 'I buy some things as a point of principle. We've got to try doubly hard, me and Henry, because we're just a teeny bit resented.'

'Because you have money?'

'That, yes, and because we don't spend every minute of every day here. I suppose, if you count up, we will spend roughly half a year here, the rest of the time at our other homes. So, whilst we are here, we have to be seen to be active in the community, although we do our bit. We keep the staff on all year and they have a doddle of a job when we're not here, keeping everything perfect. Henry likes to set them a challenge. We can turn up any time, on a whim, and if there aren't any fresh flowers around indoors and the garden's been neglected then they know they're for it.'

'Really?' Olivia smiled but Rosie seemed, worryingly, deadly serious.

She stopped to have a word with a woman who was passing by, introducing Olivia as an old friend who lived in Chester.

'Ah, Chester .. I love it,' the woman said. 'But we're very glad that Rosie has come here. She's doing so much for the church.'

'Not at all. I'm delighted to help,' Rosie said, actually touching the woman on the arm, dispensing any amount of charm.

'What are you doing for the church?' Olivia shot her an amused glance. 'The mind boggles.'

'They were hopeless. They just needed a shake up, somebody to get them started, somebody with organizational ability.'

Olivia laughed at that; couldn't help herself. 'You, I suppose?'

'Dead right. They're a bunch of ditherers, if you must know, so I've set up an afternoon session. Some of the ladies from church meet up at my house,' Rosie told her animatedly, with no trace of sarcasm. 'A sort of discussion group. Hot topics preferably – at least that's what I intended, but it's degener-ated into a gossip session and they've started exchanging recipes, for Christ's sake. Still, everybody oohs and aahs about the house and Henry's last ex never did a bloody thing, so I'm already one up on her in everyone's eyes. We intend to do some fund raising for village funds. Henry, of course, gives a sizeable donation out of his own pocket to the church but people just love any old excuse to fund raise, don't you think? It helps to have a common aim. Forges that community spirit.'

'Well, yes . . .' Olivia said in amazement, for it was more a Judith remark than Rosie.

'The campaign to save the village school is probably next on my agenda,' Rosie told her, pointing it out as they approached. 'Look at it, isn't it a lovely old building? It's been here for ever and the children stay until they are ten. The problem is falling numbers and there's a big doubt hanging over it but its the thin end of the wedge. If we lose that and the village store, then we'll just be half a village. We've got to keep both. Luckily, we've just got some new people, who have four children, bless them, and another on the way, thank heavens, so we just need a few more public-spirited folk like that. And no, you needn't look at me. There are limits to what I'll do personally.'

They laughed, neither pressing the matter further, Rosie continuing to discuss her plan of action for saving the village.

'You're turning into a regular little campaigner,' Olivia muttered, totally bemused because Rosie had always had a 'sod you' attitude to do-gooders. 'Whatever next?'

'Henry's all for it,' Rosie said sweetly, not rising to the slight challenge. 'He's a very political animal. That's what attracted me to him, I suppose. I love a power-ful man. It's so very sexy, don't you think?'

Olivia said nothing to that, not wanting to get into a discussion about Henry, preferring to keep all thoughts of Henry off-centre in her mind.

'You've certainly made a quick start, adapting to village life,' she said instead. 'I'm surprised. After all, if you don't mind me saying so, you've only been here five minutes.'

'Officially, yes, but we have spent longer than that here, Livvy, and don't forget, Henry has been part of the community for years. I used to come here before we were married. Separate rooms then, of course, and I made damned sure the staff knew that, so that in turn the whole village knew. I made Henry wait until we were married. I stopped short of padlocking the bedroom door but he was an angel and respected my wishes. He thought it hilarious but rather sweet. And God, we've made up for it since.' She lowered her voice. 'The sex, Livvy, is just fantastic.'

'Really?'

Rosie laughed. 'How is it with you two? Although I hardly need to ask, you look so blooming.'

She nodded, a little shy.

'I do see what you see in him,' Rosie mused. 'Ben is charming. He doesn't even have to try and I suppose being a surgeon is rather glamorous.'

'Not a bit of it,' Olivia said at once, wanting to correct that common mistake. 'It's not the least glamorous. It's hard work and he's under a lot of stress. After all, if he makes a mistake, just think what happens. If Henry makes one, it isn't exactly a matter of life and death, is it?'

'Don't you believe it! Business is life and death to him.'

They retraced their steps back to The Old Manor where a light lunch was awaiting them and spent the afternoon lazing about in the garden. When the men returned, they went their separate ways, she and Ben retiring to their room ostensibly to put their feet up for a while.

'Don't even think about it,' Olivia told him, seeing the look he gave her as they closed the door. 'I feel too awkward here. Rosie's flashing her wedding ring at me the whole time. She's acting like a maiden aunt and making me feel very guilty.'

'About what?' Ben asked in astonishment. 'About our being together? Our sleeping together? Don't be daft. Who is she to talk?'

'A happily married woman,' Olivia told him, pulling a wry face. 'Honestly, I could kill her sometimes. The things we used to talk about – the things *she* used to talk about. And now it's all holier than thou. Well, most of the time, anyway.'

He pulled her towards him, laughing gently, and she saw with only slight regret that he wasn't in the mood to be put off.

'You're reading too much into it, darling. Shall I tell you what I really think?'

'What?' she asked, her voice muffled against his shoulder as he stroked her hair.

'I think she's doing all this to convince herself that all's well. He was just impossible at the golf club this morning. Lording it all over the place. And worse, he let it out that I was a cardiologist and you know how I hate that.'

She smiled. 'Don't tell me. You were forced to hold court. Did everybody start telling you about their operations?'

'You bet.' He smiled too but wryly. 'Asking for a second opinion, that sort of thing, and that, darling, as you know, is very unprofessional, nor am I prepared to give on-the-spot diagnoses. I'm afraid I had to be a bit terse to put a stop to it.'

'Oh dear, poor you,' she said with sympathy. 'You need to relax. You're all tensed up.'

'Well . . .' He grinned. 'Why don't we stop talking about Rosie and concentrate on us for five minutes.'

'Five minutes. . . ?' she laughed, going into his arms.

Getting ready for dinner later, Olivia knew one thing with certainty.

She would be glad when this weekend was over.

CHAPTER FIFTEEN

Saturday evening was spent largely listening to Henry. He was a remarkably entertaining man and they listened to some fascinating accounts of media life. There was name dropping galore and they all revelled in it.

Henry and now Rosie moved in illustrious circles.

But the evening was marred by the fact that the two men just didn't get on. What prompted the animosity was difficult to say, but they were, for all the world, like two lions circling, eyeing each other up.

It certainly took the edge off yet another beautifully prepared meal.

'That was lovely, Rosie, thank you,' Olivia said, as they dallied over the cheese.

The compliment, genuinely meant, seemed to throw her and she protested half-heartedly that she could hardly take the credit as she had only supervised.

'But what a supervisor!' Henry said with a smile. 'The cook was worried for a while. She thought I might have married another Delia Smith and there isn't room in the kitchen for two cooks. Anyway,' he added, stressing the point. 'I didn't marry her for her cooking ability, did I, darling?'

At that, Rosie blushed. Actually blushed.

Giving her an encouraging smile, Olivia thought it only served to prove that, underneath the now sophisticated exterior, Rosie was the same vulnerable woman she had always been.

'Nightcap?' Henry offered them, when they had moved into the softly lit sitting-room, leaving somebody else to clear the debris of their meal. A log fire burned in the open grate and it was all so cosy.

'What can I get you?' Henry asked, pausing in front of a well-stocked drinks cabinet. 'Do you need something to get you off to sleep, Olivia?'

'Not alcohol,' she said primly, as Rosie grinned and accepted a small glass.

'You'll have to excuse Rosie. My wife operates better in a slightly sozzled state,' Henry said, passing Ben a brandy. 'Don't you, my darling?'

'I certainly do not,' she said. 'You make me sound like an alcoholic. The truth is I have a low sozzle threshold.'

They laughed, Olivia knowing it to be absolutely true.

'I like to keep my wits about me,' Rosie went on, sipping the drink. She looked lovely this evening in a pale pink silky trouser suit with wide pants and embroidered top. 'I have to, Henry, to deal with you.'

Despite the undercurrents of awkwardness, they managed to keep it all very pleasant, the cheerful banter between a happily married couple and their weekend guests almost convincing. But, catching Henry's eyes upon her, a hot gaze, as she and Ben excused themselves, Olivia was not so sure.

'Don't be late up,' Rosie said, fully reclined on the sofa. 'Remember it's church at ten. I know we're only next door but we need to get up at eight if we're to have a leisurely breakfast.'

At ten o'clock in the morning – an hour when she would formerly have been comatose – Rosie was wearing a gorgeous blue suit, pale tights and high heels that managed to make her look nearer to forty than thirty.

Olivia could hardly believe this. She and Rosie in church, Rosie looking the part. She let her attention wander, thinking largely unreligious thoughts, comforted by the fact that the others would be thinking equally unreligious thoughts. Henry, on his knees now, was probably planning the agenda for his next meeting, Rosie would be thinking about dinner and wondering if she had left adequate instructions to the woman who came in at the weekend to cook for them, Ben would be wondering how soon they could decently leave after lunch . . .

After the service, they filtered out of the sunny porch and waited patiently for Henry and Rosie to finish their regal meanderings with the church bigwigs.

'She amazes me,' Olivia whispered. 'She's certainly taken to this life with a vengeance. Swanning it up like that.'

'It's just so phoney. I'm surprised Henry was ever taken in by it.'

Although agreeing wholeheartedly with him, Olivia managed a smile as Rosie waved cheerfully at her before heading her way.

Rosie was still her dearest friend.

Juggling her feelings was not going to be easy.

The traditional Sunday lunch that followed was bristling with atmosphere.

Rosie had new furniture in the dining-room. She told Olivia that she had chucked out a mahogany dining table that the second Mrs Chambers had loved, something of a family heirloom.

'Family heirloom? What on earth did Henry say to that?'

Rosie smiled a secret smile. 'Livvy, I can wrap him round my little finger. Catch Henry at the right moment and he'll give me the earth.'

It was a lovely rich-coloured room, the dark furniture striking. It was at its best in candlelight but even in the bright sunlight of midday it glowed exotically, the richly red curtains drawn back and the French windows open to let in the warm midday air.

For a moment, she compared it with the rushed meals she and Rosie had eaten at the flat, often with plates perched on their knees. Sometimes, if they felt slightly grand, they actually laid the little table.

This was something else, and would happily grace the pages of a glossy homes magazine. Olivia suddenly longed for the cosiness of the flat, the two of them sharing a meal and confidences. They had, she realized, lost those confidences. In the brief moments this weekend they had spent together, she and Rosie had somehow kept their conversations strictly neutral. When the men were present, it was more awkward, with Rosie constantly making gallant wifely attempts to keep the peace. The truth was that Henry and Ben just did not hit it off and both she and Rosie privately wondered when the big bust-up would happen.

Over the starter, they managed to keep the conversation pleasant, Rosie mostly holding court. But as they waited for her to produce the dessert, Olivia sensed a change of mood and saw Henry watching Ben, knowing – with a sinking feeling – that he was about to say something mischevious. She tried to warn Ben but he chose not to catch her glance – whether deliberately or not she wasn't sure.

To Olivia's irritation, Henry seemed anxious to return to his pet subject; medical matters.

'In the States, doctors are going round in a state of perpetual fear with all this litigation stuff going on,' he said. 'They only have to sneeze at the wrong moment and they're liable to be sued.'

'That's a problem probably heading our way,' Ben admitted. 'I was once on a flight from the States and a doctor was needed – a pregnant woman was not feeling well – and for a few seconds I have to admit I hesitated to own up to being a doctor, hoping some other poor soul would spring forward.' He shrugged apologetically. 'For a few seconds only and then instinct took over and I had to offer to help. It's very hard, though, when you consider that if anything goes wrong you can be sued for a vast amount. And just think of the money involved if you request the flight to be diverted. It's one hell of a responsibility.'

'But nothing could go wrong, surely?' Henry asked. 'Not for a surgeon of your calibre?'

'I would hope not,' Ben said quietly, casting a glance at Olivia for support. 'But nothing is guaranteed.'

Henry's all-business smile flashed. 'I might be needing your services soon, Ben, if I get lynched as promised next month when we introduce a few changes to the work schedule. Serve them right. They've been living on their wits for too damned long. I've warned my entire staff in the production unit at Manchester that they are for the boot if they don't get their fingers out.'

'He says these things but he's a big softie really,' Rosie chipped in, looking at him fondly. 'Everybody loves him. Don't they, darling?'

'Even the people at your Birmingham network?' Ben enquired softly, the remark hitting the bull's-eye. 'I hear tell there's a near revolution planned there.'

There was a short silence and Olivia dared not look at anyone. It was no great secret. It had been in the papers. A massive reorganization that had involved a spate of sackings and a lot of shouting about big brother techniques at one of Henry's set-ups. The union was up in arms but Henry, cocky and confident, was simply staying put.

'That's below the belt, old son,' Henry said, finally roused to anger, though he was hiding it behind that ever-present smile. 'You know bugger all about that, Ben. I'll forget you said it.'

'On the contrary, I've been following developments very closely,' Ben said quietly, very still, looking only at Henry as the women exchanged worried glances. 'I like to think I've kept abreast of all the arguments. As I see it, you're going to bulldoze them into submission, make a few concessions, perhaps, and then hit them where it hurts.'

'With respect, Ben, you are a doctor, not a businessman nor a politician,' Henry said, smile gone, ignoring Rosie's little hurried protest to keep calm. 'I wouldn't dream of coming into the operating theatre with you and I would appreciate it if you'd keep out of my boardroom. There are a lot of factors involved, things you know sod all about. And, come to think of it, who are you to talk? God, the medical profession is the world's worst at closing ranks.'

'Meaning what exactly?'

'Oh come on, let's lighten up. Don't let's talk business,' Olivia said, catching Rosie's increasingly anxious look. 'It's very boring for us. Isn't it, Rosie?'

She forced Ben to glance her way and warned him with her eyes and presumably Rosie did the same with her man because it seemed the danger was past, with Rosie launching into her merry tales of village life.

Careful laughter followed the uneasy truce.

'Christ, that was a close thing,' Rosie said, pulling her aside later. 'What the hell is the matter with those two?'

'I have no idea. Ben's under a lot of pressure just now,' she said, bound to apologize because, after all, they were Rosie and Henry's guests.

'Take no notice,' Rosie said, giving her a reassuring smile. 'Big babies.'

'If she invites us again, you say no,' Ben said on the way home.

'Oh, do I?' she said, flaring at what amounted to an order.

Olivia was driving, having hardly touched the luncheon wine. Normally, when she drove his car and he sat beside her in the passenger seat, she was nervous, scared of any hint of criticism, but today her anger at the manner of their departure had knocked her nerves on the head. It was impossible to behave in a simpering manner when you were furious.

'And don't you ever do that to me again,' she answered back, managing to keep her voice level – just. 'I didn't know where to put myself at lunch. You behaved like a little boy trying to get the better of the bigger older boy. It was pathetic.'

'He's not bigger,' he said at once. 'Older, I grant you, but not bigger.'

'Oh, for heaven's sake. There you go again. Whatever. Why do you have to nit pick?' she yelled suddenly, fully aware that she was hopeless at arguing and also aware that she couldn't control a car competently while she was having a stinking row. It was unsatisfactory anyway, for you really needed to maintain eye contact, steely eye contact, for a row to have any meaning.

'Why are you so upset?' he asked, his tone mild and conciliatory.

'I should have thought that was obvious. Rosie's my friend and after all the effort she put into it, trying to make us feel welcome, going to all that trouble with the meals, it was unforgivable and very rude to pick a fight with her husband.'

'It wasn't a fight,' he said with a laugh. 'I'm sorry, darling, if it upset you but I saw red when he practically accused me of being an incompetent surgeon.'

'When did he do that, for heaven's sake?'

'When he was talking about litigation in the States. I felt he was pointing the finger at me. OK, maybe I overreacted but surely he's big enough to take a bit of criticism? He revels in it. In fact, I'd go so far as to say he enjoys a bit of a slanging match. He likes people to stand up to him. It'll all be forgotten now, you'll see.'

'I'm not so sure,' she said, remembering Rosie's anguished expression as they waved goodbye, standing there with Henry's arm protectively round her shoulder. 'We should never have gone. We have nothing in common any more.'

'I did warn you,' he said with a sigh. 'I had a feeling it would go wrong.'

'Thanks to you,' she said, crashing the gears of his beloved car as she slowed at a junction. Beside her, she felt him cringe but, mercifully, he knew better than to say a thing.

She pulled on the handbrake and waited, taking a long deep breath.

'Rosie took it all in her stride,' Ben remarked, his voice quiet and calm and irritatingly silky, letting a hand drift towards her leg and touching it gently – presumably as a means of saying sorry. To her annoyance, for she could never sustain an argument at length, she felt herself waver.

'I think poor Rosie's lost her way,' she said, her voice softer. 'Can you believe she's the leading light of the local W.I. now? She'll be making her own jam and chutneys next. I can't make her out at all.'

'Forget Rosie. Concentrate on what you're doing. You could have been out then,' he said, as she waited for oncoming traffic to clear. 'Bags of room.'

'Who's driving this car?'

'You are. Sorry, sorry, a thousand times sorry,' he said, pulling a forlorn face and allowing her to ease out safely.

'I should think so too,' she said, a very small smile struggling to surface.

By the time they were home, they were in a marginally better mood. It was too pleasant a day for continued sulks and, as they put the miles between them and the Chambers' house, their irritations eased.

It was tacitly agreed though that they would not be issuing a weekend invitation to Rosie and Henry. Olivia felt awkward at not reciprocating the invitation but it was impossible to consider entertaining at the flat, for no way would she have Henry sleeping on a futon and the flat itself held too many memories for Rosie. She would telephone tomorrow to tell Rosie how much they had enjoyed the weekend and leave it at that.

Perhaps Henry and Rosie felt much the same way, because weekend visits were not mentioned thereafter and she and Rosie contented themselves by telephoning every week when Rosie was at home, fitting in lunch now and then in Chester.

Rosie always insisted on picking up the tab, which Olivia reluctantly allowed her to do. Henry never bothered to check the platinum card he had given her and the cost of lunch simply fell through one of her money holes and disappeared without trace.

What a relief it was, Rosie said, not to have to worry any more about overdrafts. She confessed she had rarely any idea what she spent her money on when the statement arrived at the end of the month. In fact, she said with a big smile,

Henry said that her card was the equivalent of the Bermuda Triangle, except that instead of boats and planes and things it was vanishing money.

'Nasty cough, that,' Ben remarked, glancing at her across the visitor's parlour. 'Got something for it?'

'It's a lot better,' Anna said, dismissing it, although she knew that the chilly corridors and her not very warm room were not helping her recovery. Sister Matilda, who as a former accountant dealt with the finances, strictly controlled the heating bill by simply not using it, unless it was absolutely essential. Fleetingly, Anna longed for the comfort of a high tog duvet instead of a couple of thin blankets. She could ask for more, of course, but somehow that was admitting defeat when most of the older sisters managed with just one. She wondered if God appreciated such sacrifice. Her feet these days were often so cold that sometimes they didn't seem to belong to her and she ought not to be having circulatory problems at her tender age.

'How's Olivia?' she asked.

'She's fine.' He smiled at the mention of Olivia and Anna was warmed by the reaction. If ever two people were meant to be together, it was Ben and Olivia.

'I'm having trouble with obedience,' she told him with a sigh, a little irritated at herself for blurting it out. 'I can manage the chastity and the poverty.'

'Can you?' he asked, looking uncomfortable. 'I think it's a lot to ask of you. I know it's none of my business, Anna, but this Ross bloke . . .'

'He was wonderfully understanding,' she said, acknowledging to herself that it was still painful to talk about. 'I made a choice, Ben. And you needn't worry, I can manage perfectly well without sex.'

'I'm sorry, I didn't mean to pry.' He looked even more embarrassed, changing the subject abruptly. 'What do you mean exactly by poverty?'

'Simple living,' she said at once. 'It's not about starving because we have all the food we need. It's about giving up something. Material things are not important. Look round your home – how many things do you really *need*?'

'I see what you're getting at and I agree with that in principle,' he said. 'But most of us like to have nice things around us, Anna. That doesn't make us bad, does it?'

'No, of course not. But we share what little we have here and it's quite a good feeling. There is a pool of money that we can dip into when we need something but where it hurts is not being able to buy presents for you. I'm afraid it doesn't run to that.'

'Forget that. We understand.'

She nodded. 'Thank you. And please don't buy me expensive gifts either,' she added, aware that her birthday was coming up. 'So, I cope with poverty and chastity but the obedience is getting to me.'

'Do you want to tell me?'

'Well...' she took a deep breath. 'Our community is part of a much larger community with convents and houses here and abroad. We're more contemplative than pastoral in that we don't normally become involved in working outside the convent, although it's not forbidden and some of the smaller convents are heavily into social work and so on.'

'Go on,' he urged as she paused.

'We, prayerful communities like us, are a drain on the whole community resources and because of that we've always been very aware of the need to save money. Skimping and saving...' She pulled a face, thinking of the short cuts in the kitchen, where the dire tea-towel situation, scraps of the thinnest material mended far beyond the call of duty, was assuming sinister proportions. 'Our principle community is over in Canada and there's a sort of high committee there, who make decisions on our behalf.'

'So you could say it's run pretty much like a normal business?' Ben asked, looking rather surprised.

'I suppose it is. Anyway, the point is we're being told to modernize, to adjust our way of thinking, to bring ourselves up to date and...'

'You don't like that?'

'I don't like some of it,' she said. 'For instance, we've always eaten our meals in silence and now we're told that we can talk at breakfast.'

'Eating in silence would sink Olivia,' he said with a grin. 'Although I could cope with that idea perfectly well.'

'You see, the thing that concerns me is that if we choose not to talk it might look like we're being disobedient and that will never do. And yet I have nothing to say at that time of the day. I'm just so sleepy at early Office and I have to drag myself out of bed for my private early prayers.'

He laughed, reaching across and taking her hand. 'Anna, love, relax. And don't worry. I'm sure everyone will understand.'

'You're right.' She sniffed. 'It's this chest cold. It's made me a bit down and I've not been able to get out into the garden either.'

She let him tell her about the weekend he and Olivia had recently spent with Rosie and her husband. She listened intently, reading much between the lines, and vowing to find out the truth from Olivia when next she came.

'Olivia is very upset about this rift with her father,' she ventured at last, determined to have it out with him. 'Perhaps he is being unreasonable but you know what fathers are like . . .'

'I know what ours was like,' he said soberly. 'It annoys me that if we do get married now it will look like we're doing it purely because of him. I'm not sure I like being told what to do.'

'Oh dear, Ben, that's very childish.'

'Childish?' he asked, his indignation comic.

'Yes,' she said. 'Surgeon or no surgeon, you're acting like a little boy.'

There was a short silence.

'The truth is I worry about her,' he said. 'I love her so much and I worry that it's all going to go wrong if we tie the knot. We're happy as we are.'

'That's a bit cynical, isn't it? I know there are a lot of separations and divorces but there are even more very happy marriages. You and Olivia are quite perfect together.' She gave him a moment to take that in and then carried on, twisting the knife to drive out the remaining reluctance. 'She wants to get married. She wants a family.'

'I know but . . . there's lots of time.'

'She wants a *large* family and I think she needs to be married first,' Anna added, leaving it at that.

He looked a little startled but said nothing.

'How's Mum?' Anna asked after a moment, feeling the usual pang.

'Busy, of course,' Ben said, giving her a reassuring nod. 'She will come to see you sooner or later even if I have to drag her here.'

'I'd rather you didn't do that but thanks for trying.'

She passed him the letter she had written to her mother, which was their only means of communication these days. She hoped her mother read them. She needed her mother to understand.

CHAPTER SIXTEEN

Today, she and Rosie were meeting in The Crypt, a restaurant situated on the lower level of the Rows in Eastgate. The original cellar of a wealthy merchant's shop and townhouse, it had been built around 1290 and was now sympathetically restored. It was one of a variety of luncheon venues they frequented, one of their favourites in fact. There was an ecclesiastical look in the structure of the stone chamber and a distinct feeling that you were dining in church, although a wine cellar seemed the best bet for its original use.

As half expected, there was no sign of Rosie when Olivia arrived, so she ordered a coffee whilst she was waiting. It could be five minutes but it might be up to fifteen, for when she was shopping Rosie tended to forget simple things like the time, punctuality never being one of her assets.

There she was – not bad – only seven minutes late. Olivia made room at the table for her and numerous upmarket bags and, from the other tables, one or two people shot quick glances at the elegant arrival.

Rosie, smiling hugely, made no apology for being late, slipping off her silky charcoal jacket to reveal a camisole top. She draped the jacket carelessly over the spare chair next to them as the waitress approached with the menus. Olivia knew Rosie was just back from a four-day trip to Milan, shopping and relaxing, and the lightly sun-tanned shoulders confirmed that.

'I'm ravenous,' she said. 'I can't remember if I ate breakfast or not. Henry was up at the crack of dawn – early flight from Manchester – and he likes me to get up with him and make sure he has everything he needs for the trip. He's such a baby about things like that.'

'How long is he away?'

'A week.' Rosie rolled her eyes. 'I hate it. The house is so empty without him. I decided not to go with him this time because he has wall-to-wall meetings and I can't say I fancied another trip so soon, even to Paris. I need to recharge my batteries, spend a little time at home.'

Olivia smiled a little. Once upon a time, Rosie had grumbled about her lack of travel and now she was bored with it.

Their friendship was at a difficult stage. Olivia was finding it increasingly hard to come to terms with this new Rosie. She still thought of her as a friend but somehow she was no longer the *best* friend and no longer the same friend. They were trying hard but Olivia couldn't help feeling that it was all tailing off, that they were growing steadily apart, and that made her sad. She had to force herself these days to arrange these lunch dates, to stop coming up with excuses.

'How's life?' Olivia asked as they ordered their usual simple lunch of jacket potato and salad. Rosie, she noticed, was putting on weight, though not excessively, and it quite suited her.

'Great,' Rosie said. 'I am just *so* busy. I can hardly believe it but I don't miss work at all.'

'Don't you?' Olivia asked, raising her eyebrows.

Henry had insisted she give up work because he did not think it appropriate that his wife should work at the television studios for the company he owned and, rather to Olivia's surprise, the suggestion had not met with any opposition – none that Rosie admitted to anyway.

'Are you sure you don't miss it?' Olivia went on, finding it hard to believe that she had given it up just like that. 'I thought you were going places in your career?'

'Oh, come off it. Let's face it, Livvy, I'd probably have been lucky to get any further and, with all the back-stabbing and bitchiness, did I seriously want to? Sod that sort of challenge. I'm all for an easy life. It's what Henry wants – you know him, he likes the idea of me being at home and looking after him. That's what scuppered his last marriage. Henry likes his routine.' She smiled the same old mischievous smile. 'Although he is capable of wonderful surprises.'

'So is Ben,' Olivia said quickly, feeling she had to defend him but wondering just when he had last concocted any sort of surprise for her. Even her recent birthday present had been fairly predictable and he wasn't the sort of man who bought her flowers for no reason. They were beginning to settle, worryingly, into an all-too-familiar routine themselves, a sort of cosy old married couple routine with the likelihood of them ever getting married fading with each passing day. 'I like *my* job,' she added earnestly. 'And it's nice to have a bit of independence. Your own money.'

Rosie shrugged. 'I agree. But I don't have a hang-up about that. Henry and I are equal partners and he doesn't give a stuff that he earns the money and I spend it. He loves me, Livvy, and I can get away with it. It's just wonderful. It's like we're still on honeymoon. He's just so considerate.'

'But aren't you bored at home?'

'Bored?' She raised amused eyes. 'I should say not. I go for a walk every day, which keeps me fit without all the bloody gym hassle, and I've joined the flower group. I'm learning to arrange flowers.'

'I don't believe it,' Olivia said, laughing. 'You are joking, surely? You always prided yourself on not knowing a daffodil from a tulip.'

Rosie smiled a little. Her hair was cut into a new wide-angled shape, an expensive cut, and as well as the beautifully cut suit, she was wearing fine gold jewellery at her throat and wrist. Goodness, she was elegant – even Olivia's mother had noticed the last time she saw her. An improvement, Judith conceded reluctantly, and where had she been hiding her sense of style all these years?

'How's the flat?' Rosie asked. 'I'll always have a soft spot for that place.'

'It's fine,' Olivia said. 'A lot tidier without you.'

Rosie laughed, unperturbed. 'And how are things with you and Ben? Has the bastard still not proposed?'

Olivia looked quickly round as Rosie had a carrying voice.

'For goodness' sake, Rosie. You're as bad as my dad. No, he hasn't and I've decided it really doesn't matter. It doesn't matter until we decide to have children and then I shall have to insist.'

'You will have to *insist*?' Rosie queried, looking doubtful. 'Insisting is not good. I'd get married first if I were you, before you have to put a shotgun to his head.'

A lone woman in pink at a nearby table gave them a bemused glance.

'Look . . .' Olivia glanced round, then lowered her voice. 'Stay out of it, OK? It's none of your business. Just like it's none of my business why you chose to marry Henry.'

'That's easy. I married Henry because I fell in love,' she said defiantly. 'I know I used to poke fun at it, at being in love, but when it happens to you, then you have to just eat your words. When it happens, it's just fantastic.'

'Rosie Andrews!'

'Chambers, if you please.'

'How you've got the nerve . . .' Olivia leaned forward, shutting out the other diners, spitting out the words in the face of Rosie's supremely smug expression. 'Don't mess me about. You always intended this to happen. You said you were going to marry money. Well, you have and good luck to you, but the least you can do is be honest about it. There's no need to pretend you love him, not to me.'

'But I do.'

'No, you do not,' Olivia said, exasperation complete. 'You love the money, the houses, the clothes. Your brand new car.'

'Oh yes. Isn't it just too much?' Rosie sighed. 'Just imagine getting a sports car for your birthday When I saw the car keys, I thought for a minute he'd bought me a little runabout. You know the sort of thing – boring and mumsy and easy to park.'

Olivia did. The sort of thing she had.

'And then I saw it.' Her face shone with the memory. 'I was wearing my negligee at the time, barefoot, but I just got in and zoomed off, leaving poor Henry stranded in the drive looking after me with this silly smile on his face.'

Olivia could imagine it. Rosie, barefoot in her negligee, tearing through the country roads in her brand new sports car. Now that was more like it.

'Do you fancy a spin?' Rosie went on. 'Let's go to London and I'll show you the apartment. We got somebody in to do the interior and it's very modern and incredibly chic, completely different from The Manor. That's what I love about all my homes. They're all so different but each one is special and when I'm there, it's my very favourite.' She glanced at her watch. 'We could pick up a few things and be on our way in an hour. How about it?'

'I can't. I'm a bit tight for days off,' Olivia said flatly. 'And it's a bit off to leave Ben on his own at short notice. He's got a full list this week and he's always exhausted when he gets in.'

'Do him good to fend for himself for once.' Rosie shrugged. 'We could have a great time, Livvy. It's very central and we could maybe get tickets for a show. Oh, come on . . .'

It was tempting. She wouldn't have minded a few days in London with Rosie and a few days together might have eased them back into the old carefree ways. But she shook her head.

'If you're sure. . . ?' Rosie did not seem too concerned. 'I'm going anyway, the day after tomorrow. I've got some shopping to do. Henry's presenting the awards on a television show next month and he wants me to get something fabulous to wear. He doesn't care how much I spend.'

'My goodness, you've landed on your feet, haven't you, Rosie? You always wanted money and prestige and now you have it.'

Rosie sighed, giving her a hurtful glance.

'You should hear yourself. It's not like you at all. You've gone very bitchy lately. Are you sure everything's OK? You'd better watch Ben, Livvy. Men are very good at keeping things from us. Henry thinks Ben's awfully defensive about something and Henry's very good at knowing what people are thinking.'

'I don't give a toss what Henry thinks,' Olivia said tartly, recognizing that part of their problem, she and Rosie, was the fact that their menfolk did not like each other. They were therefore always put in this impossible position of defending them, even when their position might be close to indefensible.

'You hate me for marrying him, don't you?' Rosie said, giving her a sly look. A life of leisure and pleasure suited her. She was glowing and beautiful. 'Are you sure it's not jealousy?'

'Now, look . . .'

Rosie leaned forward. 'Oh yes. Don't think I don't remember every minute of that bloody awful school. The looks. OK, maybe not from you and Anna, but from everybody else. Well, I wonder what some of those poor little rich girls would make of me now? I bet they'd be all over me.'

'I'm not even going to answer that,' Olivia said, annoyed, doubly so because there was just a touch of truth in it. 'You're paranoid about it and it wasn't as bad as you make out.'

'Wasn't it?' She looked thoughtfully at Olivia. 'Or could it be that you fancy my Henry just a tad?'

'Don't be ridiculous.'

Rosie laughed. 'Just wondered. His secretary's been after him for years, poor soul.'

'Don't you mind?'

'No. He tells me about it, Livvy, and it's when he doesn't tell me things that I will begin to worry.'

'But how will you know if he's keeping something from you?'

Rosie sniffed. 'I'll know. Anyway, he deals with it – the secretary thing – by flirting outrageously with her just to keep her sweet. I am not jealous in the least and don't forget, it's me he married and, more to the point, I'm the one named in the will.'

If that sounded hard-edged and surely confirmation of what Olivia had just accused her of, Rosie did not seem to notice and they both picked at their salads a moment before Rosie put down her fork and sighed.

'What do I have to do, Livvy, to convince you? I know I used to go on about marrying a millionaire, but the truth is I really did fall in love and it wouldn't matter if Henry had nothing. I love him and I want to take care of him.'

'Huh!'

That did it. That 'huh' did it. Tipped the fragile balance.

Rosie, halfway through her lunch, took umbrage in a fashion to rival Olivia's mother. She pushed her plate aside, reached for her handbag, delved in and flung a twenty pound note on to the table. Then, without another word, she picked up her jacket and the collection of shopping bags and flounced out, as best she could in the tight-fitting skirt and high heels.

On a scale of flounces, it rated as successful enough, turning quite a few heads, leaving Olivia alone and embarrassed.

She had no real choice but to tough it out, sitting there and finishing her salad down to the very last bit of diced carrot, trying to appear unconcerned. On the table, Rosie's half-finished meal lay there.

'Can I get you something else, madam?'

She looked up at the waitress, whom she felt she knew because she regularly served them.

She detected sympathy.

Refusing the sympathy, she decided she was not going to sneak out like a distressed schoolgirl. Consulting the menu, she ordered cheesecake.

She was not going to let anybody see just how dreadful she felt. She felt so dreadful that she wasn't even sure whether or not she could face going back to the office.

What was the matter with her?

She had managed to alienate the one real friend she had ever had and for what? Just because she did not believe her. How *could* she love Henry? She had married him purely for the money and the position, as she had always said she would. So getting on her high horse now was ridiculous. As she struggled through her dessert, Olivia saw she had no alternative if they were to remain friends, albeit on a reduced level, but to offer an apology.

She had seen plenty of Rosie in high dudgeon in the past and it was usually short lived.

She decided not to mention any of this to Ben or to Anna next time she saw her. Anna was always very interested in anything concerning Rosie and she worried that Anna might speak the truth and tell her what she half suspected, that she, Olivia, was being a bit heavy handed.

It was up to her and Rosie to sort it out, for each of them to give a little. So far as Olivia was concerned, a succession of midnight feasts with Rosie at the flat, pouring out their hearts to each other, had given them the right to have a bit of a tiff now and then without it necessarily being the end of everything.

She and Rosie had known each other too long, gone through too much together and, trying to think about it rationally, she saw that perhaps she had been a little hasty in taking such a dislike to Henry when she did not know him at all.

How unkind she was being. No matter what Ben said, Rosie deserved the benefit of the doubt. Didn't she?

CHAPTER SEVENTEEN

Olivia soon put all thoughts of Rosie and her tantrum right out of her head because, the following month, the unthinkable happened.

She was pregnant.

But, before she told Ben, she needed to get used to the idea herself and for a while she walked around in a sort of dream, thinking everybody must know because surely she looked different. She certainly felt different, although Ben, busy, extra busy, at the hospital, scarcely seemed to notice her these days.

It was stupid to be worried about telling him but she knew it would change everything and ridiculously kept putting it off. Making her mind up at last to break the news, she made an extra special effort with the meal, wore a dress he liked and waited for him. He had promised to be back early and sure enough, he was. She heard the car outside, his quick footsteps and then the outer door slammed and her heart slammed with it.

'Why the hell didn't you tell me, Olivia?' his voice thundered as he came through. 'Does everybody know before I do?'

'Sit down and calm down,' she said, fussing him through to the sitting-room where coffee was waiting. 'I was going to tell you tonight. . . .'

'Oh sure, but first of all you tell your mother and my mother and Anna and God knows who else.' He stopped short, smiled a bit, ran fingers through his hair. 'I'm sorry. I didn't mean to yell at you. The truth is I'm dead-beat. It's been a bad day . . Sorry, darling.'

'No, it's me who's sorry. I suppose your mother told you?'

'She did. She rang me to congratulate me on the happy news. Unfortunately, she picked a hell of a moment. To start with I nearly didn't take the call and then I was almost sorry I had.'

'She should know better than to ring you at the hospital.'

'She's a doctor,' he reminded her. 'My secretary thought it was a medial matter...'

'The mistake was my telling *my* mum,' Olivia said, sitting with her hands on the as yet indecipherable bump, fighting down the feeling of nausea that kept attacking her. 'It slipped out and you know she can't keep a secret, so she must have telephoned your mother and yes, I did tell Anna. She was delighted, by the way, and very understanding.' She felt her mouth tremble, knowing she was close to tears.. No doubt hormonal.

'Oh sweetheart...' He put his cup down and held out his arms. 'Come here.' She went to sit beside him, nestled in his arms. 'You *are* pleased?' she asked, feeling the comforting thump of his heart.

'Now that I've got over the shock,' he said. 'How stupid not to have realized. You were sick the other morning and didn't I ask if you'd eaten something?'

'You did and I nearly told you then but you were in a rush and it didn't seem the right moment.'

'We'll get married,' he said.

'We will?'

'Give your mother the go-ahead to get things moving,' he said with a slight sigh that did not escape her. 'But try to keep her under check, will you?'

'Come on,' she said lightly. 'I am her only daughter and she's been planning my wedding for years now.'

This then was her proposal, been and gone in a flash. She thought of Henry's proposal to Rosie, of the Parisian night sky, of champagne and caviar. Rosie had given her all the details, down to what they had to eat.

'Are you sure about this?' she asked, mouth dry, feeling she ought to reject him for the very half-heartedness of it all. 'We don't have to.'

He ruffled her hair kissed the top of her head. 'I know that. Forgive me, sweetheart. Things are pretty tough just now. As if we haven't enough to do, we're expected to be accountants as well these days. If I've neglected you, I'm sorry I...'

'No. It's all right. And it will be all right,' she said, more confident now as she realized he was desperately overworked and tired and it was unfair of her to expect a romantic proposal from a man as weary as he was.

'If I seem to hesitate, it's only because I want things to stay as they are between us,' he said. 'I'm scared of things going wrong.'

'They won't. You worry much too much but you can't help that and I am proud of you, Ben. As for getting married and having a baby, it needn't change things so much...'

He raised his eyebrows. 'That's not what I've heard from colleagues.'

'Well, yes,' she conceded. 'I suppose it'll all be a bit different.'

'A baby?' he said for the first time, looking at her and tracing his finger down her cheek, pushing aside her hair. 'We didn't plan it. How did it happen?'

She shook her head. Smiled. 'You're the doctor,' she said. 'You tell me.'

Anna liked to wake at five o'clock, so as to have time for private prayer before the six o'clock communion. Afterwards, there was a half hour's meditation and then breakfast. Despite the new ruling, it was still a very quiet meal, for nobody cared for conversation at this hour. Those who tried spoke of the most frivolous things and then Anna longed for the old silence.

After breakfast, once a week, there was a general meeting, which Mother presided over, an opportunity for them to speak freely. Today, it was Sister Matilda's turn to speak on financial matters and they listened in silence, trying to make sense of the gloomy figures.

'The upshot is this . . .' Sister Matilda snapped her book shut. She was renowned for being outspoken and for retaining some of her business shrewdness, even after ten years here. 'It's a Micawber situation. As you know, we've been living for years off the original money we were given from the community fund and, although we have been frugal, we can't go on taking money from a dwindling account. If we can't find some money soon from somewhere, we're going to have to do something drastic.'

'Such as?'

Reverend Mother glanced at the questioner, an elderly much beloved member of their community, and smiled. 'I don't want to alarm you,' she said, 'but it could mean selling the convent. As Sister Matilda has just explained, we can't afford the upkeep any longer,' she added as the horrified murmurs started up. 'And there have only been four novices in the last two years. What we need is a huge increase in the number of novices . . .' her smile was slight. 'Or for one of us to win the Lottery.'

The laughter relieved the tight atmosphere but seeds of doubt had been sown. It was sobering to think that they might not be here for very much longer and Anna was glad to finally escape into the garden.

Losing the old deceased oak tree last week was a mixed blessing. The stump remained but the men had cleared the thick branches and disposed of the twigs with the minimum of fuss. The ground round about the stump, which had seemed such a small plot, now looked enormous with the umbrella of the tree's branches gone. It was now open to the sky, much lighter and, surveying it with an ever more keen gardener's eye, Anna saw the possibilities for a flower-filled bed or at least a mixed plot of shrubs and annuals.

Olivia and Ben were to be married and she was to become an aunt. The prospect delighted her, for Olivia would be a wonderful mother. She had talked excitedly about the baby on her last visit, already making plans and looking forward to moving – when they found a house they both liked of course.

Olivia wanted an old house in the very heart of the city – a tall order – and Ben wanted a new one within easy reach of it.

Oh dear!

Compromise already and they weren't yet married.

Olivia had her work cut out keeping the wedding as simple as she wanted. Keeping her mother, and to some extent Eva, reined in was extremely difficult but it seemed that things were going to work out more or less as she intended.

Before the wedding arrangements clicked into top gear, however, Olivia had something very important to do. She had to sort things out with her father and somehow thaw out the *Titanic*-sized iceberg of mistrust and resentment that was separating them. According to her mother, he was wavering now that wedding plans were being discussed, pleased that Ben was at last making an honest woman of her.

Olivia clicked her tongue in exasperation. 'Honestly, I can hardly believe him. That makes me want to cancel everything, just to spite him.'

'You wouldn't?' her mother asked, horror showing at the very idea. 'Darling, you can't. There are too many wheels in motion.'

Olivia knew that all too well. She smiled her mother's anxiety away.

'No. I want to get married. What does Dad think about the baby? You have told him, I hope?'

Judith smiled. 'Of course. He was the first person to know. Between the two of us, he's thrilled, but he's such a stubborn old fool that I think you will have to make the first move, darling. We can't have you two not speaking. It's just too ridiculous for words and your father doesn't know how to apologize. He never has.'

She decided to telephone her father before she met him face to face and, rather than risk having her mother hovering at his side, rang him at the office on one of the days he spent there.

'Who is this?' the secretary said briskly. 'Mr Hayton is due in a meeting shortly and has asked not to be disturbed.'

'This is his daughter,' Olivia said, smiling determinedly to keep her own voice pleasant sounding. 'If he could possibly spare a moment, I'll keep it brief.'

'I'll see what I can do,' the secretary said with a huge sigh, suggesting it might be easier to have a personal conversation with the President of the United States.

A moment later, her father's voice . . .

'George Hayton . . .'

'Daddy . . . it's me,' she gulped.

There followed a conversation of supreme mind-boggling incoherence on both their parts, speaking at the same time, both apologizing, both upset, both delighted that, in an instant, it was all forgotten and forgiven. Afterwards, Olivia was too happy and relieved to dwell on whose fault it was, although she did privately place the ball firmly in his court. She put it down to the male menopause slightly tipping him off the edge into unreasonableness.

What did it matter, though? It was all over and done with and she needed his help and support now with the wedding arrangements.

She wasn't getting much support from Ben, who was so busy that he scarcely had time to spend with her and was so tired when he did that he spent it yawning and dropping off to sleep.

She knew his work was important to him but was it always going to be like this? Would it be like this when the baby arrived? Would he ever *see* his baby?

Doubts. And it was too late for doubts.

The house was just below the city walls, off Lower Bridge Street. A house in a street she had passed by often, one of a row she had admired. It had three storeys, Queen Anne style, with a semicircle of black railings close up to the door and a garden – small, granted – pressed up against the railings. In front of the gate was a cobbled area before an avenue of trees that gave on to the road itself. The trees and the cobbled area made all the difference, giving it some breathing space.

It was their house.

It was very nearly perfect. It would have been perfect if it had had a large enclosed rear garden instead of a small courtyard and that, coupled with the tiny front one, meant there would be little to quench her gardening thirst. Still, for once it would have to take second place because she just adored the house. As Chester town houses went, she reckoned it was one of the best, and her mother was quite jealous, it being a stone's throw from all her favourite shops.

She loved Ben for not putting up much of a fight and going for this house, instead of one of the newer ones he would have preferred, and she vowed she would care for it and make it a home both of them could be proud of. At last, they would be able to entertain, have people for the weekend. . .

Although perhaps not Rosie and Henry. Olivia had tried to offer an apology but Rosie was not yet in the mood for accepting it and the last time Olivia had tried, she had left a no-nonsense message on Rosie's machine. She could like or lump it.

The house was empty, had been for months, and the vendors were desperate for a quick uncomplicated sale, so they took possession as soon as the solicitors completed the paperwork.

They had a late celebratory lunch in town, Olivia feeling quite light-headed at the enormity of what they had just done. In the space of a few months, weeks even, so much had changed and all for the better. She was pregnant, and happy about that, the sickness had miraculously disappeared, and now she was to live in a house she might have dreamed of.

Not forgetting Ben, of course. She was to marry the man she loved.

Life couldn't get much better.

CHAPTER EIGHTEEN

'*Farrell.* On 21st March, in Chester, to Olivia (née Hayton) and Ben, a son, Jamie George.'

Her mother had wanted to put 'Deo Gratias'. She had also wanted to put 'mother and baby both well', the weight (8lb 2oz), *and* that he was the first grandson for both Judith and George Hayton and Dr Eva Farrell, and she hoped to goodness that Olivia wasn't restricting the number of words on account of the cost.

'No, we want to keep it simple, Mum,' Olivia said, too tired for all this hassle.

Jamie George was gorgeous. A little dark-haired bundle of joy. She knew exactly what that meant now and why they said it. He was perfect, from the softly throbbing top of his baby head down to the ten little pink toes.

Just three days old and already she knew she would kill for him.

And die for him.

Olivia Farrell was still a dreamer.

Instead of listening to her mother, who was chattering madly on, Olivia was gazing out of the window on to the lawns that stretched into the distance. It was spring, that wonderful time when the trees were beginning to leaf and daffodils, lily of the valley and wild hyacinths were dotting the beds with tones of yellow and blue and pink.

The room was full of flowers. All her favourites. Ben had bought her an enormous bunch of spring flowers, as well as an antique pendant, which she remembered admiring in a shop in town. The inscription said 'For my clever girl'.

It was OK. Very few marriages were one hundred per cent perfect and she could have done with a husband who was not quite so frantically busy all the time with his mind always half on the hospital. *And* who had missed the birth to boot!

She had been very off sex, too, during the latter stages of her pregnancy, but he was so considerate that in an uncharitable moment she wondered whether he might be having an affair. She was fully aware that there must be many available young women at the hospital who would give their all to have a fling with him.

But she trusted him.

As much as any wife of a good-looking man. . . .

'Have you been listening to a word I'm saying, Olivia? You have that look on your face. You're such a dreamer. Always have been.'

'Sorry.'

She drew her attention reluctantly back to her mother, who had never stopped talking since Jamie's arrival. Anyone would think nobody else had ever been a grandmother before, although it was rather sweet that she was so excited. Visiting times were restricted to a couple of hours in the afternoon and she had already exceeded that but was waiting until she was turfed out or, rather, in this expensive private clinic, gently persuaded to leave.

'Names, darling,' her mother said firmly. 'It has to be settled once and for all.'

'Jamie George,' Olivia said, puzzled. 'It's already settled.'

Her mother clicked her tongue. 'I knew you weren't listening,' she said. 'Not Jamie's name. Our names. Eva and I. I thought grandpa or grandpop for your father. Which do you think?'

'What does *he* want?'

'He'll be told as soon as I've decided. I don't want to pester him with trivialities.'

Bewildered, Olivia nodded. 'Either.'

'Or grandfather, of course, although that is a little formal, rather Victorian. What do you think? I really would like some input here.'

'I don't mind,' Olivia said wearily. 'Anything you think fit.'

'Then it's grandpa. That's settled but it's going to be more tricky with Eva and I. She's being awkward. She wants to be called granny and I really wanted that.'

Olivia laughed. This was wonderful and so typical of her mother, who could create a debate about nothing. What must she be like in the council chamber that, now the novelty was wearing off, she only occasionally occupied these days.

'You've had months to decide this, Mum. I don't see what all the fuss is about. Eva can be granny and you can be grandma,' she said, knowing that would infuriate her mother.

'I will not. Absolutely not. Grandmas have perms and wear support stockings.'

'Then invent something.'

'I might if Eva persists in being awkward.' Judith frowned. 'It really is annoying. I'd set my heart on granny. It has the right ring. We can't both be granny, it will confuse poor Jamie when he's older. Anyway, enough of that. Have you thought any more about the nanny? I can help you interview. I have the name of an excellent agency that one of my friends used for her daughter. You must get somebody with qualifications. And, if you're to get the right person, you will have to be prepared to offer some incentives. They expect the earth these days apparently.'

Olivia sighed. They had been through all this before.

'I'm not having a nanny, Mum,' she said. 'I'm looking after him myself.'

'Well, if you insist on being a martyr to the cause,' Judith said with a little shake of her head. 'It's all very well here, where he can be whizzed away by the nurse if he cries, but once you're at home, you will be on your own. I thought you were going back to work in any case, so you'll have to fix something up.'

'I haven't decided about work,' she said. 'I have a little while before I need make a decision but, in the meantime, I don't need a nanny.'

'As you wish . . .' The sigh was deep.

'Don't forget, Ben will be there too,' Olivia reminded her gently. 'He's determined to be a hands-on father.'

'How can he be? He's never away from the hospital.'

'Well, yes . . .' Olivia sighed. 'But it's just a difficult phase. Budget problems and you know how he hates that sort of thing.'

'Don't let's get on to politics,' Judith said with a shudder. 'I've had quite enough to last me a lifetime. I'm going to stand down as soon as it's convenient. Being on the council is nothing like I was led to believe.'

Olivia smiled. She had known it was just a passing fancy.

'I've no doubt Ben means well,' her mother went on firmly, 'but I'd advise you to engage a nursery nanny at the very least for a few weeks. You need your sleep, darling, otherwise you'll look quite dreadful. You've got to build your strength up.' She clicked her tongue. 'I had a nanny for you, darling, and it was the best thing I ever did. You mustn't be afraid to admit it if you don't have maternal leanings. Not all women do. I never did. I much prefer you now that you're grown up. Babies don't do a lot for me – with the exception of darling little Jamie, of course,' she added quickly.

'Do you think I'm incapable of looking after my own baby, Mother?'

'Did I say that?'

Olivia huffed and flopped on to her piled-up pillows, too tired for a row.

Giving up on it, Judith sighed, returning to her seat by the bed and picking up the cards that were balanced on the locker top. 'Gracious me, what a heap! May I look?' She rifled through them a minute. 'There's no card from Rosie.'

'I hardly expected one. She might not even know I've had a baby. We've lost touch, Mum, as you well know. She never did forgive me for what I said about her and Henry,' Olivia said quietly. 'And I did apologize.'

'I know you did and it was very rude of her not to accept an apology offered in good faith, although why you feel you have to apologize for stating the truth is beyond me. Mind you, it's no more than I would expect from her. I thought it was a dreadful slight when she didn't turn up for your wedding. And of course she will know about the baby. Remember I have an acquaintance in the village?'

'Of course. I'd forgotten about your spy.'

'Rosie could have turned up for your wedding if she'd wanted,' Judith persisted.

'She was away at the time.'

'She was only in Paris. She could have easily nipped back for the wedding and gone back there if she'd wanted. That is no excuse.'

Olivia sighed. Her mother was right. If Rosie had wanted to be there, she would have been.

'Apparently, they've sold the property in France, so that will have brought him another pretty penny.' Judith sniffed her disapproval. 'And she's forever at the flat in London, dining out at all the best restaurants and shopping. What she spends on clothes is nobody's business!'

Olivia smiled. 'Come on, Mum, you'd do exactly the same if Dad was a millionaire.'

'Very likely but it's maddening, isn't it? Marrying for money and then pretending it's a love match. I'm amazed it's lasted as long as it has. He's nothing more than a playboy. When the man finds time to actually work is beyond me but then he's probably just a figurehead.'

'That's not true. I think he still keeps a tight grip on things.'

'They share a bedroom anyway, so at least it isn't a complete farce.'

'Mum!' Olivia laughed. 'Who on earth told you that?'

'The cleaner let it slip to my friend.'

'She's very efficient, your spy,' Olivia said drily. 'Does she send messages by Morse code?'

Her mother gave her a resigned look. 'If you're still determined on the nanny front, then I will of course be happy to come and help. If Ben won't mind my being around.'

'What do you mean by that? Of course he would be happy for you to be around.'

Judith gave her a look. 'I doubt that very much.'

'Now, Mum, don't start on that.'

'Men!' her mother said with feeling. 'It's lucky you and I get on so well these days and we must never let the men get in the way of that, darling. Promise me you won't let that happen.'

'Promise what?'

'Well, we're talking loyalty, Olivia. You will be loyal to Ben as I've always been loyal to your father but a mother and daughter relationship is something entirely different. Quite simply, I believe it to be the closest kind of relationship there is. Do you see?'

No, she didn't, not quite. And it was a bit rich coming from Judith, who had allowed Olivia to stroll through her childhood with a mother's touch of the distinctly lukewarm variety.

However, for the sake of some peace – for her mother seemed strangely troubled – Olivia promised.

Jamie was a remarkably good baby. He fed well. He put on the right amount of weight. He behaved like a little angel when she took him to the clinic, which made her feel insufferably smug.

As for his daddy, all Ben's professional expertise went completely out of the window when it came to his own baby. He thought him ridiculously forward for his age, pointing out things to her in the baby bible they had bought that confirmed it.

Maternally proud, of course, she nevertheless did not go along with Ben's very unprofessional belief that Jamie was nothing short of a genius. He was soothingly baby average as far as she was concerned and to her relief she was a perfectly normal mother herself. Not too panicky. Not too laidback. She was happy to talk to other new mums at the baby clinic but wary of comparing.

Comparisons were for daddies to indulge in.

Life went on and decisions had to be made.

Olivia might not have a nanny but she did have help in the house, someone to do simple chores, so that she had more time to look after the baby. Covering three floors as it did, it was not an easy house, as her mother was maliciously fond of pointing out.

'It's all a little bare, dear,' her mother said on one of her visits. 'Don't you think so, George?'

'Leave me out of it,' he said with a smile. 'It looks fine to me. Wait until Jamie gets older and he's got his toys all over the place.'

'He has his nursery and we plan a family sitting-room upstairs,' Olivia explained. 'That way we'll keep these downstairs rooms looking good.'

'Theories . . .' her father said, a twinkle in his eye. 'You should burn all those how-to books. Children have a habit of doing their own thing and keeping their toys in the allotted place is not one of them.'

'How many are you intending to have?' Judith asked, straight to the point as usual. 'We need to know, darling, if we're to plan for their education.'

'Give the girl a chance. She's only just had Jamie.'

'Two or three,' Olivia said, adding mischievously, 'or even four . . .'

Judith gasped. 'Good gracious, four sounds far too many. Three's bad enough. Two is perfect. Ideally, I would have liked two,' she added. 'But we were always off somewhere or other and I was unhappy with the maternity care and time just drifted on. Eventually, it was too late and I went off the idea anyway.'

Olivia decided not to go into the 'education' thing just now, but they would have to get round to discussing it before her mother upped and booked Jamie in at a pre-prep establishment, an interference which would make Ben explode.

When Jamie awoke, Judith insisted on taking him for a stroll, swaddled in a white cotton blanket, his dark hair peeping out from a white bonnet. With his scrunched up old man's face, he looked worried, as well he might under the bossy control of his granny – Judith having snatched that title from Eva.

Watching her mother go, togged up in beautiful casuals, walking in that peculiarly confident way of hers, Olivia felt as close to her now as she had in a long time. She understood her mother much more now that she was a mother herself. She could now believe the agony she had gone through when they were apart when she was little. She could see, in some way, why she had felt it necessary to be a little aloof. Over the years, her mother had let her real feelings slip only occasionally.

Perhaps her mother had been right. By standing one step away, she had allowed her daughter to breathe, to sort things out for herself. But she would so have appreciated a proper cuddle – all children deserved that.

She was not going to make the same mistakes.

Very likely, different ones.

CHAPTER NINETEEN

Life, after Jamie, took on a new pattern and, whilst Olivia still tried to find time for other things, at the moment everything revolved around him. When her parents visited, Judith liked to take Jamie out for his 'constitutional', which meant that she and her father had the opportunity, not always relished, for a heart to heart.

Olivia could always guess his mood and today he seemed a touch down.

'Is everything all right, Dad?'

'Yes,' he said hurriedly. 'Why do you ask?'

'You seem preoccupied.'

'No more so than usual. I can sort out my own problems. Don't you worry,' he said, his smile meant to be reassuring. 'Are you and Ben all right? I hope he's not still working all the hours God sends.'

'Not quite. I'm hoping to persuade him to take a holiday this year.'

'You deserve it. Where will you go?'

'I have no idea. Somewhere where babies are welcome. And preferably somewhere warm and exotic.'

'That rules out anywhere in England then,' he said with a grin. 'Try Italy. The Italians love babies. Remember when we were in Milan?'

'I remember everywhere,' she said. 'One or two places in particular.'

'Ah yes. So do I. I very much liked that brief spell in Vancouver, wonderful city, and I loved Bermuda.'

'Rosie has a home there. Did you know that?'

'Your mother might have mentioned it,' he said, sounding a bit vague. 'Lucky girl. I used to like Rosie. You two were close, weren't you? Why didn't she come to your wedding?'

Olivia shrugged. 'Who knows? I know I accused her of marrying Henry for his money which, looking back, was an awful thing to do but even so, I did say sorry and it's not enough to cut me off completely. Is it?'

'It's debatable, Olly,' he said. 'Maybe she doesn't want to upset her husband. Maybe she wants to look forward and forget her past. Will you make it up?'

'I can't see how. She's never available on the phone and she hasn't answered my letters. I did catch sight of her in town recently but I'm certain she avoided me.'

Sadness nudged at her as it always did when she thought about Rosie. She hated unpleasantness and she wished Rosie had accepted her apology but most of all she wished she had never said the things she had said. Too late now.

'If she doesn't get back to you, it's her loss,' her father said, dismissing it. 'I've found it's no use harbouring grudges.'

She gave him a disbelieving look, remembering the long road to his forgiving *her*, but there was no point in stirring things up.

'I hear about Rosie from time to time,' she told him, not quite ready to give the subject up. 'Mum has a friend who's part of Rosie's flower circle.'

'Flower circle? Good God!'

'I know,' Olivia said ruefully. 'It's hard to imagine.'

They fell silent. Sometimes, just sometimes, she wondered if she had really got it horribly wrong and Rosie had actually fallen in love with Henry.

Her father gave a careful cough to attract her attention. 'Are you happy, Olly?'

She nodded. 'What do you think? I have all this . . .' She gestured round the room, not quite so elegant and pristine as her mother's sitting-room maybe but a room where you could put your feet up in comfort without fear of disturbing the precise lay-out of the cushions. 'I am happy, Dad,' she said, needing to say it. 'Don't worry.'

'I feel I should apologize to Ben,' her father said. 'I was a bit of a stuffed shirt, wasn't I? I see now that he loves you very much.'

'There's no need,' she said quickly. 'it will only embarrass him. Why don't we just forget it.'

'Are you sure?' he asked, relief flooding through him as he smiled.

She nodded. At the moment, she would forgive anybody anything. She was the luckiest woman in the world.

She had Ben. She had Jamie. And her father.

The most important men in her life.

Ben was away, a long-standing conference that had been impossible to get out of and in fact Olivia had insisted he go. She could manage perfectly well for a few days on her own and, although she didn't say as much, she relished the prospect of having the place to herself. A bit of the slob factor was creeping in, almost inevitable to a new mum, and she was starting to live in sweatpants and trainers. She needed to take the time to give herself an overhaul.

Therefore, with Jamie settled for the moment, she was just about to soak her feet and have a pedicure when the phone rang.

It was her mother saying urgently, without the usual preliminaries, that she must see her at once.

'What, now?' Olivia asked, not hiding her irritation. 'Can't it wait?'

'Would I be calling if it could? I must see you now, darling.'

The pedicure would have to wait and hastily she tidied up, picking up baby clothes, bringing flowers in from the hall, plumping up cushions and quickly dusting the polished surfaces. By the time her mother arrived, she had the cups out and the coffee on.

'You look tired but then that's how you'll be with you insisting on doing everything yourself,' Judith said, barging past her, her long olive-green mackintosh trailing round her legs. Under it, she wore a smart suit.

Despite her appearance, immaculate as usual, there was quite obviously something wrong but Judith admitted nothing until coffee was poured and they were drinking it. Over the baby intercom, little Jamie could be heard quietly breathing.

'That thing would drive me mad,' her mother said, nodding towards it. 'It's a wonder how any babies survived in the past without the benefit of all this new-fangled technology. We just had to listen out . . .'

'You had a nanny to do that, didn't you?' Olivia asked tartly.

'Yes, darling. But the point I'm making is that a mother would hear her child anyway through a three-foot brick wall. It's a sort of telepathy.'

'I don't hear the intercom,' Olivia said.

'What's the point of it then?'

'I mean it doesn't disturb us but of course we would notice straightaway if he stopped breathing,' she said, the very words managing to scare her so that for a moment she listened with care to the gentle and comforting baby snuffles.

'Your father's left me,' Judith said abruptly.

'Left you?' Olivia clanged her cup against the saucer.

The shock left her momentarily speechless.

'Gone.' Judith made a dramatic gesture, sighed, and put her cup down. 'He left a note,' she added, scrabbling in her handbag and handing a sheet of paper over. 'At least it's written with a proper pen so he has some sense of decency left.'

Olivia took it uncertainly. 'Do you want me to read it?'

Judith shrugged. 'It's not private. He just says, if you care to read it, that he's sorry to do this but he needs a little time on his own to think about things. I've never heard anything so ridiculous. Presumably he will be in touch when he has done so.'

Olivia scanned the note. Her mother was right. That was just about what he said, ending with 'love, George', which seemed an odd thing for a man who was leaving his wife to say.

'Where's he gone?'

'Gracious me, I don't know. And do I care? He's quite obviously taken leave of his senses.'

'What shall we do? Should we report him missing?' Olivia asked.

'Why? *He* knows where he is,' her mother said. 'And I'm certainly not involving the police. This is a private matter.'

'Why has he done this?' Olivia murmured, puzzled that her mother was taking it so well. She seemed annoyed rather than upset, unless it was a front, designed to mask her real feelings. Olivia gave her a close look but Judith was giving nothing away.

'Why? You ask why? It's simply a momentary aberration that's all. It's since he retired, darling, that things have hotted up. I never realized until I had to cope with him twenty-four hours a day what a colossal nuisance he is. He hangs around. He hovers. He intrudes. He even suggested coming shopping with me.'

'Some ladies might like that,' Olivia said. 'Look, Mum, you complain about him, but surely you didn't want him to leave?'

'No. Absolutely not. And it's so very inconvenient with so many social events coming up. How will I explain it to people? We'll have to come up with a really good excuse for him being away for a while.'

'He isn't seeing someone else?' Olivia asked, daring to voice it.

'Someone else?' Judith laughed. 'What an idea! He's still extremely shy with the opposite sex, darling. There's no question of another woman, we needn't concern ourselves with that. He feels safe with me. He knows exactly where he is with me.'

'What are you going to do, Mum?' she asked gently.

'If he thinks I shall go chasing after him, begging him to come back, he can think again,' Judith said, letting out a huge sigh that could have been the foretaste of a sob.

Olivia quickly jumped in. 'I'm sure it's just a little temporary hitch,' she said, trying to soothe her mother's fears. 'Male menopause probably.'

'That's as maybe. There'll be a complete new set of house rules when he comes back.'

'Do you think that's wise, Mum?'

'What do you expect me to do? Forgive him?'

'Why not? He always forgave you.'

Judith shot her an impatient glance. 'There was no need to mention that, Olivia. Anyway, that was different. He knew I never really meant it.'

'Maybe he's just trying to show you what it feels like.'

She frowned. 'I don't think so. I'll say one thing for your father, he's utterly straightforward. Remember all that fuss before you got married? He's not scared of principles. I married a man of principle, darling.'

Just for a moment, she detected a crumpling in her mother's face as the perfectly made-up exterior trembled. She suddenly knew what putting on a brave face meant.

'Would you like to stay here tonight?' she asked, her senses sharpening as Jamie's little cry echoed over the intercom.

'Oh no, I couldn't possibly intrude,' her mother said, the refusal very half-hearted.

'You're not intruding,' Olivia said, too tired for her mother's polite games. 'With Ben away, I'll be glad of your company.'

'Are you sure?' The relief flooded her face. 'I did hope you'd suggest that. I've brought an overnight bag. It's in the car.'

'I'll make up the bed,' Olivia said, smiling, giving her mother chance to compose herself. 'You can have a long soak and then I'll bring you up a hot chocolate. You'll feel much better after a good night's sleep.'

As she went upstairs to see to the baby, it occurred to her that she was behaving like the mother, Judith the child.

It felt strange.

CHAPTER TWENTY

The house looked like a prosperous merchant's house, square and solid, warm red-bricked, a brass plaque beside the door declaring it to be the convent of The Community of The Heavenly Cross.

A small notice nearby said 'Please ring the bell and enter'.

Eva Farrell did so, opening the heavy door and stepping into a hall. There was a sweet smell from a vase of garden flowers sitting on an old dark chest and, at the far end of the hall, light flooded in from a tall narrow window that overlooked the garden.

Nervously, she waited and a moment later, magically almost with the sun shining behind her, a nun appeared in full regalia, her feet making no sound as if she was barefoot.

'Good afternoon,' she said, 'and welcome to our home. Dr Farrell, isn't it? Your daughter is expecting you.'

The visitors' parlour was a simply decorated but surprisingly pleasing room, the sun shining in through a large uncluttered window, from where the garden could again be glimpsed. A low square table and two chairs occupied a corner space and opposite a simple chair stood against the wall. There was a small period fireplace of the sort sought after and fought over by trendy decorators. The polished floor shone and for a ridiculous moment Eva imagined a nun on her hands and knees polishing it as a penance. Did they still do such things? With a start, she realized once more how little she knew, how ignorant she was.

Tea and crunchy-looking biscuits were already set out on the table in front of her and after a moment another nun entered the room, gently closed the door behind her, and smiled.

It was Anna!

They embraced and Eva patted her back, thinking how well she looked. She had worried about that, thinking that all this nonsense was some sort of cry for help, that the underlying cause was a physical or mental illness.

'I'm not here because of Ben's insisting I visit,' she said, as soon as they were settled. 'I'm here because it's time I came.'

'Thank you. I'm so pleased you did come.' Anna smiled at her, the perfect hostess, offering her the plate of biscuits, quite at home here in *her* home. 'Olivia brought the baby to see me. She's so proud of him and isn't he beautiful?'

'Wonderful. Just like his father.' Eva glanced round. 'They are treating you all right?' she whispered. 'Tell me if there's something I ought to know.'

'I am very happy, Mum.'

'Are you?' she looked at her daughter, tried to see beyond the calmness, because she had to be sure. Before she accepted it with grace, she had to be sure that Anna was sure. 'This is a beautiful place, darling. Will you stay here for ever?'

'If it is God's will,' Anna said carefully. 'I will stay in the community but not necessarily here for ever. I may be moved to one of the other houses. This is one of the larger ones and it isn't paying its way, Mother.'

'Oh, how awkward! And how unsettling for you not knowing where you'll be from one minute to the next.'

'Most of the sisters have been here for a very long time,' Anna went on briskly. 'They tell me there have been rumours of it shutting down before, many times, so there's no reason to suppose I won't be here too for a very long time, once they sort out the financial problems.'

Eva sighed. This was an Anna she knew well and she was reminded of the child that Anna had been, the stubborn streak that had so enchanted them because they thought, quite rightly, it depicted an earnest nature. She had all the qualities of a good doctor, just like Ben, sincerity and compassion in abundance, and instead she was stuck here, frankly doing no good to anyone, least of all herself.

'I've never understood why Ben and Olivia choose to visit you separately. Is everything all right between them?' she asked, suddenly concerned.

'Yes. Don't worry about them,' Anna told her with a smile. 'You mustn't think, Mum, just because of what happened to you that other people won't be very happy together.'

'I know,' she said. 'I'm afraid I mistrust men, even Ben to some extent, and if he did to Olivia what your father did to me, I would disown him.'

She clenched her fists, not wanting to show anger in this place, wondering for the first time what on earth Anna's father would have made of all this. She suspected he would never have allowed it to happen because he had always exerted a considerable influence on his only daughter and, if he hadn't died so young, he would have continued to do so.

He had been the one though to teach Anna how to say her prayers, so in a way you could say he was responsible for all this.

When he left, she accepted – when the shock receded – that he could leave her for another woman. She assumed everyone imagined that the reason for him leaving had been because their sex life was in tatters and that irritated her profoundly because it had always been very robust. No, he left because their differing personalities eventually jarred too much.

But how could he have left his little Anna?

Little Anna, who at five years old had been utterly bewildered by the whole sorry business and had kept on asking where he was and when he would be back and had he gone to be somebody else's daddy. She felt a sudden tightness in her chest as she recalled with startling clarity that little child face, something of which was still there in her grown-up daughter.

'Mum . . . are you all right?' Anna touched her arm and smiled encouragingly. 'Would you like to walk in the garden?'

'If you like.' Eva picked up her bag, standing awkwardly as Anna rose, much more graceful in the habit than she had ever been in normal clothes.

'I help with the garden,' Anna told her proudly, showing it off. 'Look over there. I love what we've achieved in that corner. Sister Bethany was always saying how dark it was and look at it now. We've managed to brighten it up. Olivia suggested those plants and wasn't she right? She takes such an interest. She told me she thinks of it as her garden even if it isn't quite hers.'

Eva dutifully looked at the cream and white display, surprised at Anna's new enthusiasm. 'It looks good,' she conceded, although the beauty of nature was often lost on her. 'At least it gives you something physical to do. What do you do the rest of the time?'

'We live a very full life. I've told you in my letters . . .'

She kept the letters, Anna's letters, up in Anna's old room at the cottage. She kept the room tidy, the wardrobe full of Anna's clothes for when she came back. After all, if she ever left here, she'd just have the clothes she stood up in, the ones she'd come in with, and nothing else.

Everybody knew about it now because it wasn't something you could keep secret for long.

She had a son, who was a cardiologist of whom she was very proud.

And she had a daughter who was a nun.

The path circled and led them back to the visitors' parlour.

A little later, shutting the convent door, she stepped out into the world, feeling very much that she was abandoning her child. Shaking off a gloom, Eva reminded herself of her new baby grandson, and all that she had to look forward to. Judith was still a blessed nuisance, of course, acting as if, as Jamie's maternal grandmother, that made her something special in the pecking order.

Eva could cope happily with that. She wasn't over-keen on babies and toddlers but would take him under her wing a little more when he was older, so for the moment she was content to let Judith have the lioness's share. Anyway, it didn't do to cross swords with Olivia's mother.

Seeing Anna today had given her some comfort.

She still thought she was misguided but at least she was content.

And how many women could say that of their lives?

CHANTER TWENTY-ONE

The ringing of the phone, around eleven o'clock, stung Olivia out of sleep. She and Ben had taken to having an early night whenever they got the chance because Jamie was still waking during the night and it was 'grab sleep while you can' time.

It was her father.

'Hello, Olly,' he said, calm as you like, as if it was one of their ordinary phone calls of old.

'Dad! Do you know what time it is?' she said, sleepily coming to.

'Eleven, your time,' he replied, his voice light and seemingly untroubled. 'I didn't think it was too late. I thought you two were night owls?'

'We used to be,' she said. 'Before the baby.'

'Oh dear. I'm sorry. Had you gone to bed?'

'Yes. Jamie keeps us up a lot still,' she said, propping herself up on the creamy-white pillow. Beside her, Ben grumbled and stirred but kept his eyes firmly closed.

'I'm sorry to have woken you, darling. Bad timing, eh? Are you all right?'

'Are *you*?' she said, suddenly realizing the importance of this call, waking up fully, whisking into frantic action in case they were disconnected. 'Where are you? Mum's beside herself.'

'Is she?' he said with a low chuckle.

'Yes, she is,' she said sharply. 'Worried sick about you. We all are.'

'I should imagine your mother's far more concerned with keeping things quiet for the moment. How embarrassing it will be for her that I've escaped and what a dreadful nuisance for her. I bet she's told everybody that I'm away on business, hasn't she?'

Olivia ignored that.

'Why didn't you ring before?'

'I've been meaning to but it's been hard. I've been travelling and I've had a lot on my mind, love,' he said. 'And I have to think it through on my own. Coming to a decision like this has been difficult enough.'

'What on earth's wrong?'

Ben grumbled again in his sleep and she glanced crossly at him. She guessed he wasn't really asleep and a bit of support wouldn't come amiss.

'Ben's worried too,' she said, giving him a dig. 'We all are. Whatever it is, it can be sorted out, I'm sure. When are you coming back?'

'That's just it, I'm not,' he said and it was said with such finality that she knew he meant it. At least, at this moment.

'You can't leave us, Daddy,' she said quietly, giving up on a determinedly pretending to be asleep husband, reaching for her wrap and slipping it round her chilly shoulders. The light summer curtains moved a little with the night breeze and the room, peach and gold, glowed prettily with its soft lamps lit. Listening to her father's voice – his anxiety just showing – she sighed. 'If you leave, it will break Mum's heart.'

He laughed. 'Oh come on, darling. You know her. She will survive and don't worry, I've left her well provided for.'

'That's not the point and you know it,' she said. 'She's waiting for you to come back. She's refusing to face up to things.'

'We've just been going through the motions of a happy marriage for a long time,' he said, sad now. 'It's best to break loose whilst there's still some time left.'

'But what about Jamie?' she asked helplessly. 'You can't leave him. He's your grandson. I want him to grow up knowing you, all his grandparents. I lost mine when I was small – remember – and I don't want him to lose you.'

'This decision is hard for me too,' he said. 'It's not an impulsive thing. It's been brewing for years, ever since the times your mother left me. It occurred to me then that she didn't love me, not if she could do that to me. Believe me, I was lost without her and then she would just swan in and take up where she left off, as if that was all there was to it. No apology.'

'You're not exactly brilliant at apologies yourself . . .'

'I know. But your mother lives with the feeling that everything *she* says and does is right. It never occurred to her at the time that her leaving me as she did caused me a lot of distress.'

'But that's the sort of thing she does, isn't it? It was never meant to be taken seriously. She likes the dramatic touch.'

'It's nothing to do with drama for me,' her father said, his voice growing faint a moment before returning to full strength. 'I shall miss Jamie but I'll keep in touch and I will see him from time to time. I hope you'll allow me to do that. It can easily be arranged and when he's older, he can come on holidays to wherever I happen to be living.'

'Dad . . ' She felt the tears starting up because this sounded too well thought out. Indeed, it was no impulsive decision. 'Who's looking after you?'

'Someone,' he said lightly. 'Don't worry. I have new shirts – not business shirts because I'm finished with all that. I am quite capable of looking after myself.'

'This is just so silly,' she said, sniffling back the tears. 'Tell me where you are and I'll get Mum to come and talk to you.'

'No. I'm not telling you where I am because I'm just about to move on, but I promise I'll keep in touch. I'll ring. OK? And you aren't to worry. I shall be fine.'

'But Dad . . .'

The line went dead.

She then had to get up to go to the bathroom and managed somehow, irritatingly, to wake Jamie as a result. It meant a feed and change and cuddle before he settled down and, finally wide-awake by now, she returned to bed armed with a tray of tea and biscuits.

Cruelly, she woke Ben.

'God!' he grumbled, squinting at the clock as the tea things rattled on the side table. 'I'm not in the mood for a tea party.'

'Shut up and drink it,' she said with a slight smile at his grumpiness. He looked adorably handsome when he was grumpy and she wished, fractionally, that she was more in the mood these days, but since Jamie it was taking time to get back to normal. Having read in her baby book that it was a natural female reaction, she was trying not to let it worry her too much but was concerned for her husband and the effect it might have on him if it went on for too long.

'What are we going to do about Dad?' she asked, once they were both propped up, drinking tea and crunching biscuits. 'Should I tell Mum that he rang?'

'Difficult one . . .' he mused. 'If you tell her, she might be cheered up that he's still alive but, on the other hand, she's not going to be thrilled that he rang you instead of her and also that he seems to be determined not to come home.'

'The trouble is I think he means it,' she said. 'I always thought he loved Mum in his way, even though she is exasperating to live with. So, why is he doing this? Has he fallen out of love?'

'He said someone was looking after him. What does he mean by that?'

'A lover?' Olivia laughed. 'I don't think so. I really can't believe that.'

'Look, sweetheart . . .' Ben brushed crumbs off the bed and put his cup aside.

'I know it's hard not to interfere but it's between the two of them. I can't say I'm very surprised.'

'What do you mean?'

'Your mother's a tough nut. She treats him like dirt. Surely you've noticed? And don't tell me it's just her way. You say she left him years ago, well, in my opinion, it might have been better if she'd stayed away then.'

'Ben! How can you?' she asked, genuinely agitated. 'You of all people know how disruptive it is when a parent leaves.'

'OK. Put it another way. Would you want somebody butting in on us if we had a problem?'

'No,' she said, catching his glance, knowing that he was now fully awake, just as she was beginning to feel sleepy once more.

She had to face up to his not liking her mother – fact of life – but what had once been easily disregarded was not so easily dismissed now. He wasn't trying much to make amends and it was beginning to irritate. They couldn't go on the rest of their lives tiptoeing over hot coals where her mother was concerned. Ben had to learn to get on with her or at the very least make some sort of effort.

'We must talk about the christening,' she said, turning her thoughts to something more pleasant. 'Sometime soon. Although Dad disappearing on us isn't going to make it easy. How will Mum explain him not being there?'

'I have no idea. One of these days she's going to have to admit he's gone,' he said. 'The christening can wait. I really don't want to get caught up in too many arrangements just now. There's no rush, is there?'

'No rush,' she agreed, although for some reason she felt there was.

In fact, she knew the reason why.

It was visiting Anna recently that had done it, for, after their walk round the garden, she had been allowed a quick peep into the convent chapel and had been quite overcome by the beauty of the silence, the faint smell of incense. There was something almost sensual about the polished wood, the smooth floor, the way the sun streamed through the windows. She had felt, quite extraordinarily, as if she was in the presence of someone – presumably God – but it was not something she felt willing to share with anyone, especially not her mother, or Ben, or Anna come to that. It seemed so private a thing.

She wanted her son christened, sooner rather than later, so that she set him on the right road.

But it would mean thinking of godparents.

The men were easy enough – Farrell friends who had both been tentatively approached – but who would be Jamie's godmother? She had let it slip to Ben that she wanted Rosie but it was a wistful, stupid thought for Rosie was hardly the sort to guide Jamie along the right path. In any case, whilst they were not speaking, it would never be.

'Hey, you look as if you have all the worries of the world on your shoulders, your very silky, sexy shoulders . . .' Ben said with a grin, pushing back the wrap and the narrow strap of her nightgown and kissing them. 'Relax, won't you? What's to worry about? You have me and Jamie and your father and mother will come to their senses soon enough.'

'I know.' She leaned into him, feeling sleep drawing in on her. 'I'm very tired,' she warned, catching his look.

'I'm only offering a cuddle, Mrs Farrell. Nothing more until you're ready.'

'Thanks, darling.' She snuggled into his arms, grateful that at least she had him.

He was such a darling, being so considerate, a smashing daftly doting dad, that she would be ready soon for a full return to the sex side of their marriage.

But not yet.

CHAPTER TWENTY-TWO

On days when she wasn't on council duty, Judith often came round in the afternoon and took Jamie out for his walk.

And today was no exception.

It was Ben's outpatients' clinic day, always a hassle and a half, and Olivia was going shopping whilst her mother looked after Jamie.

'I won't be long,' Olivia assured her, anxiously scanning her baby's face. 'Does he seem a bit flushed?'

'No. Wait until he starts on the teeth then you'll know what flushed means,' her mother said ominously. 'Off you go and enjoy yourself. And buy yourself something glamorous, for heavens' sake. You've been neglecting poor Ben lately.'

'I have not,' she said, at once up in arms.

'Glad to hear it.' Her mother smiled slightly. 'Can we talk a moment?'

'What about?' she asked, suspecting a long melancholy grumble about her father and what she would do to him when he came home.

'About Ben,' Judith said. 'I know he's fearfully busy but we need to fit in a meeting sometime, Ben and I, just the two of us.'

'A meeting?' Olivia laughed. 'You're obsessed with meetings, Mother. This is family. You have no need to arrange a meeting.'

'Maybe not. But you can be too informal. We need to sit down, Ben and I, and discuss why we're not getting on. I find myself increasingly frustrated by it. If we set aside twenty minutes, we can get to the bottom of the problem. He doesn't like me,' she added, a brightness in her eyes. 'I'm so proud of him and what he does but he doesn't like me. What have I done to upset him?'

'You've done nothing wrong, Mum,' she assured her, suddenly very annoyed with Ben for making things so obvious.

Judith rubbed tiredly at her eyes, smudging the generous amount of mascara she still used. 'I'm being stupid, I know, but what with your father leaving and everything . . . well, it's getting to me.'

'I'll get Ben to talk to you. Why not come for dinner on Friday? And I'll find some excuse to leave you together so you can talk.'

'Lovely idea, darling. Although you mustn't go to any trouble.'

'Of course not,' Olivia said, already regretting the impulsive invitation. It would mean poring over meals, doing a table decoration, so that she wouldn't look a complete hostess-failure in her mother's critical eyes.

'That makes me feel much better. I feel that if only we can talk and get it off our chests, all will be well. Now, off you go and enjoy your shopping,' her mother said, standing beside her and looking into the mirror in the hall. 'You look fine. Not quite so peaky as you did. Motherhood suits you.'

Maybe it did but it was a pain in that you were totally unable to shut off from it, she thought, as she wandered the shops. She felt, without Jamie, as if she was missing a limb and kept glancing at other women with babies, wishing he was here with her, which was very self-indulgent, when he was perfectly happy at home.

There was a special dinner coming up and that's what she was shopping for, something exciting and ultra chic and definitely not black, for everybody else would surely be wearing it.

She settled for a gorgeous off-white crepe number, slinky with a broad belt. Rosie would approve, she found herself thinking, as she checked it out in the changing-room. Just for a moment, she thought she heard her voice from an adjoining cubicle but, even as she stiffened at the very idea, she realised with a great relief that it was not her.

Were they being completely stupid, the two of them?

What did it take to say sorry?

Anna had said as much to her but then sometimes Anna could be a pain too. Everything was black and white with Anna. Right and wrong. No shades of grey.

However, perhaps it was time she took the initiative and apologized again and this time she would mean it.

She would maybe try ringing Henry, find out the lay of the land before telephoning Rosie herself. Checking her watch, she decided it was time to get back home. Her mother would have taken Jamie out for a walk and then it was his nap time and with a bit of luck they could have a coffee in peace.

Olivia was to recall later that, during her shopping trip, she heard the sound of an ambulance siren, cringing inwardly that someone was in trouble, never imagining for a minute that it was her mother and Jamie.

But then, that sort of thing always happens to other people, doesn't it?

The details emerged later, statements from horrified onlookers but the gist of it was that a lorry driver had died at the wheel of his cab and it had careered downhill right into the path of Judith and Jamie.

'Get out of the way!' someone had yelled, for it seemed that Judith was frozen with fear.

Judith Hayton had used all her strength at that moment, looking fixedly ahead, according to a witness, and shot the pram out of the lorry's path, checking it was out of harm's way before surrendering to the inevitable.

It was all so quick. Seconds to react before being thrust into the wall.

Afterwards, Olivia's neighbour, a pleasant woman called Sally, whom she was only just beginning to get to know, rang the hospital to speak to Ben to tell him the news because Olivia was numb and dumb with shock, clutching little Jamie, who had escaped without a scratch, to her breast.

Sally returned from using the phone to say that she had left a message as, at the moment, Ben could not be located. In fact, she went on sheepishly, he wasn't expected in today at all and his deputy was taking the clinic.

Olivia nodded, not understanding. She relinquished a now silent Jamie to the care of Sally, who put him up in his cot for his nap, and when she came back down, Olivia had the kettle on.

She was so proud of her kitchen, country chic in the heart of the city with copper pans, dark green Aga and lots of pine. She stood watching the kettle in that gorgeous kitchen and wondered when she would cry.

The last time she and her mother had talked about Dad, Judith had tried her best to be upbeat.

'It's more a bore than anything else now,' she said. 'If he ever bothers to come back, I shall very likely kill him. It's put me in such an embarrassing position with everybody. I'm not sure I can keep up the pretence much longer.'

'It might have been easier if you'd told the truth in the first place,' Olivia gently pointed out. 'But I'm sure people will understand your motives.'

'Yes. I shall say I was reluctant to face facts, when the truth was I was simply giving him time to come to his senses,' her mother said. 'As it is, I'm no longer sure I would take him back were he to come back on his knees. I have been humiliated quite enough.'

'You're like children sometimes, the pair of you,' Olivia said, driven to exasperation by it all. 'You blame him for walking out but you must have suspected something was wrong. Don't you talk to each other any more?'

'Does any married couple? Do you and Ben?'

'Yes. About most things.'

'I love George,' her mother said unexpectedly, eyes bright for a moment. 'I really do. But he has been the most irritating man on earth to live with. The things I did for that man. The sacrifices I made . . .'

Olivia smiled. 'What sacrifices?'

'What sacrifices?' Her mother's smile was tight. 'Well, I gave up my job for one thing. I felt I had it in me to go all the way in my career but when I married your father, what alternative did I have but to resign? He was going places and he needed me as a support.' For a moment, the old bloody-mindedness surfaced. 'If you don't put your foot down straightaway, you've had it. Anyway, there we were traipsing off all over the world. Romantic-sounding European cities and exotic climes are all very well for holidays, darling, as you well know, but living there is quite another matter. And leaving the house and leaving you behind, virtually abandoning you at school, was a nightmare. I have never forgiven myself for that.'

'It wasn't so bad and it wasn't their fault if I failed the exams. You talk as if I'm permanently damaged by the experience and I'm not. I have some happy memories of it.'

'Yes, well . . .' Her mother glanced sharply at her. 'Thank heavens you're a well-adjusted sort but you used to look so small and sad when you visited us and seeing you off on to the plane when you had to go back was sheer torture. I don't believe I ever quite forgave your father for subjecting me to that. You can probably imagine how difficult it was, now that you have Jamie.'

Yes she could.

'That was why I was brusque with you, I suppose,' Judith continued thoughtfully. 'Because I dare not be otherwise. If I'd started crying, for instance, having second thoughts, when it was time for you to go, what good would that have done? It was easier just to give you a quick hug and pat you off and be quick about it. When I got back, the house would be so silent without you. I saved my crying for later, darling.'

'So did I.'

Olivia watched the kettle steaming and Sally, taking charge, had the tea made and biscuits on a plate before she had time to come to her senses.

'The policewoman said she wouldn't have felt a thing,' Sally said softly, sitting beside her on the sofa. 'That's a relief, isn't it? And wouldn't she be so pleased that Jamie was safe?'

Olivia nodded, wondering why Sally, such a petite lady, should choose to wear dresses designed for a giantess. Her mother had commented on it with a click of her sometimes caustic tongue, saying that they ought to do the basics of style as a compulsory school subject because some people had no idea how to present themselves. It could affect your whole life, Judith insisted. Dressing appropriately could get you the job you craved or the man of your dreams.

Her mother should have been president of the style Mafia.

Her mother . . .

It took a minute to realize that Sally was holding her hand, looking terribly sympathetic.

'Are you all right?' she asked softly. 'Do you want a brandy?'

She shook her head. 'My father . . .' Her mouth was dry and she had no idea why she was blurting this out to Sally, whom she hardly knew. 'He and my mother were temporarily separated. I'm not sure where he is just now. He'll have to be told.'

'You don't have a number for him?'

She shook her head.

Sally pressed a cup of hot sweet tea into her hand. 'Drink this,' she said. 'And don't worry about your father. We'll find him.'

'Ben . . .' she sipped a mouthful of the tea, then put the cup down. 'Where did they say he was?'

'They didn't,' Sally said, looking a little shifty. 'I'm sure there's a perfectly good explanation.'

'Oh yes.' Olivia smiled. 'There will be.'

'Are you sure you're all right? I'll stay until Ben gets back.'

'No really, there's no need. I'm fine.' But, as she sat down and eased her head back, the room suddenly swam, and clearly she was not.

When she came to, looking up into Sally's anxious face, the reality of it hit like a stone.

She had lost her mother. Her mum was dead. And it was time to face up to it.

'Chester grandma (58) sacrifices life for baby grandson' screamed the headline, accompanied by a photograph of the wrecked truck, whose driver (51) had collapsed and died at the wheel minutes before impact.

Not only did they get the age wrong, they also called her 'grandma'. At least the photograph of her mother was a flattering one, chosen by Olivia, so that was something. The reporter had asked after her father and she had waffled away the question, saying he was abroad on business and they were trying to contact him at this very moment.

For some reason, the fact that Ben was a cardiologist made his eyes light up but, sadly for his report, there was no dramatic follow-on such as Ben doing miracle life-saving surgery on his mother-in-law.

The truth was Judith had died instantly at the scene.

Whether or not she had known in that instant that Jamie was safe, nobody would ever know, but Olivia hoped and even prayed that she had.

CHAPTER TWENTY-THREE

Her father, voice shocked and funny, contacted her as soon as he heard the news, saying he would be right home. She believed him when he said that he had been going to come home anyway, that the little rebellion was over, that he had seen it for what it was – an old man's folly. He had sent flowers only yesterday, he said, her favourite roses, and wondered if Judith had got them.

Holding hands, they went round to the house together and it was a strange experience. Somehow, the house had managed, within a few short sad hours, to lose its warmth, its soul. It was still the same house but it was like an empty shell, a show house. Looking round, Olivia had no idea what her father would do now, stay here or move on, but it was much too soon to talk about it.

They braved the first few difficult days together, finding it better if they talked continuously of her, marvelling at what she had done, looking at little Jamie and thanking God. Anna came to see her to offer her condolences and seeing her in civvies was easier in a way because it was unofficial and she could say what she wanted to say without worrying about offending the nun's habit.

She was able to tell Anna that things were not well between her and Ben. The tragedy had rocked them both and it had particularly infuriated her that he was nowhere to be found when he was most needed.

'Where the hell were you?' had been the words she had greeted him with that evening. 'You weren't at the hospital. You'd think, wouldn't you, that when I really needed you, you might have been there.'

'We should talk,' he said quietly. 'I have some explaining to do.'

'Not now,' she said, shaking her head wearily. Her head was full of tears but they wouldn't come out. All she could think about was her mother. All she could see was the crushed mangled body, the air, the life, squeezed out in an instant.

Ben, as far as she was concerned, and *his* little problems could take a running jump – he was acting very oddly and if he was having an affair, the very worst scenario she could think of, then she would face it later.

He tried to come over to cuddle her but she turned aside, much too tight inside, thinking of funerals and guests and the wake. She owed it to her mother to do something splendid – she would never forgive her otherwise – and she must buy a new black outfit, something sensational, one her mother would be proud of.

'Roses . . .' she murmured. 'Mum always loved roses. Pink ones. A bit conventional but she loved them anyway.'

'Are you talking about a wreath?' Ben asked with a rueful smile.

She nodded, mind already elsewhere. 'We must go ahead with Jamie's christening as soon as possible after the funeral. It's what Mum would have wanted. She was starting to go on about it and she'd sounded out the vicar. She was talking about a little buffet afterwards and wondering who we should invite . . .'

'I've asked Rosie to be godmother.'

She turned to stare. 'You've done what?'

'The other day. That's where I was. I've been trying to tell you but you haven't been listening. I was with Rosie that afternoon. I phoned her a week ago and she said she'd think about it but she sounded unsure, so I thought if I went to see her, I might be able to persuade her.' He sighed. 'There was no point in telling you beforehand. She might have said no.'

'And? What did she say?'

'Yes. She'll be happy to do it. And she wants you to take Jamie to see her. Of course, this was before all this happened.'

The phone call, when it eventually came, was unexpected.

'Livvy. . . !' Rosie said, sounding as thoroughly wretched as she used to when she had had one of her famously lousy days at the studio. 'Oh my God, what am I to say to you? You poor, poor darling! And poor, poor Judith.'

Olivia's heart was still stuck in a solid lump. Like a block of ice. And no amount of Rosie's anguished expressions could shift it from its agonized perch. The hurt was physical. Heartache. She had lost her mummy and as far as she was concerned, she was the only person in the whole world to have suffered such a tragedy.

'Thank you for your card, Rosie,' she said stiffly.

'Oh Livvy, I'm so sorry we couldn't be there at the funeral.'

'That's all right. Thank you for the flowers.'

'How ... how did things go?'

'Very well. Lots of flowers. The vicar was very kind. We sang "Jerusalem". You know Mum, she adored it. And then we got those caterers in, the ones Mum liked.'

The pause was heart wrenching.

'Oh good,' Rosie managed to say at last.

Olivia remained silent, unable to help, but Rosie ploughed desperately on. 'I know I teased her but I was fond of her. She was such a wonderful snob of the old school. And so elegant – God, did she know how to dress!'

'Yes. She was wearing Jaegar separates when she died.'

Rosie gave a nervous laugh. 'Look, darling, has Ben told you that he asked me to be Jamie's godmother and that I said yes?'

'He has. I did think we'd have the christening soon but I don't feel I can face it at the moment. Thank you for offering.'

'Is that a no then?' Rosie asked doubtfully. 'Don't you want me to be his godmother? I'd make a bloody good job of it, Livvy. I'd take it very seriously and when he gets older, I won't shirk telling him all about women and how to treat them.'

'Thanks, Rosie' she said with a gulp, strangely moved. 'I'm sorry. How could we have let things go on like they have for so long? Stupid, isn't it?'

'My fault,' she said glibly. 'Look, Livvy, I know it's trite but this is the worst time for you. It will ease a bit.'

Olivia smiled a little. People meant well and even Rosie had joined them on the consolation bandwagon.

'Look, darling,' Rosie went on, sounding increasingly desperate, 'Henry and I are going to spend a few weeks at the house in Bermuda. I've had a word with Ben and he's happy that you and the baby come and visit, in a couple of weeks when you've had time to get over things.'

'Get over things?' Olivia felt her voice rising with anger and despair. 'My mother was killed protecting my baby, Rosie. So you could say it's all my fault. If I hadn't had Jamie, then she wouldn't have been taking him for a walk that day and if I'd never met Ben again, I'd never have had Jamie so you could say it's his fault too.'

'That sounds completely daft,' Rosie said with a quick nervous laugh. 'If the driver of that lorry hadn't suddenly had a heart attack and died then he'd have just driven on by, wouldn't he? So talking about blame is useless.'

'I'll never get over it,' Olivia sighed, not into arguing although what Rosie said sounded eminently sensible. 'And a trip to Bermuda is not going to help either.'

'OK,' Rosie said hastily. 'That came out wrong. You know me. What I meant was it might help. We can talk. It will be like old times.'

'It's very kind of you but may I think about it?'

'By all means,' Rosie said, sounding resigned. 'But if you change your mind you only have to say the word. And the whole trip's on Henry, so don't dare book economy class.'

'I am perfectly able to pay business class myself. There's no need to treat me like a pauper.'

'Sorry. What I meant was . . . Oh, please try to come, Livvy. It will do you good.'

She had no intention of going but she supposed, ungraciously, that it was nice of Rosie to think about her.

To her surprise, though, Ben and her father were in conspiratorial mood, already knowing about the suggested trip, giving it their wholehearted approval.

'Off you go,' her father said, helping her with the awful job of sorting through her mother's clothes. It was a task that had to be done sooner or later and it would never get any easier. At least the job was made easy by the meticulous colour-coded system her mother had used to catalogue her collection.

'Give me one good reason why,' she said. 'Deserting you and Ben doesn't seem a particularly good idea and travelling across the Atlantic with a baby seems a dreadful idea.'

'You can manage that,' he said with the slightest of smiles. 'You did it when you were a child. Do it, Olly. It will do you the world of good. And you loved it there. Remember?'

'Mum didn't.' She pulled a daffodil-yellow suit from its hanger and put it on the nearly new designer pile.

'No. She was a home bird, darling. I feel so guilty for dragging her off to places she didn't want to go. If only I could turn the clock back . . .' He glanced at her shrewdly. 'Is something wrong with you and Ben? I know you're upset but you're giving him a hard time.'

'Nothing's wrong,' she said impatiently. 'What on earth gave you that idea?'

'You're neglecting him,' he said. 'You're not letting him help you through this. You need a prop and it shouldn't be me. It should be him. Do you understand?'

'You think I'm being selfish?'

'Since you ask, yes I do. How do you think he feels? He very nearly lost his baby too. Don't forget that. We should try to let it help, the fact that Judith saved Jamie's life. Oh, we'd all like to think we'd do the same thing given the chance. But would we? I would have been too slow for one. If it had been me pushing that pram then we'd both have been gone. But it wasn't me. It was Judith and she had the guts and the ability to get Jamie out of it.'

She saw his eyes bright with unshed tears.

'Dad . . .'

'I'll be all right in a minute,' he said, voice shaking. 'It's just that . . . if only she'd got my flowers before she died. Then she would have known I was coming back.'

'I think she must have got them,' Olivia said. 'She was excited about something. She told me that. She was going to buy a new outfit and . . .' She stopped, knowing it was silly to go on.

He smiled a little. Squeezed her hand. Shook his head.

'Thanks for that,' he said. 'But there's a terrible flaw to it all, love. If she did get them, where were they?'

He looked tired and old and oh how very much she loved him.

She felt her own lip trembling, felt the tears at last loosening, felt the block of ice melting.

Fell into her father's arms.

Ben could not get over quite how devastated Olivia was. He had never seen her looking like this and although he was familiar with grief and the effects on the family, this was suddenly different because it was personal, it was his grief.

The manner of his mother-in-law's death made it somehow worse not better.

He found himself overwhelmingly grateful to her, to the woman whom he had not tried to get to know properly, whom he had very nearly despised. He had dismissed her as lightweight, a mere clothes freak, a person who, despite her stab at the councillor job – and he even queried her motives for that – was essentially shallow. He could not forget how she had upset his mother before the wedding. Eva, who professed to be a toughish nut, had been upset when Judith had tried with elephantine lack of tact to help her choose an outfit, for 'we can't have you turning up in one of those suits of yours, darling'. On a more sinister level, Judith had tried to use him occasionally in his professional capacity to organize some queue jumping – something he told her straight he was power-less to do and wouldn't have even if he could, not for a favour for his mother-in-law.

'Well, thank you very much, Ben,' she had said to that. 'At least we know where we stand.'

So, he was guilty, wishing he had had the opportunity to smooth things over, to have that chat with her that Olivia had told him about.

And now it was too late.

Seeing Olivia's set face, the mask she now presented to the world, and worse, to him, he tried to skim off the veil of misery and get to the bottom of it all.

'I know you're angry and upset, darling,' he told her, 'but it's more than that, isn't it? You've got to tell me. What on earth is the matter?'

'The matter? You have to ask that?' she laughed bitterly. 'I should think it's perfectly obvious what's the matter to anyone with an ounce of sensitivity.'

'Are you calling me insensitive?' he asked, more sharply than he intended, but that cut him to the core. 'God, Olivia, that's a bit rich,' he muttered.

'You're insensitive where *I'm* concerned. You're not the least bit bothered by my mother's death. It means nothing to you. She saved your son's life and you feel nothing. And why? Because you never liked her, that's why.'

'What are you talking about? That is not true. You're way off the mark, darling. I can't believe what Judith did and I'm so grateful for what she did that, if she were here now, I'd hug her to bits for it. And I'd take back all the unkind thoughts I might have for her. But she's not here, is she?' he added gently. 'And you have to realize, sweetheart, that this is grief talking. You're taking it out on me because I'm the closest to you. And I don't mind. Shout and scream all you like if it helps.'

Olivia dreamed of her mother.

Always the same dream.

She, Olivia, was in this shopping mall, where they had arranged to meet at this expensive boutique. And she could never quite find it. Then, looking round, she saw her mother, in bright pink, on the upper level. She waved to her and started up the escalator but when she got to the top, she was gone ... always gone.

She would wake, heart pounding, unrested, with Ben tensely asleep beside her.

Once upon a time, she would have cuddled into him, shaped herself into the angle of his back and found comfort in that, but not any more.

They slept, both of them, on the edge.

She was too angry to pray. The vicar had suggested it might help but he was wrong. God had let her down. God was indifferent to her feelings, allowing her this pain. The only time she felt any degree of comfort was when she was in Jamie's room, in gentle darkness, looking down at him, at his softly breathing body, the owl and the pussy cat mobile swaying softly in the breeze from the half-open window.

Stroking Jamie's face, Olivia found some small consolation.

CHAPTER TWENTY-FOUR

The clouds were high in the sky, fluffy and inconsequential, and they chose to walk therefore in the garden, rather than stay in the parlour taking tea.

They sat, Anna and Olivia, on the warm stone bench and said not a word for a very long time. Olivia had muttered 'don't you dare mention God or that brother of yours to me' at the beginning and then felt guilty for the words.

Anna felt no discomfort in the silence, but then she was used to silence.

Next to her, she felt Olivia's sorrow, the sharp pain transferring to her, as she tried to imagine what it would feel like to lose her own mother in those tragic circumstances.

She waited. In no hurry. She had had bad news herself this morning, for the decision was made and the convent was to be sold. The sisters would be transferred, deposited here and there, in twos and threes, amongst the other houses of the community. A sad, difficult day but she had no intention of burdening Olivia with the news.

'What's the matter with me, Anna?' Olivia said at last, sighing through the words. 'I'm being an absolute bitch with Ben and I don't know why. I'm accusing him of not liking mother.'

'I'm sure he understands. Grief does funny things to us.'

'I know I'm hurting him,' Olivia said slowly, as it dawned. 'But I can't seem to help it, Anna. I feel so guilty. Mum wanted so much for Jamie. She wanted to see him growing up.' she paused. 'I don't know why I've come here. Why *have* I come here?'

'Because you need someone to listen,' Anna said.

'Rosie wants me to visit her in Bermuda. Did Ben tell you?'

Anna nodded. 'Yes. I'm pleased you two are reconciled. I'd love it if she were to visit me.'

'I don't know what to do about it. About visiting her. It's this thing with Henry. How could she marry a man for his money?'

'Olivia . . . you're very *angry*, aren't you?'

'Wouldn't you be? I've not long ago had a baby and now I've lost my mother in the most horrible circumstances. How would you feel?'

'Probably like you. I do get angry sometimes.'

She smiled, seeing Olivia's look of surprise. Yes, nuns were allowed to be angry! And they too felt petty and irritated and out of sorts – all the normal human foibles – and yes, the younger ones did suffer PMT and mood swings. The point was they had to learn to control such feelings, to try to put others first and it wasn't easy. 'I'm sorry about your mother . . .' Anna waited a minute, took Olivia's hand in hers, struggling to come up with the right words.

She took her time, gazing a while at the flowers that grew nearest the bench, yellow lilies that she knew as sultan's cap, yellow with vivid orange centres and a powerful scent. The orange stained and she had to be careful brushing past in her habit or the laundry nun complained.

'I've planted chrysanthemum in my front garden,' Olivia told her softly. 'They smile, open out, when the sun shines. I love flowers that have a reaction like that. It makes you remember that they're a living thing, as much as we are.' She paused and sighed. 'It's strange but I never noticed them for days after it happened but then, yesterday, I was going out and they were just there, glowing, and I remember being surprised that they were still there as if nothing had happened. I wondered how on earth they dared show their face, frankly.'

Anna felt she knew what that meant but was reluctant to explain that God had chosen to touch her at that moment. 'Your mother died doing something heroic, something she would have wanted to do,' she said. 'Don't you think that any grandmother would do the same? And just think how proud Jamie will be of her one day. Think of her courage and it will help you.'

'Thanks . . .' Olivia managed a smile and squeezed her hand.

'God bless.' Anna hugged her a moment. 'Take care,' she said, before walking away.

Sister Matilda was in fighting mood and, after supper, she said her piece.

'We should prepare a business plan. It's something we ought to have done years ago,' she told them. 'We have a lot to offer here. We have a beautiful convent, a lovely garden in the very heart of the city. We have empty rooms and we could do bed and breakfast, offer meditation weekends.' She glanced at Anna sharply. 'You have experience of this, Sister?'

'A little,' said Anna, thinking of the retreat in Scotland and Ross. 'It's amazing how happy people are to accept the simple life for a while . . .'

'Exactly,' Sister Matilda said firmly. 'It's considered trendy. And, from an economic angle, the more we charge, the better.'

'Alas, Sister,' Mother broke in, voice gentle as ever, 'I fear your business mind is taking over from your serene one. You know my feelings. Retreats are springing up all over the place and I have a great admiration for them and for the good they do. But it isn't for us; it never has been and it never will be. This community was not founded on that basis and I wonder just how it would affect the general working of our community to have strangers present. We cannot take that risk. It's out of the question.'

'It's that or sell,' Sister Matilda said with some exasperation. 'There's no way we can continue as we have been doing for all these years. We live in the modern world even though we may wish we did not. And in the modern world, it's all about paying your way.'

She had prepared a business plan anyway and they received it with lukewarm interest. Anna felt, as did most of the others, that it was already decided and that nothing would change it. In any case, Mother, backed by the community hierarchy, was against it and so that was that.

As Reverend Mother intoned before they withdrew to their rooms for private prayer, they really needed a generous benefactor, no questions asked, who would put up a considerable sum so that they might remain here quietly, fulfilling their lives with prayer.

Sister Matilda's face was a picture.

She and Jamie were travelling business class, courtesy of Rosie and Henry, stopping short of the first class they had wanted to arrange.

After miles of open ocean interspersed with food and drink and sheer boredom, it was a relief to see the green of the subtropical island beneath, as they swooped down, landing smoothly on the tarmac.

It was September and the Bermuda air was still baking from the heat of summer, temperature hovering at around 28 degrees even in the late afternoon. Rosie was at the airport to meet her, waving furiously as she came out of the customs hall, greeting her with a warm hug.

'Good to see you, Livvy,' she said softly.

'And you . . .' Olivia managed, still feeling the exhilaration she always felt from a safely accomplished flight.

'And this is Jamie . . .' Rosie cooed over the baby a minute, before channelling them out to a waiting car. 'You look thin. We'll soon fatten you up and get some colour into your cheeks.'

'Stop acting like my mother, for goodness' sake,' Olivia said, too sharply, her mood instantly mellowing as she caught the doubt in Rosie's eyes. 'Sorry. You'll have to forgive me. I'm behaving very badly these days. Anyone would think I'm the only woman in the world to have lost her mother. Mum would have been appalled. She was very keen on keeping a stiff upper lip. Anyway, they're all glad to see the back of me.'

'That is absolutely not true but we'll talk about it later,' Rosie said, helping them into the car, still cooing over little Jamie who was wide awake, happily unaware that he was now supposed to have baby jet lag. 'I've just passed my driving test,' Rosie told her. 'Crazy, isn't it, that they don't recognize a British licence. Don't worry, I'm a very careful driver these days. You have to be at this snail speed.'

Olivia said nothing, as it hadn't seemed to occur to Rosie that driving was not something she cared to chat about. She had always been a nervous driver and passenger – as if she had had some sort of premonition – and a runaway lorry killing her mother had not helped.

She was tired and not capable of taking in anything of the short journey to Rosie's house. Tomorrow would be soon enough to explore again. But the heat and the pretty pastel-coloured houses with the sparkling roofs and the glimpse of sea and sand were sufficient to rouse her spirits just a fraction.

'Do you like it?' Rosie asked, anxious as ever, as they approached the pink house.

'It's lovely,' Olivia said, gazing at the stretch of simple but stately garden with its dotted palms and massed hibiscus. 'It's all very grand, Rosie.'

'I know that. Do enjoy the garden, I know you're into that. The gardener despairs of Henry and me. Henry has no interest at all and I don't really care so long as the grass is cut. Here, let me take your bag.'

'It's all right. You needn't treat me like an invalid,' Olivia said, regretting the brusque words at once. She was bereaved, true, but other people managed to get through bereavement with a touch more grace.

'Come on in.' Rosie swung through the door into the cool of the interior. There was a broad expanse of pure white tiled floor, unrelieved by rugs, with white walls, white shutters, black and white furniture with touches of green and a lot of shiny-leafed plants. 'There's the porch . . .' Rosie said, opening the shutters to show her, still comically anxious to impress. 'It widens out beside the dining-room so we can dine outdoors,' she added with a smile. 'We like to take breakfast there before it gets too hot.'

Olivia nodded, still amazed at Rosie's capacity to be the lady of the house, amused at Rosie talking of informal eating, remembering Rosie of the plate-on-the-knee school of dining.

'I'll show you your rooms first and if all you want to do this evening is collapse into bed, that's fine by me. I just want you to do things at your own pace, Livvy. If I start getting on your nerves, you know me well enough to tell me to shut up and sod off and leave you alone. I've put Jamie in a little room off yours. Is that OK? If you want him in with you, do say. And Christabel, our Filipino, will look after him. She's looking forward to it and she's a gem, absolutely one hundred per cent trustworthy.'

'But...' She stopped, not sure if she wanted to trust Jamie with a stranger.

'We thought it might be a good idea if you had some time on your own. You'll see plenty of baby but he shouldn't be out too much in the sun anyway with his tender skin.'

Olivia nodded, admitting defeat. So long as Jamie was fed and watered and cuddled, he was happy and yes, she would appreciate some time on her own. Rosie looked fabulous, rich and fabulous.

She wore her hair in a new shorter style with a feathery fringe, a golden blur of curls. Her trouser suit was palest primrose, a glossy heavy material, superbly cut and stunning as only the most expensive items can be, the trousers wide legged and trailing at just the right length over lemon mules. A few gold bracelets, a glitter of chains round her neck and pearl earrings completed the outfit. Sunny and attractive and every inch the wife of a multi-millionaire.

She was a far cry from the Rosie of old and, suddenly and unexpectedly, it was the Rosie of old whom Olivia craved, the old Rosie of the tatty dressing-gown and down-at-heel slippers.

The guest bedroom was prettily if sparsely furnished, the main feature being the enormous double bed, the expanse of pink carpet and the white and rose-pink American-type bedcover. The walls were graced by a couple of impressive paintings and the remaining furniture, a desk and chair and a small sofa, had been carefully selected to blend in perfectly.

There was an adjoining shower room and the views from the bedroom were of the shelving garden with a glimpse of the turquoise sea beyond.

A polite knock signalled the arrival of the tea brought in by a maid, who chatted non-stop in the time it took her to place the tray on a table, telling her she was of Portuguese origin and that she had worked for Mr Chambers for many years now and what a charming man he was, with such a sweet new wife.

Pleading tiredness, Olivia got rid of her finally, taking the tea over to the chair by the window. She had been introduced to Christabel, to whom Jamie had taken an instant liking, and she had whisked him away without any protests.

True to her word, Rosie did not disturb her. She took a shower then, feeling tired, slipped into a cotton nightshirt and into bed. The room was pleasantly cool, the buzz of the air conditioning muted, although the whistle of the tree frogs soon started up their night chorus outside the window, reminding her of where she was.

Dog-tired from the flight, she experienced a mixed set of dreams, of her mother here in Bermuda, of her standing on the steps of the house in Warwick, of her perfume.

She awoke with a start.

Panicking because, for a few seconds, she could not recall the dream.

Doubly panicking because she realized it was late. Goodness, how many hours had she slept? And what on earth was the time, the real time, the English time? And what would Christabel think of her, abandoning Jamie like this?

In his little annexe next door, Jamie – many hours adrift in his little world – was fast asleep and Christabel was busy putting his things away in the drawers. Olivia checked him, wondering how much Christabel knew of the circumstances, realizing as Christabel murmured 'what a lucky little boy he is' that she knew the lot.

'Good morning, Livvy,' Rosie said, coming into her room with a smile. 'Sleep well?'

'Yes,' she said gratefully. 'Christabel said she would attend to Jamie and she did. She's wonderful with him.'

'Henry sends his apologies but he's had to dash off already, so he'll see you this evening. Tea and toast will be up in a minute,' Rosie said, plonking herself on the bed. 'And then you and me can have a big long talk. I'm going to help you get through this, Livvy, if it's the last thing I do.'

Olivia tied the belt of her gown. 'I'm hardly going to be a bundle of laughs,' she warned. 'You and Henry deserve a medal for inviting me. You know I never knew what people meant when they asked how someone was taking a death.'

'Oh yes, I've heard that one. She's taking it very well, they say. How can they know? There are public faces, aren't there, and private ones.'

Olivia agreed. 'I'm taking it badly, I've heard told. I suppose that means I'm letting my feelings show. I feel just terrible, Rosie. I miss her so much when most of the time she irritated me.' Her eyes filled again with the ever-ready tears. 'Look at me,' she sniffed, grabbing a tissue. 'This is doing no good. I've got to pull myself together.'

'Who says? Just take one day at a time.'

She nodded, pausing as the tea and toast arrived. 'You're right. If I can just get through today in one piece then . . .'

Rosie smiled and patted her hand. 'Livvy, I want to say something about that day at The Crypt. All that fuss.'

'Please don't. There's no need to dredge that up.'

'Oh but there is,' Rosie said firmly. 'I know I was angry but I should have let you apologize afterwards. That would have been the graceful thing to do.'

'It was my fault,' Olivia said, awkward with this. 'I had no right to say those things.'

'And I should have understood that – because of what went before – you were bound to think I'd married Henry for very cold and calculated reasons.'

Olivia found a smile herself, from somewhere. So, it was to continue. Oh well . . . She tucked into the toast, finding herself surprisingly hungry after all.

'What shall we do today? Just say if you want to do anything in particular or go anywhere special,' Rosie told her. 'I don't want you to think that I'm bullying you into doing things you don't want.'

'I'm happy to do whatever you want. Don't ask me to make any decisions, Rosie. Just get hold of me and take me places.'

'Right. And then this evening, Henry wants to take us out for dinner but we'll see how you feel. Now . . .' She rose and wiped crumbs off her mouth. 'Get yourself ready and we'll be off. It's going to be another gorgeous day, damn it to hell. It never varies, boring sunshine the whole time.' She grinned. 'And I for one am not complaining.'

'I remember you look like a beetroot at the first hint of sun,' Olivia said. 'How do you cope?'

'Don't you start,' Rosie grumbled lightly. 'Henry's always on at me but I do take care, darling. I spend a fortune on sun blocks *and* I wear a hat outside.'

She dressed in a long wraparound skirt and skimpy top, unfussily doing her hair and, remembering what Rosie had said, putting on her own sun cream. She was pale, eyes dull, the pain deep within still showing outwardly. Willing herself to smile at her reflection, she did so but it was a false smile, meaning nothing.

'Right, let's go,' she said aloud, picking up her bag and going downstairs.

The morning heat was already overpowering and she could feel that remembered dampness against her neck and throat, the humidity that her mother had hated.

She stood on the porch, waiting for Rosie, closing her eyes and just absorbing the atmosphere. Something stirred in her memory, deep, a childhood memory, and opening her eyes she saw a bank of showy red-pink oleander nearby.

She wandered over and found herself drawn further into the garden, walking amongst fallen blossom, stopping to examine plants unknown to her, thinking this time that she must remember to tell Anna about them when she got back home. She watched a lizard as it sat on a stone nearby, very still, watching her with its beady eye. It was a pale turquoise, almost see-through, and she knew, from past experience, that it would not move so long as she looked at it but, as soon as she looked away, it would be gone.

'Livvy, come on – you can daydream later.'

Turning, she saw Rosie waving at her, and went to meet her.

CHAPTER TWENTY-FIVE

She let Rosie get on with the driving and let her eyes take it in, one thing after another jogging at her memory. Some things were the same, a few more houses perhaps, definitely more cars, but Rosie drove carefully, giving Olivia plenty of time to absorb details.

'The house we stayed in when I was a little girl was around here,' she told Rosie as they drove through Warwick parish. 'Goodness, there it is. It's still there, still the same colour.'

'What did you expect?'

'I don't know. It's just a surprise, that's all.'

'Do you want to get out and take a closer look? We can sneak round the back and have a shifty.'

'No. Let's leave it,' she said, seeing it slipping by and taking a backward glance.

'Nearly all the ex-pats rent, so we reckon we're so lucky to own property here,' Rosie said, carefully slotting past a scooter rider before resuming her sedate pace. 'Henry bought at just the right time but then he is very astute. It's more difficult to buy now, with all the red tape.'

Red tape? She swallowed, recalling her mother and her hatred of it. 'Do you get many people coming to see you?'

'You mean family?' Rosie laughed. 'A few. But mostly we're on our own.'

'Do you see Henry's daughter?' Olivia asked.

'Absolutely not. She's still incensed at his marrying me. She wants for nothing and I wouldn't care if Henry had cut her out of his will but he hasn't. If it were me, I'd cut her off without a penny for being so damned unbending and so nasty to me but you know me, I'm unsentimental when it comes to cash.'

'I'm not sure I do know you any more, Rosie. You may not realize it but you've changed.'

'Money changes people,' Rosie pointed out. 'It's bound to. Think about it – it's the one thing that normally bugs you because you never have enough of it. Remember me with all that moaning about the overdraft and all that bore about making economical meals...'

'*I* made them,' Olivia reminded her with a short laugh. 'All you did was open a tin and you thought that was a big deal. It was me who juggled the budget, eked out the meat and so on... You know, in a way I miss that. It's certainly a challenge.'

'Bugger that kind of challenge,' Rosie said stoutly. 'Ideally, I like to dine out. Henry is taking us to this horribly expensive restaurant tonight.' Her glance was sharp. 'Feel up to it? Just say, for God's sake, if you don't and the two of us can have egg and chips up in your room.'

Olivia smiled her thanks, realizing she was beginning to be able to put on a public face, so that soon it might not be so obvious to people that she had recently suffered a terrible tragedy. She concentrated firmly on the sights, looking across the water, shimmering in the sun, dotted with boats, hearing Rosie chattering on, saying that they might take a ferry from here sometime over to Hamilton.

'It's like Venice,' she said eagerly. 'Such a wonderful view approaching by water.'

'Venice? When did you go to Venice?'

'That's where we were when you and Ben got married,' she said.

'Oh, I thought that was Paris.'

'No, Venice. Planned before we got your invitation, I'm afraid,' she added, quickly and unconvincingly. 'I was so upset to miss it. I wanted to make it up to you and turn up looking fantastic but it was not to be. Sorry.'

'Venice is such a romantic city,' Olivia remarked, thus implicitly accepting the late apology. 'I love it.'

'Hamilton's more your cardboard cut-out city,' Rosie laughed. 'But it has its own style, even if it does look like kids have coloured in the little buildings with those big thick crayons. I like it.'

She cursed, but mildly, as they got stuck behind a very slow-moving car, waiting patiently for an appropriate moment to get past.

'Your driving's improved,' Olivia said. 'You're not so impetuous as you were.'

'Oh God, that sounds awful. As if I'm turning middle-aged,' she said with a mock groan. 'People are generally careful here. And if there are accidents, at least, because of the slow speed, they're rarely the sort where people get killed.'

There was a short shocked silence as she realized what she had said.

'Livvy – I'm sorry, that was stupid of me.'

'It's all right,' Olivia said quickly. 'Goodness, I can't have people going round forever worrying about upsetting me. I just have to get used to it,' she added, feel-ing Rosie's hand briefly and comfortingly on her knee.

They were nearly at their destination and, within a few minutes, Rosie had parked the car and they were stepping out into a medium-heat oven temperature. They intended to look round the Arts Centre and maybe do a spot of shopping. Today, with no cruise ship in dock, it was quiet.

'First things first,' Rosie said, digging into her bag for her purse. 'An ice cream, I think.'

They sat on a bench to eat them. On the next bench, there was a woman with a baby and Olivia caught the look Rosie gave her, the same look she had given little Jamie.

'Do I detect a little brooding?' she asked. 'Oh come on, Rosie, you can tell me.'

'Actually, no,' Rosie said. 'I could be tempted but it's really not on for us. Henry has Sophie after all and he doesn't want to start over. And it wouldn't be fair for me to cheat on him, would it? It would be so easy to forget to take the pill but I shan't do that.'

For a moment, they sat in silence and then, shocking herself, Olivia found herself saying that she might be leaving Ben.

'Might you. . . ?' Rosie asked, seemingly nonchalant. 'Why would you do that?'

'Because of what happened,' she said. 'He never liked Mum. I thought it didn't matter but I now realize it mattered a lot.'

'Now, hang on . . . There isn't a clause in the marriage contract that says you have to like your mother-in-law, is there?'

'No. But I hate it that he never tried.'

'Henry doesn't get on with my parents.' She shrugged. 'But then I don't much like them either. . . .'

'You don't mean that, Rosie,' Olivia said, a little shocked.

'Maybe not. But what I am trying to say is that you mustn't forget where your priority lies.'

'With your husband,' Olivia said stonily. 'I know, I know.'

'It's the silliest reason ever for wanting to leave him.' Rosie regarded her, calm and cool. 'Sudden deaths are horrible to face. You need each other. And don't forget the most important thing, Ben loves you. If you could have heard him when he phoned me about the christening. And don't forget what he was trying to do that day. He was coming to see me to try to persuade me to do the one thing that would really please you. I was very offhand when he first phoned and a lesser man would have given up then but no, he kept right on phoning until he wore me down.'

'I know what he was trying to do but that's nothing to do with it,' Olivia said, reaching into her bag and pulling out a squashy sunhat, plonking it any old how on her head. Rosie managed to be coolly elegant in lilac, a long loose dress with a matching broad-brimmed cotton hat.

'We'll move into the shade,' Rosie said, directing her along to a spot below a tree. 'Have you told him you might be leaving?' she went on, when they were once more settled. 'Or are you just leaving him to guess?'

'He knows I'm feeling pretty fed up but we'll discuss it when I get back.'

'Stay with him. I've seen a lot of marriage bust-ups. It gets very grim, very selfish, and those people who say they remain good friends are liars. You end up hating the sight of each other.'

'It'll be horrific if I go, horrific if I stay. I'm sure we can come to an agreement about details,' she said, without conviction, realizing she hadn't thought about that.

'Don't rush into something stupid,' Rosie said. 'I've heard this can happen after an unexpected bereavement. It's got some sort of name. Instead of drawing together, you suffer separately and draw apart. I think if you can accept that this sort of thing is not unusual, you can work through it. Otherwise, it's just a nonsense. How is your dad, by the way?'

'Stuffed with guilt but that's hardly surprising, is it? He was coming back to her and then she goes and gets herself killed . . .' She felt her voice tremble and took a deep steadying breath.

'Sod's law, that,' Rosie said calmly. 'He has to put that out of his mind. Of course she knew he was coming back. Tell him that. Tell him she told you she was expecting him back any day. It's only a little white lie.'

'I'm hopeless at lies, white or otherwise.'

'I know. Henry says he always knows exactly what you're thinking.'

'Does he?' She found that worrying for sometimes, where Henry was concerned, she wasn't entirely sure she wanted to know herself what she was thinking.

Excusing herself once they were home, Olivia went firstly to check on her little son, who was being expertly pampered, and then to have a rest, finding the completely different surroundings oddly soothing. She lay partly relaxed, aware though that the panicky rapid beating of her heart could start up any time. Grief could too. It could strike anywhere, when she would be suddenly reminded of her mother and her mother's sacrifice and the tears would turn on like a tap.

The table was booked for eight and, busily getting ready, Olivia heard Henry arrive downstairs. She paid careful attention this evening to her appearance for there was little else to do but fuss and she had an idea that, if she lost interest in her appearance, she would lose it completely.

She bathed, soaking in the enormous hot tub, dressing in oyster silk undies, one of the beautiful new sets her mother had bought her as some sort of comfort present, a smart deep pink suit with a shorter skirt than usual and a matching camisole top. She had bought it after Jamie's birth as a celebration suit, one size too small so it was a huge incentive to be slim enough to get into it.

After some consideration, she wore her hair up with wispy tendrils escaping, a style that she knew flattered her, and she took ages choosing the pink lipstick that would best go. She could not compete with Rosie, jewellery wise, so she settled for a pair of sparkly stud earrings, complete fakes, and towering heels to give her confidence.

There!

She went downstairs to find just Henry there, Rosie still not ready.

'Olivia . . .' Henry rose to his feet and advanced towards her, bronzed and fit looking, although just now he had a concerned expression. Holding his hands out wide, he sadly shook his head. 'What can I say? I scarcely knew your mother but I am so sorry, darling. So very sorry. How *are* you?'

'Fine,' she said brightly. 'Coping.'

'That's my girl.'

He bounded across the room, gave her a hug and, because she was not ready to be touched by anyone, she had some difficulty with it, although no doubt he meant well for once.

'You're strong,' he said, ending the embrace with a light kiss on the cheek, the beard tickling gently against it. 'You will cope. We hope you will relax whilst you are here. Rosie is thrilled you agreed to come. Don't disappoint her. Just go along with all she's got planned for you. She's got a full calendar organized.'

She nodded, noting from his brief glance that he heartily approved of her choice of outfit, although he made no comment, reserving that for his wife who appeared directly, wearing an utterly gorgeous cream dress, the neckline dipping to show off the diamond pendant nestling between her breasts. Her hair was a golden-red halo round her head, her eyes sparkling.

She looked every inch a million dollars.

'How lovely you look!' Henry said, eyes only for her so that, watching them, Olivia was suddenly overtaken by an uneasy inkling that these two people did truly love each other or, at the very least, Rosie loved him.

The evening weather was pleasantly warm, cooler than the day, and as they were driven into town, Henry said that by the end of the week, it might turn. A tropical storm was hovering and threatening to hit. The thought made her shiver and she offered up a silent prayer that it would pass by or at the least its edge would just trim the island as a mere gale. Tropical storms were too close to hurricanes to laugh off.

The restaurant, when they finally reached it, was one that Rosie and Henry frequented often from the manner in which they were greeted and shown to their table in a surprisingly cosy and crowded dining-room.

Olivia remembered some of the speciality dishes from before, for she had been taken out just the once by her parents before she flew home, after a tortuous lesson in table etiquette by her mother.

'How about a Rum Swizzle first?' Henry suggested. 'Or a Dark 'n' Stormy?'

'Do you want to get me sozzled?' Rosie asked him sweetly. 'I think I'll just stick to wine with the meal. How about you, Olivia?'

'Why not?' she said, surprising herself, but suddenly the thought of dulling the senses appealed. 'A Rum Swizzle, please.'

Rosie made an instant dynamic choice from the menu, Olivia and Henry, sipping their drinks, taking a little longer. At last they were ready, Henry choosing lobster from Maine, Olivia settling for ubiquitous fish chowder soup followed by a succulent-sounding lamb dish.

The lighting was subdued, conversation a gentle hum, and she was glad of that. The relaxed atmosphere suited her, the punchy rum cocktail softening the edges of her tension. And perhaps Henry had been got at by his wife, for to Olivia's relief, Ben's name was not brought up at all, other than in passing. Nor did they speak about Judith and the manner of her death, that subject discreetly set aside as if it had never been. She did not want to talk about it and yet perversely she did, feeling it a slight to her mother's memory that they did not.

They talked instead of life at The Old Manor and village life generally, which could easily form the basis of a major new soap, according to Rosie.

'The things that go on,' she told them, eyes shining with mischief. 'Henry misses most of it being at work but honestly, you would be amazed. The postmistress knows the lot. Affairs galore. The most unlikely people having them at that. The place is an absolute minefield of sex and depravity.'

Henry laughed. 'Don't you believe it, Olivia. The postmistress has my wife down as a very gullible listener.'

'Why would she make things up?' Rosie asked, looking a little annoyed. 'And I'm not that gullible, Henry.'

'She makes things up so that she can laugh behind your back, darling. I don't like her and I don't trust her. And you should take care what you tell her about us. I hope to God you don't talk to her about us?'

'Of course not,' Rosie said, but a faint colouring of her cheeks suggested otherwise.

Point taken, Henry dropped it.

He reached over and touched her hand, a little gesture of apology, which Rosie seemed to accept, but not for the first time in their company Olivia felt uncomfortable with them, a little concerned that Henry should put Rosie down sometimes. Maybe it was just his way and meant nothing but if her husband did that to her she would be blazingly angry – but then Ben never would, for he was, if nothing else, scrupulously fair.

Henry, seeing that Rosie was silent, steered the conversation to stories about his work, the non-controversial aspects. Then, as Rosie relaxed, they talked about their recent trip to New York, the shows they had seen, the sights they had ogled, the fantastic hotel they had stayed in.

Olivia mostly listened for Henry was apt to control the conversation with his deep lulling voice but she was fascinated and a little bemused by the amount of travelling Rosie had done since she married Henry. She was certainly making up for lost time.

'Dessert?' Henry asked, as they were given a few moments to relax following the main course. 'I can recommend the trifle which I think they added to the menu purely for my benefit or the syllabub . . . Come on, Olivia, what will it be?'

Normally, she might have objected to the tone, a little bossy, but she was just glad to have the decision made for her and chose the trifle. Rosie, watching her figure, declined and went off to the ladies room, so that for a few minutes they were left alone.

The people at the nearest table had just departed, so they were in no danger of being overheard, but it was still a total and complete surprise when Henry said what he did say.

'May I be frank with you?' he asked, touching the stem of his wine glass. 'May I say something that might very well shock you?'

'Goodness . . .' She smiled nervously. 'What on earth can you say that will shock me, Henry?'

He smiled. Disturbingly, Henry had a way of making you look at him. At close quarters, the blue eyes held you and it was hard to remember that he was in his fifties. There was about him a vitality that was ageless and the aura of power that oozed out of him was infectious, making people sit up and notice him. Henry, she realized, was as much a head-turner as his wife. And no, people were not looking at him and thinking what a lecherous old soul he was. No. Men probably envied him and wondered how the hell he did it and women must think what a lucky woman Rosie was.

The thought made her feel confused and, seeing his eyes still on her, she tried a stupid diversion by letting her napkin slide off her lap, taking her time dipping under the chair to retrieve it to give herself a moment's breathing space.

Missing nothing, Henry gave a low chuckle.

'Ben was never the man for you,' he said in a low voice, looking at her closely, until he had her undivided attention. Henry could have easily done the voice-over on some erotic chocolate commercial. 'A beautiful woman like you needs cosseting. It needs a man of my years, of my experience, to do that. Look at Rosie – isn't she blooming these days?'

'Yes but . . .' She tailed off, not knowing what he was up to, not knowing what to say.

'However, I never realized quite how shallow she is,' he went on, glancing quickly at the door to the powder room which remained shut, not surprisingly for, knowing Rosie, she would be giving herself a complete make-over.

'Shallow?' Olivia echoed uncertainly.

He nodded. 'The fluffiness appealed to me at the start and, you know her, she has a first-class honours in retail therapy, which I found amusing. I thought my first two wives were bad enough at spending my money but Rosie is something else.'

'That's not very nice, Henry, and I know you're only teasing,' she said with a small laugh, trying to lighten things up as she caught his gaze, which could only be described as meaningful.

'When I first met you – remember that, Olivia?'

'Vaguely,' she admitted, although in fact she remembered every detail.

'It was at some reception or other at the studios, the launch of Chameleon, I think, a very boring affair. You were there as Rosie's guest I remember.'

'Not exactly.'

He ignored the interruption. 'You were with Rosie. Chatting to her. And you had cream on the end of your nose.'

'I didn't?' she said, horrified all these years on. And Rosie hadn't said a word!

'Just a dab,' he said with a smile. 'I wanted to lean across and lick it off.'

'Did you?' she said, and it was such a sexy thing to say, so unexpected, that she avoided looking at him, looked round helplessly, willing Rosie to come back to rescue her. This man was flirting with her – *flirting*.

'From that moment on, I was utterly entranced by you but, because I thought you were with someone, I did the decent thing and backed off. I've never know-ingly stolen a woman from another man...' He smiled a little as the powder-room door opened, delivering the final amazing coup de grâce, even as Rosie, freshly made up and looking very glamorous, walked towards them, threading her graceful way through the room. 'Olivia, my darling, I want you so much.'

And then he was on his feet, helping Rosie back into her seat, ordering coffee and looking relaxed.

'I hope he hasn't been boring you too much,' Rosie said, everything about her sparkling, make-up freshly applied, her hair newly fluffed. 'You haven't, Henry, have you?'

'Not a bit. Olivia finds me utterly fascinating. Don't you, darling?'

'Well...' She managed a smile, directed at Rosie, not knowing what to say, not as adept as Henry at the subtle art of lying through his teeth.

'Oh dear. I did bore her,' Henry said with a laugh. 'And here I was thinking I had made yet another female conquest.'

'You don't need any more conquests,' Rosie told him, looking at him with such a look of love that Olivia felt most discomfited. 'You've got me.'

Sitting there, seething inwardly at the sheer nerve of the man, it was all Olivia could do but get up and walk out but she had had enough of fine gestures and it would get her nowhere.

CHAPTER TWENTY-SIX

In the car on the way home, Olivia sat in the back with Rosie, Henry sitting beside the driver. Rosie was chatty, still not good with alcohol, even a small amount, and Olivia tried her best to respond, but all she could think of was what Henry had said, all she could do was stare at the back of his head, at the hair which was greying – wouldn't you just know it – in a very attractive manner, the strong profile, the powerful, athletic shoulders.

How dare he say what he had said to someone recently bereaved? How dare he? If she told Ben, he would be on the first plane over to have it out. This was just the touch-paper Ben needed. Ben would fly in, all guns blazing.

The thought of that, combined with a bit too much alcohol, produced a subdued laugh that caused Rosie to look her way and give her an encouraging smile.

'That's right, Livvy,' she said, leaning towards her, 'just you concentrate on enjoying yourself and it will help. Isn't that restaurant too fantastic? Was it very expensive, Henry?'

'Since when do you care, my sweet? Yes, it was far too expensive, even by Bermudian standards, but for the two most beautiful ladies on the island worth every penny.'

Rosie laughed. 'Isn't he wonderful?'

Henry half turned but it was Olivia he looked at and she turned away quickly, before he could read anything into her expression.

Once home, Rosie set off at an inelegant run to the bathroom. Henry, after dismissing the driver in that rather curt way of his, put his arm on Olivia's elbow as they went indoors, an innocent enough gesture and yet, in view of what he had dared say, bubbling with meaning.

She excused herself, going up to check on the baby, who was sleeping soundly and taking a moment's breather before returning downstairs to face Henry. It was no use hiding from this. It had to be sorted out and quickly.

'That was a lovely meal. Thank you,' she said carefully, slipping off her jacket, which he retrieved and tossed on to one of the hall chairs. Rosie reappeared in a robe, looking a little the worse for wear.

'Livvy, I am whacked and slightly woozy,' Rosie said, yawning hugely. 'I am going to bed,' she called to Henry. 'Don't be long.'

'I shan't. Olivia and I will just have a nightcap,' he said, tossing his jacket aside also and loosening his tie. 'A brandy, Olivia?'

'I really don't think . . .' she said quietly, waiting until Rosie was gone before she iced her voice. 'I think it might be a good idea, Henry, if we forgot what you said in the restaurant. I'll put it down to the wine and the candlelight.'

'Sit down, Olivia,' he said and it was said with the usual authority so that, against her will, she did just that, on the squashy white leather sofa that faced the wide window. Outside, beyond the lantern-lit terrace, there were a few twinkling lights, a crescent moon in a dark sky, although Henry clicked a switch somewhere and blinds descended as elegantly as a theatre safety curtain to block it out, giving the room a cosy intimate glow.

'You've got a cheek,' she told him, her fury igniting again as she supposed he was doing this, clothing the windows, dimming the light, as the prelude to a romantic interlude. Here, in this house, with Rosie upstairs!

'Olivia, please don't worry,' he said, pouring himself a brandy when she vehemently refused. 'I merely wish to talk, that's all. We haven't talked, you and I, in ages. How are things with you and Ben after this dreadful thing with your mother?'

'I'm not sure that's anything to do with you,' she said stiffly, determined not to discuss her marriage problems with this man.

'Absolutely not. I apologize,' he said instantly. 'However, bereavement takes people in different ways. Antagonism to the person closest to you is just one of them.'

She looked at him irritably. Hadn't Ben said almost the same thing? They must have been reading the same counselling book.

'Really,' she said tartly. 'And how would you know, Henry?'

'We suffered a most dreadful bereavement, my first wife and I . . .'

'Oh!' It was absolutely not what she had expected to hear and she was so surprised she could think of nothing to say.

'We were childhood sweethearts,' Henry said with a slight smile. 'And we married young and had a baby straight away.'

She sat very still, not daring to breathe almost, seeing his changed expression and aware that this was hard for him.

'Our baby died at six months, a heart problem, and yes, I do still think of her sometimes, even now, close on thirty years on. She was called Mary Rose . . . ' His smile faltered. 'She was the most exquisite baby ever, far more beautiful, I have to say, than Sophie when she arrived.'

'Oh . . .'

'They say losing a child is the very worst grief but how can we measure it and how dare people say such a thing? Your grief is different from mine,' he went on with an encouraging smile. 'Different in that you are coping with several lots of emotion all at the same time. You are distraught to lose your mother, relieved that Jamie escaped, guilty to feel that way, and very proud too of what your mother did. What a mixed bag! No wonder you're feeling totally at sea. And you know something, Olivia . . . after all these years I still find it extraordinarily difficult to talk about Mary Rose.'

This changed everything. He spoke with sincerity, not the mocking tongue-in-cheek kind that he would use in his business world but the genuine variety. Thirty years ago and it still got him.

'I'm only telling you this to explain that you have to pull together, not let it pull you apart. It nearly killed my wife. We grew out of each other, I suppose. For a while after we lost the baby, she was very much on the edge, but then she was pregnant again very quickly with Sophie and that gave her something else to think about.'

'I always wanted a large family,' she said. 'But I'm not so sure now. I don't know why. I can't explain. I can't explain why I'm blaming Ben for everything either.'

'Don't blame him. It could have been anyone – the truck was out of control and your mother just got in the way of it. You're taking it out on Ben as if he was the driver.'

'The driver died at the wheel,' she said quietly. 'Heart attack.'

'Well, then, absolutely an accident. Poor soul, he wouldn't have wanted that to happen.'

'Why are you suddenly being nice to me?' she asked, indicating that, after all, she would take up the offer of a brandy. 'After what you said in the restaurant, I should pack my bags and leave tomorrow. Either that or just laugh in your face.'

'You could but you won't do either,' he said, confident to the point of certainty. 'Will you? You're much too nice. You don't want to upset Rosie, not when you two have just made it up. She was miserable, you know. Inconsolable.'

'So was I. It was stupid. One of those little-girl quarrels when you feel you have to hurt your very best friend.'

'I gather you accused her of marrying me for my money?' he asked lazily, legs stretched out as he sat on the sofa opposite. From this distance, in the kindly half light, he did not look his years and, just for an awkward second, she felt a faint shiver of pleasure at the attention such a strong, important man was giving her. 'She doesn't like to be told that, even if it might be true. She believes herself to be in love with me. I've always found that such a charming notion.'

'And you? Do you love her?'

'I loved my first wife Doreen,' Henry told her simply. 'The fact is *she* divorced me, although people tend to think of it as the other way round. She's never remarried but she seems happy enough on her own and there's no chance of us ever getting back together. Sophie visits her . . .'

She felt his sadness, and allowed him a moment to recover.

'Since then, Olivia, I've been searching for that feeling again and not finding it. My second marriage was a total disaster from day one, apart from almost milking me dry. As for Rosie, I have fun with Rosie. She makes me feel young.'

'Then you don't love her?' She felt a sadness for Rosie, and no triumph that in a way she had been right. 'I'm sorry I upset her and I'm sorry it took so long for us to get back together,' she said, suddenly seeing Rosie launching herself out of The Crypt in that Oscar-winning huff.

'So you should be. Rosie is delightful and I was utterly captivated by her,' he said. 'But it was rebound stuff, I'm afraid. She was such a contrast to my second wife and I confess I was flattered by her attentions. Plus, she's very interesting in bed.'

The words echoed round the room and Olivia found herself peering towards the door nervously as if Rosie would suddenly burst in.

'That's hardly an appropriate remark,' she said coldly. 'I don't care to discuss such things, Henry.'

'Don't you? That is such a pity because I think you'd be rather interesting too. A man can always tell that about a woman. You don't realize it but you give off all manner of clues, send signals. And I can see right through you, Olivia. You are very nervous of me and I know why. It's because you can't trust yourself.'

'I beg your pardon.' She put down her glass and rose shakily to her feet, searching for a stray shoe in the process, which rather destroyed her intended elegant removal from the room. 'I'll pretend I didn't hear that. Goodnight, Henry.'

His laughter, unconcerned, followed her out.

*

She did not dream of her mother.

She was too upset by that damned cocky, confident Henry to dream of anything except a mixed jumble but she woke surprisingly refreshed, ready to face the day, wondering if she had interpreted him correctly. And yet how otherwise could she interpret it? He had made a pass and she would have to say nothing, do nothing, except keep it from Rosie.

A tiny bit of her had to admit she was flattered. After all, every woman likes to be told she is attractive and, if it's someone other than your husband, all well and good provided you do nothing about it.

Well, there was no danger there.

She would keep out of Henry's way, make sure she limited their time alone, not do anything to entice or excite him. Sending him signals? What was he talking about? She would stick with Rosie and she would come to no harm.

She spent time with Jamie, bathing and dressing him, under Christabel's affectionate gaze, taking him into the garden for a stroll round in the early morning gentler sunlight. Then, happy to pass him to Christabel's care, she showered and dressed in a long black cotton dress and black sandals, for the next visit on Rosie's agenda, a trip to the other end of the island.

Rosie, blissfully unaware of the events of the previous evening, of course, talked happily about Henry's plans for the day, which amounted to golf, golf, golf on one of the numerous courses.

'So he doesn't work when he's here?' Olivia asked, desperate to keep talk about Henry to a general level.

'Officially he's on holiday but he never is in practice,' Rosie said. 'He's brought stuff with him and he's in constant touch with the team at home, ready to fly out at the slightest whiff of a problem. I don't think he'll be able to retire, not ever.'

'That was the problem with my dad. His work was his life. He had no other interests, not real interests, and he just lost it. If I'm honest, I suppose Mum was no help. She got a bit caught up with the council job, although she was losing interest in that.'

'And he thought that she didn't understand him?' Rosie sighed. 'Typical scenario, that. I sometimes think we know a lot less about the people closest to us than we could ever imagine.'

Olivia gave her a quick worried glance but Rosie was giving nothing away, humming a tune as they entered the town, still humming it as she killed the engine once they were in the car park.

'We'll act like proper tourists,' she told Olivia, changing into high-heeled mules and putting on a large-brimmed straw hat. 'And then we'll have a coffee and, later, we can lunch, outside if you like, overlooking the harbour.'

They strolled, suitably slowly, into the square, casting an eye over the stocks and whipping post where an enactment was taking place. A small crowd was gathered to witness it but they, having seen it all before, watched only a moment before walking on.

'They had it right in the old days. Humiliation but no actual harm. We should never have got rid of that idea,' Rosie said with a grin. 'Nobody likes to be humiliated. I can think of a few people I'd like to do that to. Can't you?'

'Oh yes. One of my bosses at the office. A few of the ladies Mum knocks around with . . . used to, that is,' she added quietly.

'You can put that first love of mine on the list. I'd put him on the ducking stool as well. Give him a thorough soaking.'

'That's all a long time ago, surely. Do you still think about him?'

'Ah! That would be telling,' she said, not quite hiding the shadow that appeared on her face. 'But, seeing as you ask, yes, I do. He sticks in my mind, Livvy. He'll never go away. I suppose part of me still loves him a bit, even though I love Henry a lot more.'

Olivia thought of Henry, of what he had said to her last night, and said nothing about it. How could she?

'I do love Ben, Rosie,' she said instead. 'But I sometimes wonder, would he have bothered to marry me were it not for Jamie?'

'Not that old one.' Rosie glanced at her. 'You do worry about the daftest things, don't you?'

Although it was getting hotter, they continued their walk through the historic narrow streets and just prodding at the past in Olivia's memory as it did, it was a small comfort. She was back to being a child again and that summer she had been a happy one.

Over a pot of Earl Grey and cakes, Olivia even found herself watching two women nearby, quite obviously mother and daughter. They had the same nose, tilted their heads the same way, the same genes slightly rearranged.

'It will get better,' Rosie said, catching the direction of her gaze. 'Oh sod it, I swore I'd never utter those words. Henry said not to. He practically gave me a lecture before you arrived, telling me what not to say. You know, behind all that business thing, he's pretty sensitive.'

Olivia nodded. 'Yes. He told me about his baby . . . the one he lost.'

Rosie stared, cream from her cake on her lips. 'What baby's that, then?'

'The one who died at six months. A daughter Mary Rose...' Olivia said slowly, as it dawned he might not have told her.

'Oh yes...' Rosie licked the cream off her lips. 'I believe he did once mention it but he doesn't talk about it much. It doesn't quite go with the tough business image, does it? It's supposed to be a secret, so I'm surprised he told you. I expect he thought it would help. After all, he's got over it and he went on to have another daughter.' She bit into her cake, apparently unconcerned. 'What's up? You look tired. Maybe the heat's been a bit much.'

'Can we go back? I'm missing Jamie.'

'Sure.' Quickly, Rosie finished her tea. 'At least you had a relationship at the end which is more than I have with my mother. Be grateful that you two made it up, Livvy.'

She was. She just wished it hadn't been so close to the end that they had finally come to some sort of understanding.

A tropical storm alert was on for tomorrow, Henry told them when they got home. Offices in town were to be closed and a warning issued to stay indoors. Nothing to worry about, he soothed, as Olivia let out a little cry of alarm.

'Great!' Rosie said. 'I hope this time it's a decent one. The last one was a damp squib. I've experienced worse winds driving up the M6.'

They laughed but Olivia felt her stomach lurch.

She wished she was home.

CHAPTER TWENTY-SEVEN

By next morning, the storm was approaching fast and to Olivia's horror, Rosie was keen to drive to the shore to see the waves.

'Are you mad?' Olivia asked. 'We've been told to stay indoors.'

'That's purely a precaution, so that the authorities can say "I told you so" if anything goes wrong,' Rosie said, peering out excitedly at the darkening clouds and the freshening wind. Olivia had no idea how wind might be measured but it looked as wild already as any of the strongest winds at home. 'I've heard the waves breaking the reef are quite something. I want to see. I'm not asking you to come with me. Nor Henry. He's like you. He thinks I'm daft.'

'But he's not going to stop you?'

Rosie smiled. 'How can he? He's not like that. I do what I want.'

It seemed they were on their own now, abandoned. News from the airport was that one flight had attempted to land but failed and had returned to New York. All flights, in or out, were now suspended and they just had to stick it out until the storm passed. Olivia felt sharp fear for herself and Jamie and wished Ben was here. Ben was very good with her little fears.

'Hey, you mustn't worry,' Rosie said coming over to her. 'I forgot how much you hate storms but I thought you would have grown out of it by now.'

'I know. I'm acting like a big baby. Stupid, isn't it?'

Rosie hugged her. 'No. Just a bit daft, that's all. We cope with all manner of storms at this time of year, tail ends of hurricanes too, and sometimes the real thing. We haven't sunk into the sea yet.'

Olivia wished she hadn't said that but Rosie was right. It was just a storm, for heaven's sake. It would have its windy way with them and then whisk itself away to gather strength to bother somebody else on the Carolina coast.

Olivia watched Rosie depart, shivering as she peered out at the garden which was taking a real battering, the palms waving fiercely as the wind lashed them. Suddenly, the whole place looked different.

She spent some time with the baby, playing with him, but he was tired and hot and she soon gave up trying to keep him amused and popped him gently into his cot. At once, he snuggled down, looking at her a moment with Ben's eyes, before shutting them. And that almost reproachful look of his was a sharp reminder that he was Ben's child, every bit as much as hers.

'Good morning, Olivia. Never mind that we think her utterly insane, Rosie has an adventurous streak in her. Surely you know that?'

She whirled round to see Henry in the doorway, cool and calm and looking smart as usual in slim beige trousers and a black open-neck shirt. She was in two moods about Henry today. She wished she was three thousand miles away from him, but, at the same time, she was glad he was here with her this morning. Something of Judith must be in her because she had a horror of making a fool of herself in front of the staff. They were so nonchalant about storms but then their attitude was carefree verging on idle. Charming in its way but she wondered just how they would cope in an emergency.

'How bad do you think it will get?' she asked anxiously, as if Henry was an authority on the weather.

'A little worse but not much. It's not hurricane rated and it's not hitting us head on,' he told her with a smile. 'It's just giving us a little nudge, that's all. Don't worry. You're safe.'

'I hate thunder and lightning,' she said, giving a daft little squeal as the room brightened in an instant with a white flash, followed just a few seconds later by the crack of thunder. 'Childish, isn't it? At school we used to say it was just God moving the furniture around in heaven.'

He smiled. 'Yes, I've heard that one. Nice idea.'

Her worried smile was fleeting and she pulled the loose cardigan closer, even though it was not cold.

'Come through to the drawing-room and I'll ask for coffee and cake. We can sit together and talk. Take your mind off it.'

'All right,' she said, too damned scared to argue and coffee sounded a nice idea.

'Times like this I wish I was back home,' Henry said, once they were settled, the coffee and some cakes brought through to them. 'But, tomorrow, it will all be forgotten. The sun will come out and everything will feel nice and fresh and we'll all say, "That wasn't so bad, was it?"'

Another flash and less time this time before the crack of thunder.

Olivia jumped, and spilled her hot coffee all over her skirt.

'Damn, how silly. . . !'

Henry took charge, taking the cup from her, and thrusting some tissues into her hand, before she hurried upstairs to change.

'Come up with me,' she asked, as she did so. 'Just stand outside the door.'

'Anything you say.' Smiling at her fears, but not with any malice, Henry followed her, standing as instructed outside the door.

She changed into another skirt at the speed of light, not even noticing whether or not it went with the cream tank top. At a time like this, who cared? Another flash and deep shuddering roll and the rain seemed to intensify against the windows, hammering now on the roof, visibility across the garden practically zero, the palm trees by the gate whipping from side to side. She could hardly believe the ferocity of that wind, and wondered if any of the trees would crack under the pressure.

She hoped Rosie was OK, standing there on the very edge of the wild ocean. What a stupid thing for her to do.

She opened the door to find Henry standing right there, leaning against the door-post. The flash this time was terrific and she whimpered, falling against him in her terror. 'Oh God, I hate it. I wish it would stop. When is it going to stop?'

'Ssh.' He held her close. 'It's nothing to be ashamed of. We all have our fears. Personally, I'm not madly keen on spiders. Sophie is scared of thunder too. When she was little, she used to come into our room and creep under the covers with us.'

Held thus, comfortingly in his arms, strong capable arms, she relaxed as she heard him mention his daughter.

'I'm all right now,' she said, moving away. 'Sorry for making a fuss.'

'You're a little overwrought,' he said quietly. 'Not surprising, given the circum-stances. And I apologize for last night. It kept me awake, thinking about it. It was unforgivable of me but you looked so beautiful in the restaurant. So beautiful and so sad and Ben seems to be doing nothing to help. He ought never to have let you out of his sight, not at a time like this – I wouldn't have let you go.'

'I insisted on coming. I needed some time alone. To think things through,' she said, not wanting him blaming Ben. 'And Rosie wanted me here too.'

'You may have insisted but, if I were him, I would have said no.'

She managed a sort of laugh. 'Now that is not true. Rosie says you let her do what she wants.'

'I'm talking about you, darling, not Rosie,' he said, and something in his voice made her look up at him, into eyes that were suddenly warmer and rather obviously sending a message.

'Me. . . ?'

He nodded, cupping her face in his hands, drawing her very close once again, but this time not for reasons of comfort.

The kiss, when it came, was inevitable, she supposed, reflecting soberly on it later. At that moment, in a storm-stupid daze or something, she actually wanted him to kiss her, almost willed him to.

As kisses go, it was a good kiss. A very good kiss.

Deprived of that sort of love for so long – and it was largely her fault – the kiss created a sudden sharp urgency in her, a need that travelled like the speed of light up and down and sideways and – oh, just everywhere!

She wanted, and she made it pretty clear, to prolong it and just go with whatever happened after that. Fortunately for her, he had a modicum of self-control.

'There . . . ' he said, drawing away and smiling in to her eyes. 'That wasn't so bad, my darling, was it?'

Sanity prevailed and she felt herself flush.

'Sorry, Henry,' she murmured, avoiding looking at him. 'I can't think why . . .'

'Let's go downstairs.'

Back in the drawing-room, fresh coffee had been brought through.

'Sit down again and this time, for God's sake, relax.'

Easier said than done and she told him as much, wincing at the next flash and crack, but keeping hold of her cup gingerly all the same.

'Losing our child ultimately cost us our marriage – my marriage with Doreen,' Henry said after a while, completely relaxed in the chair opposite. 'I think you should know that and be aware it can happen. She never got over losing the baby and she allowed it to dominate her life, shutting me out. Oh, we carried on for years, had Sophie as a replacement, but the trouble was she wasn't Mary Rose, you see. Poor Sophie went through life being told that "Mary Rose, who was with the angels, wouldn't have done that". Doreen would never let it go. But with us it was a little different, hardly sudden, hardly completely unexpected either, because Mary Rose was ill. As I said, it was a heart problem but . . . do you want to hear this?'

She nodded. 'Please . . .'

'It was routine surgery, the doctor told us, as routine as heart surgery can be, I suppose. But we were given to understand that she stood a good chance of not only getting through the operation but also of making a complete recovery. We made the mistake of trusting him.'

He took a long moment before he carried on and she waited, not daring to speak, in case it broke the spell.

'The operation took longer than we'd been told and, after a while, Doreen began to worry. We were worried from the start of the operation of course but she began to be seriously concerned. At two-thirty, she looked at the clock and calmly announced that Mary Rose was dead. I told her not to be so jumpy. Time went by. And then . . .' He turned away, fist clenched. 'The surgeon came in and Doreen took one look at his face and just screamed. Howled. I've never heard anything like it before.' He sighed. 'It was the days before litigation otherwise I'd probably have given him the run-around but, as it was, we just accepted that something had gone wrong and that she had died on the table. At two-thirty, incidentally.'

She understood.

She suddenly understood.

'It's delicate surgery,' she said slowly, feeling she must make some excuses for Ben. 'There can be no guarantees even today when techniques have improved. And with a child too . . .'

'Forget it,' he said simply. 'But I'd go so far as to say that if we hadn't lost her, we would still be together. We let it get to us. Anger. Frustration. Bitterness. Think about it. It would be such a shame if the same thing happened to you and Ben.'

'From what you said last night,' she said, 'I would have thought you would be quite pleased if my marriage collapsed.'

'Why? Good God, why? So that I might divorce Rosie and marry you?'

'Well . . I don't know,' she said, stumbling through her embarrassment. 'I don't know what's in your mind, do I?'

'Not another divorce,' he said with a shudder. 'Financially, it's crippling, even for someone like me. And Rosie insisted on a pre-nuptial agreement, bless her little heart. We're talking a million plus if this goes belly up and I don't give that sort of money away easily. In fact, I rarely give money away, Olivia. That notion is for fools.'

'Really?' Olivia bristled. She had always suspected he was all for himself so why should that be a surprise? 'I'm glad you have no intention of divorcing Rosie – she doesn't deserve that – but why say those things to me, Henry? Why . . .' She hesitated a moment. 'Why kiss me like you did just now?'

'Simple. You wanted me to.'

She looked down. Not arguing.

'I kissed you also because you looked so beautiful and I thought you might make an excellent mistress,' he said, a smile in the voice. 'Back home, we live close enough to conduct an affair in relative comfort and I don't think either of us has the stomach for divorce. I am very discreet and Rosie would never suspect a thing. Liaisons are so exciting, my darling. Love in the afternoon, that sort of thing. And with me, it would be conducted in some splendour, no hole-in-the-corner stuff. Stolen love. Forbidden love. It adds an edge.'

'Does it?' she asked faintly, not wanting to believe him even if, somewhere at the back of her mind, deeply lodged, she did find the thought turbulent and exciting.

Henry laughed, as if he could read her mind. In fact, she was beginning to wonder if he *could* read her mind.

'Much as I would love to seduce you,' he went on, 'I suspect you will stick with Ben through thick and thin, even if you're no longer madly in love with him. Maybe I've misjudged you. Maybe you are not the sort of woman to engage in a fling.'

'You have a colossal nerve,' she said, managing a laugh to dilute the significance of his remark. 'Mistress? I've never heard anything so ridiculous. And yes, you're probably right. I will stick with Ben, no matter what, although I think you're wrong about us. We still care for each other.'

'Well said. However, caring is not the same as loving. I've always found it's best to walk at that point. The one thing that keeps a marriage going, Olivia, is sex. Yes it is. And, when desire goes, then that's it. There's no point in trying to resurrect things. Once there's a barrier, it can't be moved. Ever.'

He was right but she was not inclined to agree with him just now, still smarting from the suggestion that she might become his mistress. She wasn't that sort of woman. Mistresses were by definition outrageous and sexy and did things that a wife did not. Didn't they?

'My sweet, beautiful woman . . .' Henry said softly, coming over to sit close beside her.

'Don't call me that,' she muttered, but half-heartedly for it was a lovely thing for him to say and just now there was a lot of compassion and fellow feeling in his face.

'I know just how it feels to lose someone you love. You've suffered so much, my darling. Would you like me to hold you?'

She nodded, close to tears, allowing him to stroke her face gently and smile down at her. It felt good, the comfort she had refused to let Ben give her.

'I've got to go home and talk to Ben,' she said, roused suddenly from her stupor. 'This is nonsense. What on earth am I doing here when Jamie and I should be at home?'

The silence was long.

'I think I'm falling in love with you, Olivia.'

'Now wait . . . Rosie is my friend. Don't be like this, Henry.'

'Why not? Why ever not?'

He was very, very close, kissing distance, and, in this light, his eyes were warmer and his smile was special, for her, and she had a sudden quite awful desire for him to kiss her again but this time it might be impossible to stop. It was a long time since she had made love, had sex, whatever you liked to call it, and the need was suddenly great.

She was starting to melt; common sense was deserting her.

'No.' She leapt up, astonished that she had allowed this to happen. Allowed things to progress to this extent when the damned man thought he had it made. Well, he could think again! How dare he take advantage and how could she be so simple minded?

'Now you're behaving like a teenager,' he said with a grin. 'God, woman, relax!'

'It's you who's acting like a teenager!' she yelled, cowering momentarily as the lightning lit up the room in a fierce white glow. 'Coming on to me like this. What do you expect me to do? Cheat on Rosie, who might be back at any minute?'

'Ah!' The smile persisted, his composure unruffled. 'So, it might be a different tale if she was out for the whole day?'

'No, it would not.'

'You don't fancy me one little bit?'

'At the moment, Henry, I don't even fancy my husband,' she told him, the unpalatable truth hitting her like a bullet, as her misery overtook her.

'Pity. A night or even an afternoon of passion might help. Briefly, anyway,' he told her. 'You can relax now. The storm's passing over . . . short and sweet.'

So it was.

Outside, they heard the swish of wet tyres as Rosie arrived back.

'Not a word,' he said.

'You are a swine, Henry,' she said, although it was hard not to admire his sheer audacity. Mistress! Well, that was a first. Wait until she told Ben.

On second thoughts, it was definitely not a subject for marital discussion.

Rosie burst in, completely soaked, wet hair plastered against her face, eyes shining.

'It was fantastic,' she said. 'Absolutely fantastic. You should have seen the waves. What have you two been up to?'

Olivia smiled stupidly, not knowing what to say.

Henry had no such problems.

'I've been taking Olivia's mind off the storm,' he said. 'I've been distracting her. I kissed her and even offered her the position as my resident mistress but sadly she turned it down. Didn't you, Olivia?'

Rosie giggled. 'Henry, you're a fool. Olivia, don't take any notice of him.' She ran fingers through her damp hair. 'I'm going to have a hot bath and then put my feet up. That experience has worn me to a frazzle.'

'I'll come up too,' Henry said, taking her hand. 'Rub your back for you. Will you be all right, Olivia, if we let you do your own thing for a while?'

'Fine,' she croaked. 'I'll sit and relax. I can hear the baby if he cries.'

As they exited the room, Henry turned and looked at her. And winked.

CHAPTER TWENTY-EIGHT

Ben was distraught. Sitting opposite Anna in the visitors' parlour, he tried to concentrate on what she was telling him, on *her* evident distress. But all he could really think about was the phone call from Olivia.

True, telephone calls, particularly long distance, were difficult and it was impossible to say exactly what you wanted to say but she had seemed so *very* distant, her voice a little odd, answering his questions in an abstracted way, telling him about this and that, telling him – nothing!

He ought never have let her go. It had been a grave error. Rosie, whom he had never understood, was a disturbing influence on Olivia and likely to put all manner of strange thoughts her way. He didn't like it. He didn't know why he didn't like it but he just didn't. Unease gripped him like a vice.

'Stop worrying about Olivia,' Anna said, breaking into his thoughts. 'I know it's been quite dreadful for her but she'll be much better when she gets back.'

'I hope you're right,' he muttered. 'I miss her. Jamie too. I can't wait to see them again.'

'You will. Very soon,' she assured him and looking at her calm, quiet face, he forced himself to think about Anna and her problems instead. Having to sell off the convent was a bit extreme. Sadly, it would very likely go to a big developer, a prime site for a small number of houses, smack bang in the centre of the city. The convent itself would probably be demolished and this garden, this garden that Olivia loved so much too, would just disappear.

'I have to agree with Sister Matilda,' he said thoughtfully. 'She sounds like she has a good business mind.'

'Yes but the community is a bit stuck in its ways,' Anna said, glancing round a minute, as if they were being bugged.

Ben found himself smiling at the very idea. Bugged in a convent!

'There are options open to you. This is one enormous place,' he went on. 'And you do rattle around a bit in it. It doesn't have to go to a developer. You could offer conference facilities, a big meeting-room and lots of single accommodation. I think companies would snap it up. It has a nice ring to it, a few days in a convent. There's plenty of scope...'

She shook her head. Resigned.

'It's hopeless. How could we function like that? We're not exhibits, Ben, to be looked at. Nor is our community active in that sense. It's a prayerful one. We exist to pray...'

He sighed and she caught it, looked up.

'I know that's hard for you to grasp. We're not extravagant, Ben. Far from it. But it's not a bottomless pit and, setting aside our personal views, it makes sense with so few of us that this place is sold off and we move on.'

'Will that upset you?' he asked, watching her closely. 'And for God's sake...' He cringed at the words he had thoughtlessly used. 'Sorry. But be honest with me, Anna. Will it upset you?'

'Yes. It will,' she said simply. 'I find it so peaceful here and at last I'm learning how to pray. It's a great joy, Ben.'

He nodded, accepting it. To his surprise, his mother seemed to be getting used to it a little more. They ought to support Anna and he was ashamed now of the way they had bullied her into trying to make her change her mind. What right had they to do that?

'I wish I could help you,' he said, meaning it. 'But what can I do? Would you like me to talk to Reverend Mother to try to persuade her to keep some options open? Perhaps she might listen to an outsider.'

'No, please don't do that,' she said. 'And I'm sorry I've burdened you with it. You have quite enough to worry about. And, we must remember, Ben, in the end God's will be done.'

He very nearly responded to that, wanting to shake sense into her and wondering what had happened to her sense of outrage, to her fighting spirit.

But maybe it was time he left her to it.

They, she and Rosie and the baby, were enjoying a simple picnic lunch in Par-la-Ville Gardens, popular with office workers from the nearby streets.

'I envy you, Livvy,' Rosie said, looking at Jamie who was smothered in sun lotion and cool under the canopy of his pram. 'At least you know where you are these days. Unless you completely cock things up, you have Ben and Jamie and a nice life back home.'

Olivia looked at her in surprise. 'And you have Henry and your house – houses – so you're not doing too badly either.'

'I never thought I'd say this,' Rosie went on thoughtfully, 'but it gets a bit much sometimes. Flitting from one place to another and being able to spend whatever you like takes some of the fun out of it. Do you remember me saving up for two whole months to get that pair of gold evening sandals I coveted and then, just when I'd managed to save enough—'

'They'd sold out of your size,' Olivia said with a grin.

'Today I have three pairs of gold sandals,' she murmured, moving her purchases on the bench to make way for someone to sit down.

And she had just bought several dresses and a silk wrap.

'Perhaps you need something to do,' Olivia told her gently. 'Something to use up your energy, I mean. Something outside the house.'

'Yes, you're probably right. Being a lady of leisure is hard work and sometimes the hours do drag.' She cast a glance Olivia's way. 'There's something in the offing. I'm dying to tell you but it's been going on so long and I'm scared it will go wrong if I tell anybody yet.'

Olivia smiled. Rosie loved secrets.

'I love Henry, don't get me wrong,' Rosie went on hastily. 'And he adores me. Aren't I lucky?'

'Yes . . .' Olivia said, bending down to adjust her sandal and keep a grip on her composure.

Rosie carried blithely on. 'But he's so busy all the time and sometimes I get the feeling he's just palming me off. He throws money at me instead of attention. Do you understand?'

'We're never satisfied, Rosie. Mum was always grumbling about all the travel she had to do and then, when Dad retired, she complained about him being around all the time, giving her too much attention.'

Rosie nodded, apparently satisfied, although Olivia found she was now worrying herself. Last night, at dinner, she had caught one or two glances from Rosie to Henry, difficult-to-interpret glances but worrying for all that . . . and as for herself, she had hardly dared look at him in case he read anything into it. It had, despite the wonderful food, made for an awkward meal. And she had finally had to tell Rosie that she was taking an earlier flight than originally intended, news which Rosie received calmly.

'As it's my last day tomorrow, would you mind, Rosie, if I go off by myself?' she asked, hardly liking to ask because Rosie had been so kind in transporting her everywhere. It was deliberate, of course. A concerted and kind effort to keep her so busy that she scarcely had time to stop and think. And, in the strangest way, it had worked.

'By yourself?' Rosie sounded doubtful. 'Where to?'

'I'll take the bus,' she said. 'Don't worry about me. I can take care of myself.'

'God, the bus! I've never set foot on a bus since I met Henry.' With a flourish, Rosie threw the remains of their sandwich lunch into a waste basket. 'Let's finish our shopping.'

'I need to change Jamie first and then can we pop into Marks and Spencer for some knickers?'

Rosie groaned, rolling her eyes heavenwards. 'I don't believe it. She comes all the way to Bermuda and has to go into M&S for knickers.'

'Home comforts,' Olivia murmured with a small smile, reaching for the baby bag that contained all Jamie's worldly needs.

She left Jamie in Christabel and Rosie's care next day. Taking the bus was a novel experience and she wanted to walk along the beach at Warwick Long Bay on her own without Rosie chattering on beside her, for she wanted to relish the experience one last time, certain she would never come back. There were now too many memories that she might care to forget. But she needed to see the beach once again, to walk where she and her mother and father had often walked, to lay the ghost for ever.

After the storm, the weather had returned to normal. Hot and humid. Sweltering already in her thin cotton dress, she walked from the bus stop to the beach.

Holding her hand to her eyes to avoid squinting at the sun, she looked the length of it, the blue sea, the waves now gentle, splashing against the pink coral sand, little evidence of the vicious storm remaining, aside from some tossed driftwood. Beyond the reef, there was the deeper blue-green of the ocean proper. As she stood there, she sank a little into the hot sand, walking slowly on at last and hearing her mother's voice rattling on about the damned heat.

And there, in the shimmering distance, somewhere at the junction of sea and sky, she *was* there, anchored in the heat haze.

'Mum!' she said to herself, the sand soft and awkward to walk in, the scene blurring even as the tears flooded her eyes.

Shallow, snobbish, short tempered, downright rude .. Her mother had been all those things and yet, when it came to the terrible crunch, she had not hesitated for, if she had, they would be mourning Jamie too.

If only she had lived long enough for her to tell her what a wonderful thing she had done. If only she had lived long enough for her to tell her how much she loved her.

If only that.

The heat prickled and tingled against her skin as she headed ever on towards what she knew was simply a mirage, an effect of burning sun and sparkling sea. Aware of her own slightly laboured breathing, she was walking as in a dream, that agonizing dream where you are trying to get somewhere and never ever arrive, not in this world anyway. Bare toes sifting through sand, thinking about her mother sitting on a rock in her yellow dress, thinking of herself and the little girl she had once been.

Her mother's voice floated lazily through the hot still air: 'It's so small, it's claustrophobic. And the heat and those infernal roaches, darling . . .'

When she looked again, it was just sand and sea and sky.

Her mother was gone.

She telephoned Ben when she got back to Rosie's, just to say that they were on their way home.

It was good as always to hear his voice. He was fine, he told her, and her father was too. They had spent quite a bit of time together – quality time – and were at last, a bit late in the day, getting to know each other. He talked of Anna, telling her of the problems she was facing at the convent, obviously worried on her behalf but helpless as to a practical solution.

'Can't wait to see you,' he said, closing the call at last. 'I love you . . .'

'See you soon,' she said, replacing the receiver gently and whirling round to see Henry standing in the doorway.

'Sorry, didn't mean to startle you. Everything OK?' he asked.

'Everything's fine, Henry,' she said, waiting for her heart to settle from its very obvious lurch.

And everything would be fine, she told herself later, nuzzling her baby to her; everything would be fine as soon as she had put a few thousand miles between them.

CHANTER TWENTY-NINE

She told Rosie about Anna and the problems at the convent.

To her surprise, for she hadn't intended it, Rosie was a little annoyed, jumping to the conclusion that somehow Olivia was asking for money.

'Do you know about my project?' she asked suspiciously. 'Has Henry been blabbing?'

'What project?' she asked.

Rosie stared hard at her.

'Sorry, Livvy.' She ran her fingers through her hair. 'I shouldn't be telling you this but I've got big plans When I get back, I'm going to buy a theatre.'

'A theatre?'

'Yes,' Rosie said impatiently. 'Just listen. You know how I've always wanted to be a singer?'

Olivia nodded. 'Yes, but . . .'

Rosie ploughed on. 'My original intention was to start up a sort of theatre school for young hopefuls. Fame Academy type thing. But then I came across this old theatre and that was that. I'm going to do it up. We've got some important actors already willing to do cameo performances. I want new playwrights, new talent. Henry has a lot of contacts and so have I from the old days.'

'Are you going into acting then?'

'Jesus, no. Too much like hard work. I am overseeing,' she said grandly. 'I shall be the patron, the fairy godmother, the woman with the money.'

Olivia nodded, trying to take it in. 'But what do you know about this sort of thing, Rosie? it sounds a huge undertaking.'

'It is. And I know nothing but I really want it to work. And you needn't look like that,' she added, dangerously flushed. 'It's not some little wifely thing to keep me occupied. It's been brewing for ages. Henry insists I do it properly, get a plan and some figures and so on to show that I'm serious about it. He's told me if I cock it up, I'm on my own. He's funding me and I daren't tell you how much. It would scare you to death. It scares me.'

'He must think it will work . '

'It's got to or I'll never live it down.'

'Well . . good luck,' Olivia said, not quite able to take it in.

'I've worked hard to get this money,' Rosie went on, strangely defensive. 'Henry doesn't give big sums away lightly. I've prepared plans and been in touch with all sorts of people and it's *my* project, Olivia. I'm not giving that money to Anna if that's what you're asking me to do. Sodding worthy causes can take a jump.'

'I wasn't. I didn't even know about your theatre.'

'You still don't until things are signed and sealed. And I'm not asking Henry for any more money either, even for Anna. He's not into religion and he thinks she's a crank. No way would he donate as much as a fiver.'

She tried to avoid Henry next day but, because Rosie was booked in for a hair do which she didn't want to cancel, she found herself in the house alone with him, strictly forbidden to mention 'theatre'.

'Sorry you're leaving a little earlier than expected,' Henry said, as the two of them ate a light lunch out on the sun-dried porch. There was a slight cooling breeze and out in the harbour, white-sailed yachts bobbed and slid through the blue water. 'I'm probably going to follow you home fairly quickly. There are things to do and I've been out of touch too long. Deputies have a nasty habit of stepping in when that happens too often. And, in any case, I'm itching to get back to work. I never thought I'd say it but I'm bored with golf.'

'When we get back, Rosie and I want to keep in touch, Henry,' she said, hoping he understood what she was trying to say without her having to spell it out.

'But you want me to keep clear?' he asked, pushing the dish of fruit towards her. 'That's perfectly all right, darling. I have infinite patience and believe me, I always get what I set out to get. Eventually. I'll leave the timing entirely up to you. All it takes is a phone call. I'll let you have my private number.'

'Timing up to me? What do you mean?' she asked, declining the fruit but taking some cheese and crackers.

'Whenever you decide to take me up on my generous offer to become my mistress,' he said with a big smile. 'It's not a joke, Olivia. I really mean it. You only have to say the word.'

'For goodness' sake,' she hissed, because the maid had just finished attending them and could easily have overheard. 'Can't we even have lunch without you making these ludicrous suggestions? I don't know what's the matter with you.'

'They are not ludicrous and you know that,' he said. 'You are a sensual woman, Olivia, and just looking at you drives me mad. You and I would be quite perfect together.'

'Stop it,' she said, pushing the chair back and standing up. 'I want to make one thing quite clear, Henry. When we do get home, I don't want you bothering me. There will be no meetings, not between us, but I don't intend to let things spoil between me and Rosie, not again.'

'Sit down,' he said easily. 'And don't fuss. Of course I won't bother you if that's what you want. I will wait for you to come to me. As I say, I have incredible patience.'

'And incredible nerve,' she said, sitting down, almost seeing the funny side of all this despite herself.

And yet, as she packed her bags later, hearing him laughing with the newly coiffured Rosie, she reflected that, because of Henry, because of his audacious behaviour, the pain had lessened, just the minutest amount, for the simple reason that it was impossible to be outraged and terribly sad all at the same time.

Perhaps Henry knew that, too. Perhaps it was just a clever way of helping her. Perhaps he didn't really fancy her at all. And somehow that was faintly disquieting.

Ben was touchingly delighted to have them back. He and her father had spent a lot of time together in her absence and things were better between them.

'I'm doing my best to make amends,' he told her earnestly. 'I know I treated your mother badly but I can't do anything to change that, can I?'

'No,' she told him flatly. 'You can't.'

'You look better,' he said, watching as she unpacked. 'It did you good, the break.'

She nodded. 'Rosie was great. Fussed me of course but took no nonsense either.'

'What about Henry?'

She felt herself flush, and turned away so that he could not see. 'All right. It was all a bit sad really. He told me about a daughter he lost. Years ago but he still thinks about her. A little girl who died during a heart operation.'

There was a short silence.

'I see,' Ben said quietly. 'Oh God, I think I see. Poor Henry. Look, Olivia, if you want to try again, we could invite them for the weekend. I promise I'll behave,' he added with a smile.

'Goodness, no, I'm not up to a Rosie and Henry visit,' she said. 'Maybe later.'
Maybe never.

To Ben, Olivia was distant still. Yes, the holiday had done her good for she was
looking better, lightly tanned and healthy, but she was still a little lost. Still
haunted.

He went to see Anna, his duty visit. Ben was sorry, very sorry, but the visits
felt like that simply because of the austere qualities of the convent. He did not
like clutter in his life, far from it, but a certain amount of frippery was not only
pleasant but essential to harmonious living. Olivia had got it just about right in
their home. After his busy working day, it was a haven and he loved it.

'She's better,' he told Anna, who had enquired after Olivia. 'And she says that
Rosie sends her love too.'

Anna nodded, pleased at that. 'I like Rosie,' she said. 'She was always such a
livewire and I used to envy her that. I was always so solid, even as a child.'

'People don't change,' he said. 'What was Olivia like?'

Anna smiled. 'A good friend. Quiet and shy. Often had her head stuck in a
book. Madly keen on gardening. Very bad at sport.'

He laughed. 'She hasn't changed much.'

'I never believed that Rosie married for money,' Anna went on. 'She's not so
selfish. I think of her as generous, warm hearted.'

'I never said she was selfish,' he said, feeling she was offering a rebuke. 'And I
haven't a clue what her motives were in marrying Henry. Olivia's convinced it was
for purely monetary reasons . . .'

'I know she is.'

They lapsed into silence, thinking about that.

'Are you all right?' Ben asked. 'Is anything happening yet about the convent?'

'No. We're praying that somehow we'll save it.'

'You might have to do a bit more than pray,' he muttered. 'Something more
concrete like finding yourself a benefactor.'

'Reverend Mother wonders if we should ask around, approach a few local
businesses, invite them to make a contribution . . .' She blushed. 'I think it's a
dreadful idea, quite unworthy of us. Begging is not the answer.'

'Don't worry,' he said awkwardly, reaching to touch her shoulder, wishing he
could embrace her but the habit was strangely repellent to him and he hesitated.
'Oh, I nearly forgot. I have something for you. A gift from Olivia. She hopes you
like it.'

Anna took it, a big glossy book about Bermudian houses and gardens. 'This looks lovely,' she told him with a smile. 'Tell her thank you.'

'Things are not right yet. She's still not really with me,' he told her suddenly. 'She blames me for what happened.'

'She has to blame someone,' Anna said in that matter-of-fact way of hers. 'And it might as well be you. I thought she might have blamed her father, though. After all, he did leave . . .'

'We seem to have a knack in this family of running off – we men. But I don't intend to do it, to leave Olivia. Although the way things are just now, I am scared she might leave me.'

'How silly! Of course she won't. She loves you. And she has no real reason to leave.'

'I've heard about marriages breaking up for no reason to speak of. The problem is it's so simple with you, Anna. Black and white. Right and wrong.'

'No. There are grey areas, Ben. Can't you see I'm fighting my conscience just now? I want to stay here. I don't want the convent to be sold. I worry that, if I have to move, I might lose faith and that scares me to death.' She shuddered suddenly, looking at him with the old Anna eyes a moment, with doubt. 'And yet I shouldn't expect life to be always sweet, should I? What right have I to expect that?'

'You'll come through,' he said gently, feeling a sudden unexpected deep affection for this woman, this sister of his. 'Life is tough, it throws things at you. You have your faith. I envy you that. I wish sometimes I had your faith. I'm at the cutting edge, doing what I do, and I often see the moment life slips away from the body, but it stays on a purely practical level for me,' he finished, feeling somehow he needed to try to explain. 'I don't really believe in God.' Anna just smiled.

'Don't let Olivia go. Hang on to her.'

He intended to.

'Thanks so much for the gardening book,' Anna told Olivia with a smile when next she visited. 'There's a tree that sheds its leaves in the spring. Isn't that odd?'

Olivia nodded. 'The fiddlewood. Yes, it is odd. What's odd, though, is that now I'm back home I love the gardens here – this garden especially – so much more. We do ourselves down. Our English gardens are superb and we have such a talent.'

'Some of us,' Anna commented drily.

'Do you remember Mr Johnson, the gardener at Slyne Hall?'

Anna shook her head. 'Not really. But I remember you talking about him. Didn't he give you a book once?'

'Oh yes. I still have it. He could have been fired for that.' She grimaced. 'And we'd take a dim view of it now, wouldn't we, chatting up little girls like he did? And yet it was so innocent.'

'Sweet innocence,' Anna said thoughtfully. 'Ben's worried about you. I know it's been dreadful for you, Olivia, but what happened to your mother was an accident. He wasn't responsible. You must forgive him.'

'I know it's not his fault and I don't know why I'm blaming him but I am. I can't seem to be able to forgive him for not liking my mother. Isn't that awful?'

'I could quote you passages from the Bible about forgiveness,' Anna said. 'But I doubt you would appreciate it. God will show you how. And you'll know when he does. That's all I can say.'

'Oh Anna, don't preach at me.'

'Sorry.' She hesitated and then smiled. 'May I give you some good news?'

'Of course. What is it?'

'We have a reprieve for the convent,' she said quietly. 'Reverend Mother told us this morning. We have a benefactor who has given a substantial donation so that we can keep going for many years to come. No strings attached. Sister Matilda has investment plans up her sleeve at this very moment to make absolutely sure we don't squander the money.'

'Oh!'

'Isn't it wonderful?' Anna said. 'We are so relieved and we are to hold a special service this evening as a thank you.'

'Who is this benefactor?'

'I have no idea,' Anna said, touching the cross at her breast. 'I believe only Mother knows that. He wishes to remain anonymous.'

'He?'

'Or she. As I say, we have no idea.'

To her consternation, Henry answered the telephone at The Old Manor.

'Oh!' she said, feeling her heart flutter. 'Rosie said you were away.'

'My meeting was cancelled,' he said brightly. 'Lovely to hear your voice, Olivia. For a minute there, I thought you were ringing to take me up on my offer, although if you do decide to do that, use my private number, for God's sake.'

'I take it Rosie's not there,' she said, ignoring him. 'We're supposed to be meeting for lunch tomorrow and I'm going to have to put her off. I'd forgotten it was baby clinic day and I must have Jamie checked and weighed.'

'How is the little fella? And Ben, how is he?'

'They're both very well, thank you,' she said tightly.

'No doubt delighted to have you back. I bet you didn't say a word about what went on between us, did you?'

'Nothing went on, Henry,' she said, catching sight of her flushed reflection in the mirror. 'I saw sense before anything went on.'

He laughed, low. 'Not quite, darling. That was a kiss and a half.'

'You are the limit,' she went on, more amused than angry. 'How *many* women have you propositioned?'

'One or two and my secretary is hanging in there just waiting – a charming, capable woman but she's not my type. I like a woman of quality. Like you.'

'You think money and power can buy anything but it can't, Henry. It can't buy me.'

'Can't it?' he asked smoothly.

'What makes you think I want a fling?' she asked, half smiling, in a way enjoying the banter, for she now knew it was all talk. Just talk. Cocktail party bravado. A mild flirtation trapped in a corner. Forgotten the instant you left the room. Henry, mindful of Rosie's pre-nuptial kicking in, might very well run a mile if she were to approach him. 'I'm married to Ben and, before you ask, we're getting it back together,' she said, remembering his attempt the other evening to get things back to normal. 'I was just upset by what happened to my mother and I had to blame someone. Like you said, it could have got to us, come between us, but I'm not going to let it. Thanks for that.'

'Good for you, darling, but as I've told you, I was never proposing that we divorced and got married. I'm merely offering you some fun.'

'Give me one good reason why I would want a fling.'

'Call it intuition, my darling,' he said. 'And I'm an optimistic man.'

'There's no talking to you,' she said, knowing she should cut this conversation dead. 'Can I ask you something, Henry?' she went on, firming her voice. 'Is Rosie going ahead with this theatre thing?'

'She told you about that, then?' He laughed. 'I'm leaving everything up to her, Olivia. I haven't the time to mess about with cock-eyed schemes that'll end up down the pan within a couple of years. It'll keep her amused in the meantime . . .'

'So you're not involved at all?'

'No, other than supplying her with the money.' A wariness crept into his voice. 'What is this? The third degree?'

She shut up. She was no nearer knowing if Rosie was the mysterious bene-factor. After what she had said about charitable donations, it seemed unlikely, but how many people had that amount of money to play with? And also, as the problems of the convent had hardly been broadcast even to local radio, who would know about them?

'I've got to go, Olivia. Busy as hell. I'll tell Rosie you called, give her your message. She'll be sorry to have missed you,' he said. 'And remember, you can give me a call any time, night or day. Think of me as your private emergency helpline.'

CHAPTER THIRTY

Olivia and Rosie were lunching in town at a new restaurant Rosie had discovered.

Olivias's father was looking after the baby, proving to be rather adept at this grandfather business, insisting that, once you got the hang of it, there was nothing to this baby lark.

'I miss the sun,' Rosie said, giving a shudder, looking out on to a damp, dull day. 'But it's good to be back in some ways and Henry's much happier when he's working.'

'Did you know that someone's given the convent a huge donation?' Olivia asked in a low voice. 'A mysterious benefactor apparently . . .' She waited for a reaction. 'It's solved all their problems at a stroke.'

'That's good.' Rosie started on her quiche salad, pausing to glance questioningly at Olivia. 'Mysterious benefactor? How curious! I hope you're not thinking it's me.'

'It did cross my mind but I thought it was too good to be true,' Olivia said with a wry smile. 'I wonder who it is.'

'How should I know? It's definitely not Henry. I did mention it, told him about Anna, and he gave it extremely short shrift. So long as they have the money, does it matter who it is?'

'No. Ben's delighted. I haven't seen him so happy in a long time. Now that he's accepted that Anna's where she wants to be, he's more relaxed about the whole thing. So is Eva.'

'Which is more than I am,' Rosie said with a shake of her head. 'Can you believe it? Anna, of all people? She was always so – well, so *sensible*.'

They laughed, although Olivia felt a touch uncomfortable that Anna, dearest deeply-sincere Anna, should be dismissed so lightly.

'You and Ben must come for the weekend again.' Rosie said, when they had finished their meal. 'And this time we'll have a great time. No male sulks.'

Olivia smiled. 'Lovely, thank you. We must fix a date.'

She would think of an excuse later.

Shortly after Olivia returned from Bermuda, Ben found himself in the smart foyer of a hotel waiting for Henry.

He was doing this for Anna and, indirectly, for Olivia too. It was essential for the well-being of the 'family' that all members of it were happy, happy as they could be anyway, and having Anna upset and unhappy was not in the scheme of things if he could help it. As for Olivia, she was at her happiest when she was talking about that blessed garden and it would tear her apart to see it razed and brand new houses put in its place.

So, he had made up his mind to do the unthinkable. He was going to ask Henry for money to help save the convent, aware that he might very well laugh in his face or worse, subject him to the deepest humiliation before laughing in his face.

But, what did that matter, a little humiliation, if there was the faintest chance that it might work? Henry might have a better nature and he was about to find out, he thought, rising as he saw Henry enter via the revolving door and head his way.

He looked good, tanned and most definitely not suffering from jet lag, and he had only returned from Bermuda a couple of days after Olivia.

'Good to see you, Ben,' he said cheerfully, shaking hands. 'Have you ordered coffee?'

'It's on its way,' Ben said, motioning him to a seat. 'Good trip back?'

'The usual. Bit of a drag, the overnight flight. Still, I'm back now and I need to stay home based a while to get things sorted out. How's that lovely wife of yours?'

'Fine,' he said carefully. 'She enjoyed it very much. She looks better too.'

'Good. Sun and sand work wonders.' Henry waited as the waiter served their coffee and then leaned back in the chair and looked at him quizzically. 'To what do I owe this pleasure?'

'First of all, thanks for meeting me at short notice,' Ben said, aware that this man was about as busy as he was. 'Good of you. And thank Rosie for me for all she's done for Olivia.'

Henry nodded. Waiting.

'I'll come straight to the point,' Ben said, taking a deep breath. 'I need a favour from you, Henry.'

'Do you? Go on.'

'You know of course that my sister's a nun,' he said. 'My sister Anna.'

'Yes. They were all at school together. Funny old business that. What the hell got into her?'

Ben shrugged. He wasn't going into all that. 'The point is they're going to have to sell up, sell off the convent, probably to developers, unless they can find some money to keep them going for a while longer.'

'I see.' Henry was impassive.

'Since you're the only millionaire plus that I know . . .' Ben smiled slightly. 'I'm coming to you. Can you help?'

Henry reached for his cup of coffee and took a sip. 'I can help, but the question is why should I? I've already given my quota to charitable causes this tax year and I make it a rule to give so much and no more. I don't need any more publicity because marketing-wise we're on the up so, you tell me, Ben, why should I help? Especially a convent, which to me is dubious anyway. Now, if you'd come to me and asked for some money for your unit, I might have seen my way to giving you a donation.'

'Then I take it the answer's no,' Ben said quietly, determined to take it on the chin, not to beg.

'Regrettably, yes. I haven't made my money from being foolish with it,' Henry went on, flicking an imaginary speck of dust from his finely cut trousers. 'I've enough problems just now keeping my wife's spending in check, believe me. And this doesn't appeal, frankly. I'm not into helping nuns. I'm sorry for them, poor deluded souls that they are, but they're hardly going to find themselves out on the street, are they? I really don't feel I can help.'

'Right, if that's how you feel, I'm sorry I bothered you,' Ben said as gracefully as he could, accepting it. It had been a long shot anyway but worth a try. And now he was stumped.

They finished their coffee unhurriedly, switching to general chat, and parted with a handshake and a smile. Yes indeed, they must get together sometime for dinner – they would have words with their respective wives.

Hurrying to his car, Ben slipped into it and gripped the steering wheel tightly a minute, letting loose his tension and anger.

The bastard!

Henry told Rosie over supper that evening, telling the tale with great glee, amazed and amused that Ben should ever have thought he would hand over his hard-earned cash to save a convent.

'Save the convent...' Henry said with a laugh. 'Save a bunch of loony women? Why should I? Now, if he'd asked me for a donation for his unit, I might have agreed to that.'

'Did he ask you for a donation for that?'

'No, he did not. I was waiting for him to ask but he didn't. Mind you, if he had asked, I was going to say he'd have to wait until next May, for the next financial year,' Henry said, tucking into his meal. 'And, you needn't look like that, Rosie, I haven't made my money by giving it away right left and centre. If you want to donate, darling, it's up to you.'

'I don't have any money,' she said, ignoring his hearty laugh. 'It's all tied up in the theatre. Anyway, I wouldn't give it to a nuns' home either. I mean to say, there's charity and *charity*.'

He looked at her with narrowed eyes.

'You're learning,' he said.

They walked, Olivia and Anna, in the garden, delighted that it was to remain and that the convent would stay as it was – for the foreseeable future, anyway.

'We have plans for the garden. Would you like to come and help?' Anna asked her. 'The gardener is retiring shortly and I'll have to do it on my own. Sister Matilda is still being very tight with the funds and, if we could get somebody like you who wouldn't want payment, then it would be so helpful. Also, I haven't really a clue what I'm doing yet. I need your help.'

'I'd love to,' Olivia said, looking round at the soft autumnal shades, a little darkening here and there suggesting the approach of chillier weather. 'I'm itching to get really into a garden, one like this. I could walk here, walk round the wall, and my neighbour will be delighted to look after Jamie a couple of afternoons.'

'Good. Then that's settled,' Anna said with a smile. 'Come over here, I want to show you some new roses I'm going to plant. You must tell me what to do with them.'

They were potted roses, about a dozen robust-looking plants.

'Yet another gift from our benefactor,' Anna said, as Olivia bent to look at the labels. 'It will be a pink bed and it's going to look lovely next year I'm sure.'

Olivia straightened up.

She agreed with Anna. It would be lovely, for these shrub roses were beautifully scented.

All the same variety.

'Mary Rose.'

*

They sat, she and Rosie, either side of Anna, on the stone slab bench in the very heart of the garden, sharing a bag of chocolate creams that Rosie had brought with her in her voluminous snakeskin handbag.

'I smuggled them through the door. I wasn't sure you'd be allowed,' she said to Anna, offering her one. 'I thought you lived on bread and gruel.'

Anna laughed. 'You'd be surprised. It's nice to see you, Rosie. Looking so well at that. You're very elegant.'

'I can't take any credit for that. It's all down to Henry,' Rosie said with a smile. 'He's just wonderful, Anna. So generous. I'm so lucky. He adores me.'

She shot a smile at them both and Olivia felt her own smile freezing on her face, worried that Anna, looking closely at her, might suspect something.

'Now that we're back together, the three of us, we must keep in touch,' Rosie went on. 'None of this hit-and-miss affair. I mean to say, if Livvy and I hadn't met up by chance at that party that day, we might never have got together. Think of that.'

Yes. Think of that.

'Of course, with you two being related now . . .' Rosie passed the chocolates round and they each took one. 'It's easy for you but you won't get rid of me so easily. I shall make quite sure that we don't lose touch this time. We have such a lot in common.'

Anna smiled, looking at each of them in turn.

'What exactly?' she asked. 'Apart from our being at school together?'

'Well, you could say we all share Henry, couldn't you?' Rosie said, struggling to find a common denominator. 'He's my husband. He's Olivia's friend – I hope,' she said, casting a sly glance Olivia's way. 'And he's . . .'

'Our benefactor?' Anna said.

Rosie's silence was the answer.

'Well, well . . .' Olivia said, pretending complete surprise. 'How wonderful!'

'I told you, he *is* wonderful,' Rosie said a little sharply. 'He doesn't want any fuss of course and nobody, absolutely nobody, is to know.'

'It's Ben. He's to blame,' Anna said with delight. 'Thank goodness for Ben. Mum told me he was going to ask Henry if he could help—'

'Ben asked Henry for help? And you let him?' Olivia felt her heart pound, before glaring at Rosie. 'Did he?'

Rosie nodded, looking uncomfortable. 'Keep quiet about it because Henry refused him but then he must have had second thoughts.'

Olivia looked at her thoughtfully. 'Have you told Anna about your theatre?' she asked. 'It's so exciting. Rosie's doing up a theatre . . .'

'No, I'm not,' Rosie said, shuffling on the seat, stretching out her little leg to examine her shoe. 'That's all off, Livvy. Fell through. Literally. The bloody floor collapsed.' She drew a sharp breath and apologized to Anna. 'I backed out. Anyway, it was a load of drivel, me thinking I could do that with absolutely no experience whatsoever. Henry was right. It would have been skittled in a year.'

'So you're still sitting on all that money?' Olivia asked brightly.

'U-huh. Something else will turn up.' She paused, blushing as a nun walked or rather drifted by, nodding and smiling at them. 'This place gives me the creeps, Anna,' she said. 'God knows how you stick it.'

Anna laughed, taking Rosie's hand and giving it a little exasperated shake.

Olivia shut off, not really listening now as the others chatted on, turning her thoughts to this evening.

She had booked a table at Ben's favourite restaurant, the baby-sitting was all arranged, and all they had to do was get themselves there and enjoy it. There was a new dress and new nightgown, and she was already tingling with anticipation. And she had arranged it all before she even knew about him asking Henry for help, a wonderful gesture, which simply reinforced what she had really known all along.

Her husband was a very special man.

She had a lot to make up and one thing was sure, she was in no mood for sharing *him* with anyone. He was hers and she was keeping tight hold from now on. How she could ever for a minute have imagined herself with Henry was now a complete mystery. Temporary insanity caused by sudden sharp bereavement was probably the best way to describe it.

A bell clanged and Rosie jumped, stuffing the bag of chocolates away guiltily – a diminutive figure still, looking like a teenager.

'I'm summoned to prayer, girls,' Anna told them, rising to her feet, still heavy and clumsy but less so in the gracious folds of her habit. 'I'll walk back with you.'

As they walked back, they passed the newly planted out rose bed, Anna pointing it out to Rosie, Olivia remarking on the lovely variety of rose, Rosie saying nothing.

Anna left them at the parlour entrance and, somewhat subdued, they watched her leave.

They went out, closing the door on what Olivia now regarded as partly her garden, her lovely secret garden, shutting the door on Anna's world, entering the real one, pausing just outside the door, as if they were uncertain what to do next.

'I know what you're going to say,' Rosie said. 'So say it, please.'

Olivia smiled at her. 'It could be a coincidence, the choice of rose. But I don't think it is. And since there's only you and Henry know about Mary Rose, the benefactor must be one or the other of you and somehow I don't think it was Henry.'

'All right,' Rosie said impatiently. 'It was me but I'll kill you, Livvy, if you ever breathe a word. And, so far as Henry knows, I've still got nearly a million in my account.' She grinned suddenly. 'It's like old times. I'm very nearly in the red. Or will be when this is cashed . . .' She rifled in her bag and pulled out a cheque. 'Here. And don't fuss. It's for Ben's heart unit. And then, if Henry ever finds out, I can claim that I did it all for his baby daughter. That's why I chose that particular rose. Then he might just forgive me.'

Olivia glanced at the cheque. 'Good heavens! Rosie, I can't take this.'

'It's not *for* you,' Rosie said. 'It's for the unit. And don't ask why I'm doing all this. I must be insane. Or perhaps I'm trying to prove something. Just take it, Livvy, don't argue.'

'Thank you.' Olivia tucked the cheque away. 'What are you trying to prove?'

'Maybe that I'm not shallow,' she said quietly. 'That I do think of other people sometimes, particularly my friends . . .' Her eyes were remarkably bright suddenly. 'When you get down to it, sometimes friends, real friends, friends you have known for ever, are all you have left. You see, Livvy, I adore Henry but he doesn't love me.'

'Rosie, I'm sure that's not true.'

'Oh come on, do you really think I didn't know that he'd made a play for you? I saw the way he was looking at you in that restaurant that evening. The conceit of the man trying it on with *you* of all people. I mean, it should have been obvious that he was backing a loser there,' Rosie said with a short laugh. 'I hope you told him where to get off.'

Olivia said nothing for there was nothing to say.

'You might be interested to know that he has a mistress at this very moment.'

'How do you know?' Olivia asked, her voice sounding strange as she tried to cope with all this.

Rosie shrugged. 'Don't ask. I just do. All I know is she's a long-legged blonde. I could kill him if I didn't love him so much. He can't help it, it's just the way he is. But he won't divorce me, I'll make damned sure of that. He's well and truly stuck with me.'

Olivia put her arm a moment round Rosie's shoulders, feeling under her the weight of Rosie's misery.

From the chapel came the sound of chanting, a comforting throb, and, nearer at hand, the sounds of the city beckoned. Just here, on the convent doorstep, it seemed like no-man's land and it was, for a moment, seriously tempting to step back inside to escape from the real world.

But she couldn't leave Ben or Jamie.

'Cheer up . . .' Olivia said.

'You're right. I hate being miserable.' Rosie shrugged off Olivia's comforting arm. 'It must be going in there.' She gestured towards the convent. 'Crazy or what? She seems happy enough and I suppose I can just about understand why she did it and there might be something in that celibacy thing. It would make a nice change.' She smiled suddenly. 'No, the thing that would do it for me, the one thing that I absolutely couldn't tolerate, would be having to exist with just two sets of underwear. Now that is not only utterly impossible, it's also bizarre.'

They laughed, the mood lightened.

'For God's sake, let's live a little,' Rosie said, setting off, heels tapping furiously. 'Come on, Livvy, what are you waiting for? Let's hit the town.'